OVER THE GARDEN WALL

A CARTOON NETWORK ORIGINAL

VOLUME THREE

OVER THE GARDEN WALL Volume Three, January 2018. Published
by KaBOOM!, a division of Boom Entertainment, Inc. OVER THE
GARDEN WALL, CARTOON NETWORK, the logos, and all related
characters and elements are trademarks of and © Cartoon Network.
(S18) All rights reserved. Originally published in single magazine form as
Over the Garden Wall Ongoing No. 9-12. © Cartoon Network. (S16) All
rights reserved. KaBOOM!™ and the KaBOOM! logo are trademarks of
Boom Entertainment, Inc., registered in various countries and categories.
All characters, events, and institutions depicted herein are fictional. Any
similarity between any of the names, characters, persons, events, and/or
institutions in this publication to actual names, characters, and persons,
whether living or dead, events, and/or institutions is unintended and purely
coincidental. KaBOOM! does not read or accept unsolicited submissions of
ideas, stories, or artwork.

BOOM! Studios, 5670 Wilshire Boulevard, Suite 450, Los Angeles, CA
90036-5679. Printed in China. First Printing.

ISBN-13: 978-1-68415-060-1, eISBN: 978-1-61398-737-7

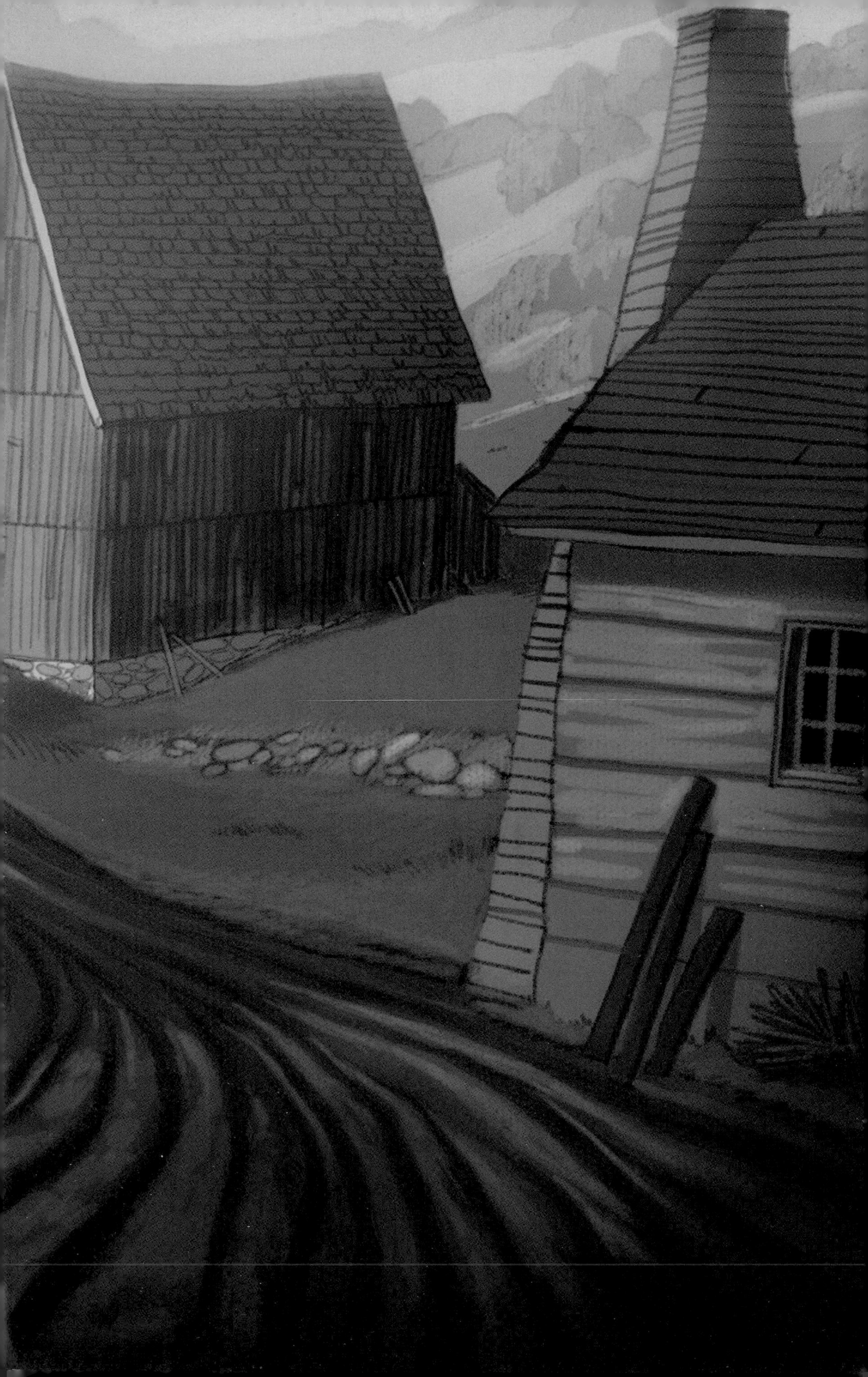

Over the Garden Wall™

A CARTOON NETWORK ORIGINAL

Created by Pat McHale

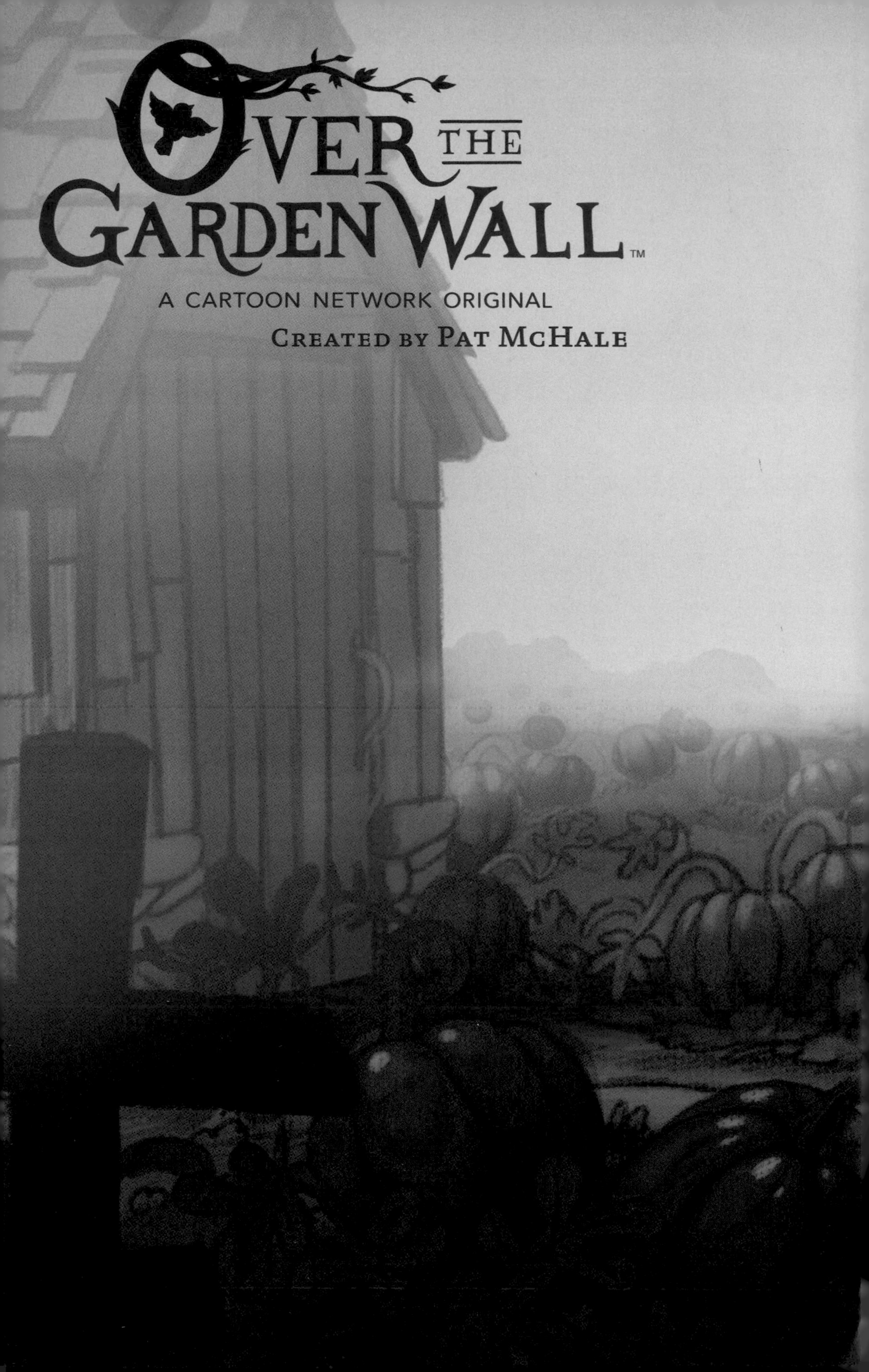

"Hunt for Hero Frog: Greg"
WRITTEN BY DANIELLE BURGOS
ILLUSTRATED BY JIM CAMPBELL

"Hunt for Hero Frog: Wirt"
WRITTEN BY KIERNAN SJURSEN-LIEN
ILLUSTRATED BY CARA McGEE
COLORS BY WHITNEY COGAR
LETTERS BY WARREN MONTGOMERY

"Kitty Goes To School"
WRITTEN AND ILLUSTRATED BY
GEORGE MAGER

COVER BY KIERNAN SJURSEN-LIEN

DESIGNER KARA LEOPARD
ASSISTANT EDITOR MATTHEW LEVINE
EDITOR WHITNEY LEOPARD

WITH SPECIAL THANKS TO MARISA MARIONAKIS,
JANET NO, CURTIS LELASH, KATIE KRENTZ,
PERNELLE HAYES, ADRIENNE LEE, STACY
RENFROE, AND THE WONDERFUL FOLKS AT
CARTOON NETWORK.

HUNT FOR HERO FROG

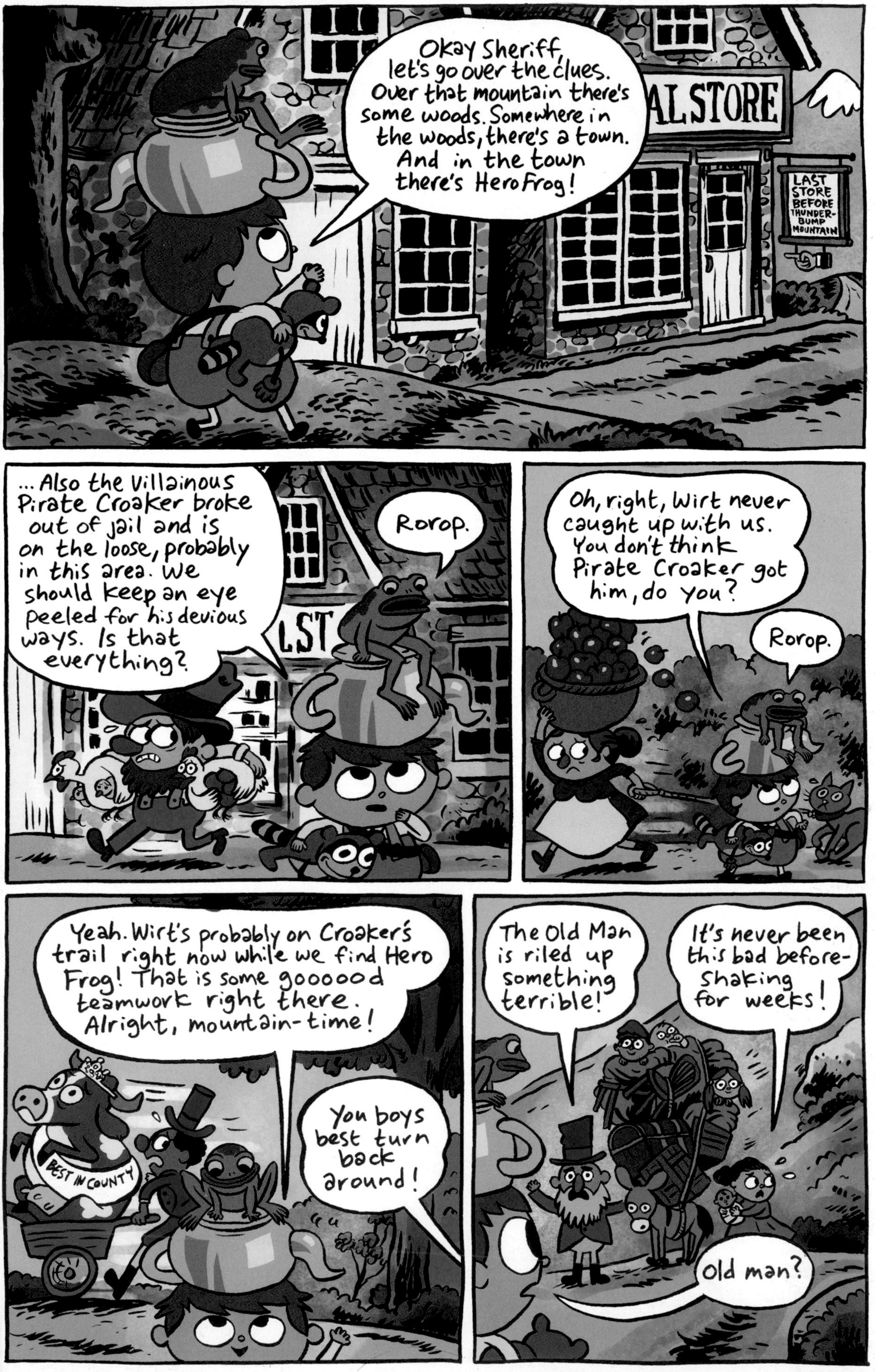

Okay Sheriff, let's go over the clues. Over that mountain there's some woods. Somewhere in the woods, there's a town. And in the town there's Hero Frog!
AL STORE
LAST STORE BEFORE THUNDER-BUMP MOUNTAIN
...Also the Villainous Pirate Croaker broke out of jail and is on the loose, probably in this area. We should keep an eye peeled for his devious ways. Is that everything?
Rorop.
LST
Oh, right, Wirt never caught up with us. You don't think Pirate Croaker got him, do you?
Rorop.
Yeah. Wirt's probably on Croaker's trail right now while we find Hero Frog! That is some goooood teamwork right there. Alright, mountain-time!
BEST IN COUNTY
You boys best turn back around!
The Old Man is riled up something terrible!
It's never been this bad before- Shaking for weeks!
Old man?

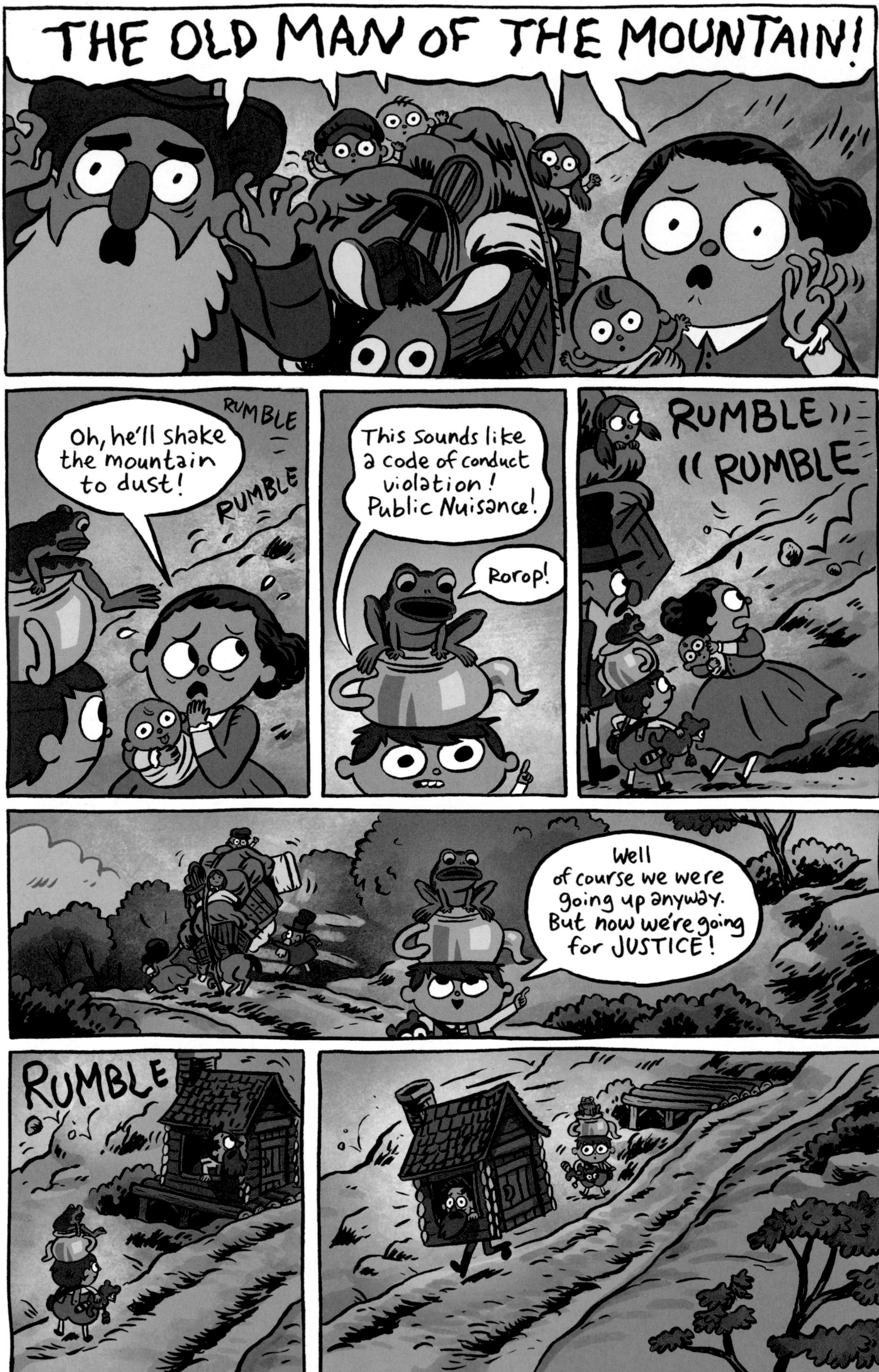
THE OLD MAN OF THE MOUNTAIN!
RUMBLE
Oh, he'll shake the mountain to dust!
RUMBLE
This sounds like a code of conduct violation! Public Nuisance!
Rorop!
RUMBLE
RUMBLE
Well of course we were going up anyway. But now we're going for JUSTICE!
RUMBLE

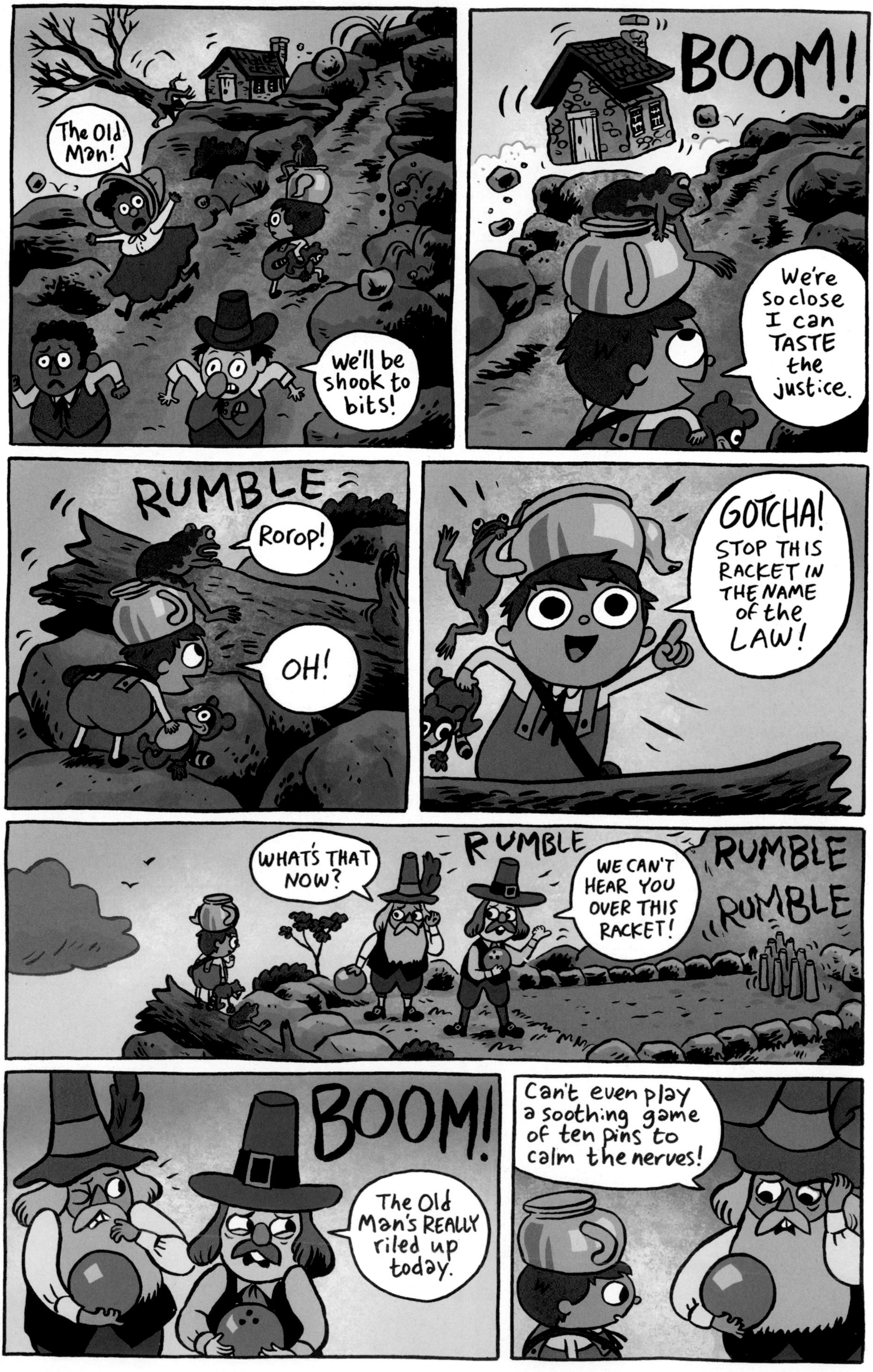

The Old Man!
We'll be shook to bits!
BOOM!
We're so close I can TASTE the justice.
RUMBLE
Rorop!
OH!
GOTCHA! STOP THIS RACKET IN THE NAME of the LAW!
WHAT'S THAT NOW?
RUMBLE
WE CAN'T HEAR YOU OVER THIS RACKET!
RUMBLE
RUMBLE
BOOM!
The Old Man's REALLY riled up today.
Can't even play a soothing game of ten pins to calm the nerves!

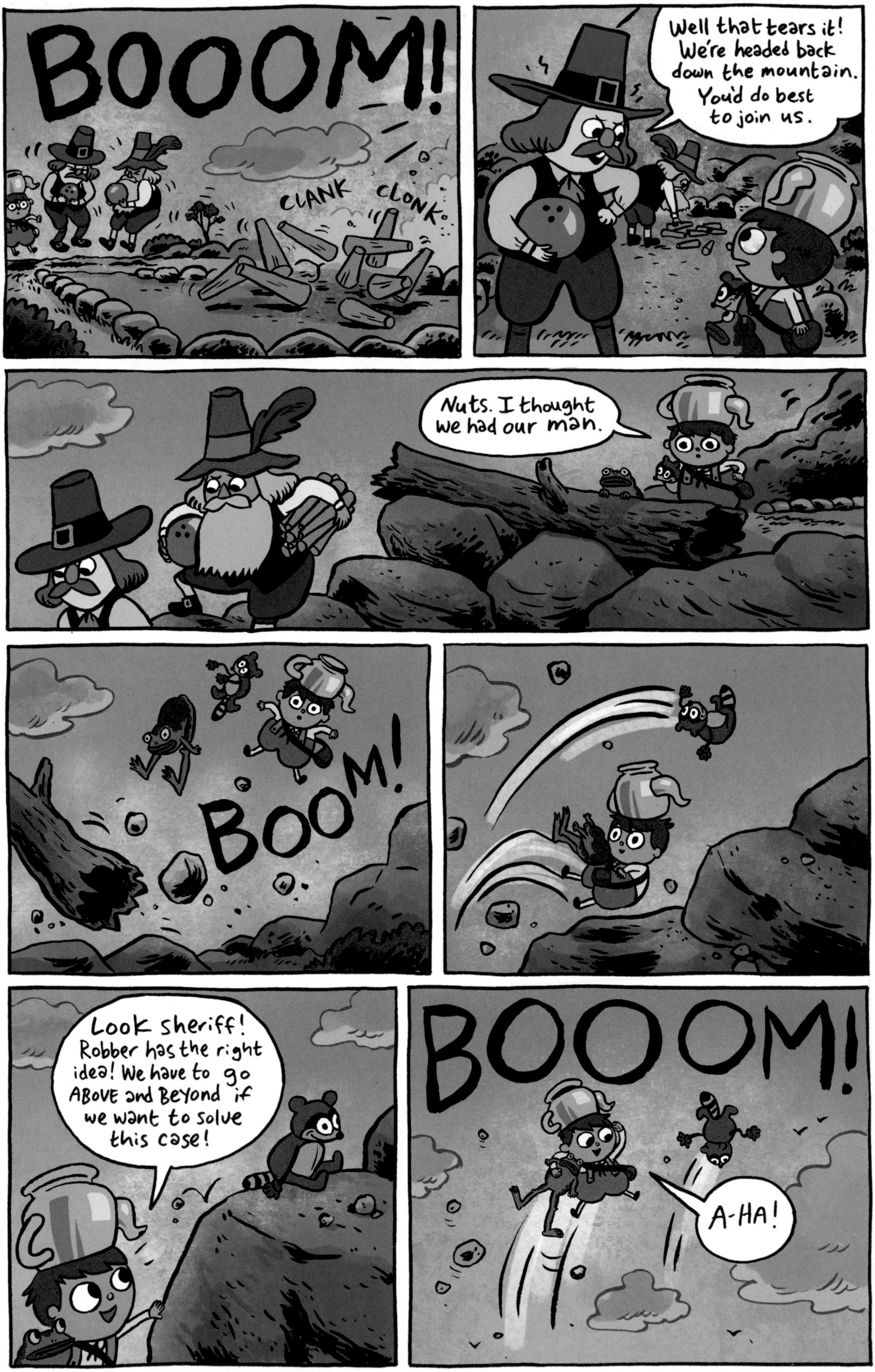
BOOOM!
CLANK
CLONK
Well that tears it! We're headed back down the mountain. You'd do best to join us.
Nuts. I thought we had our man.
BOOM!
Look sheriff! Robber has the right idea! We have to go ABOVE and BEYOND if we want to solve this case!
BOOOM!
A-HA!

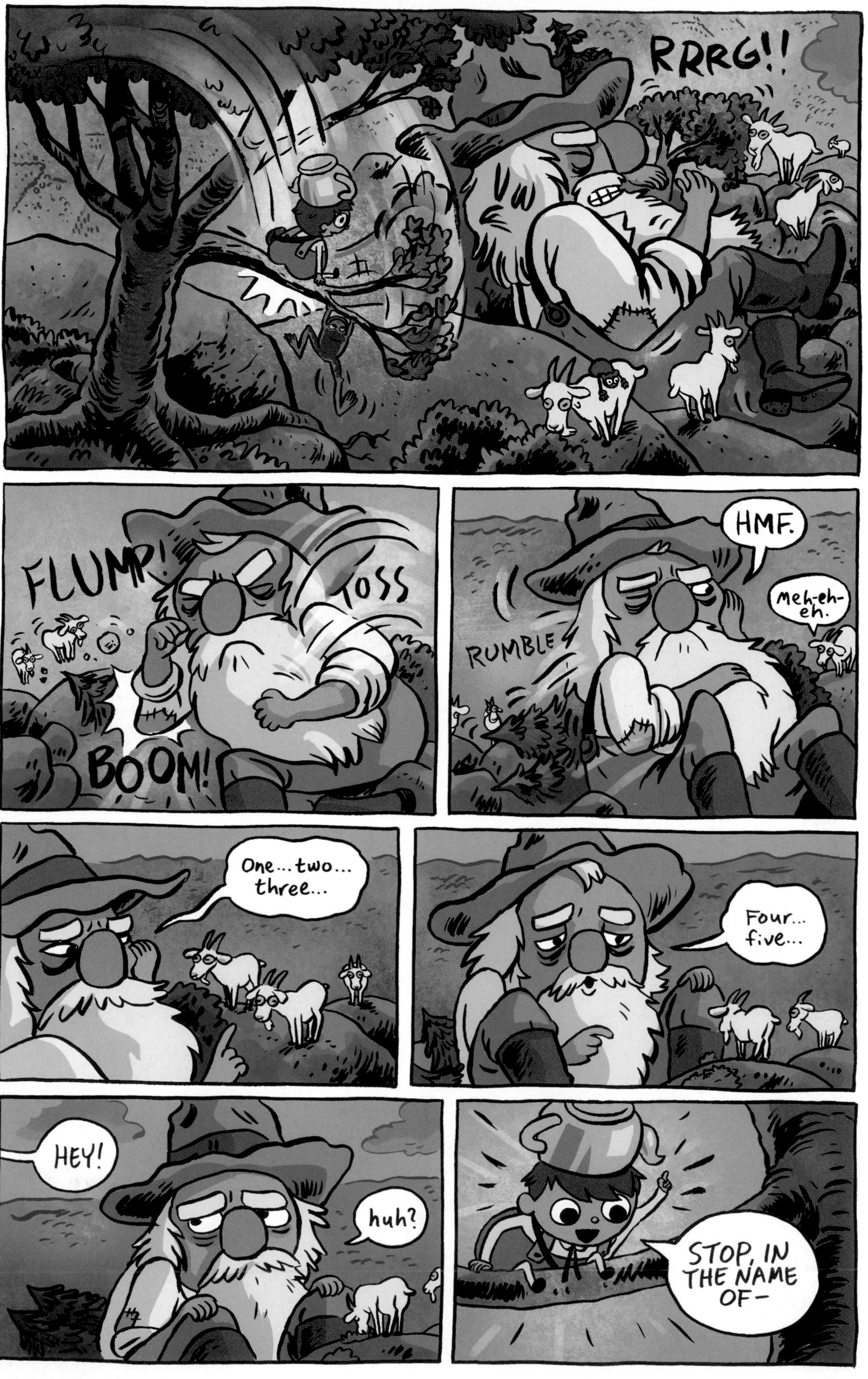
RRRG!!
FLUMP!
TOSS
BOOM!
HMF.
RUMBLE
meh-eh-eh.
One... two... three...
Four... five...
HEY!
huh?
STOP, IN THE NAME OF-

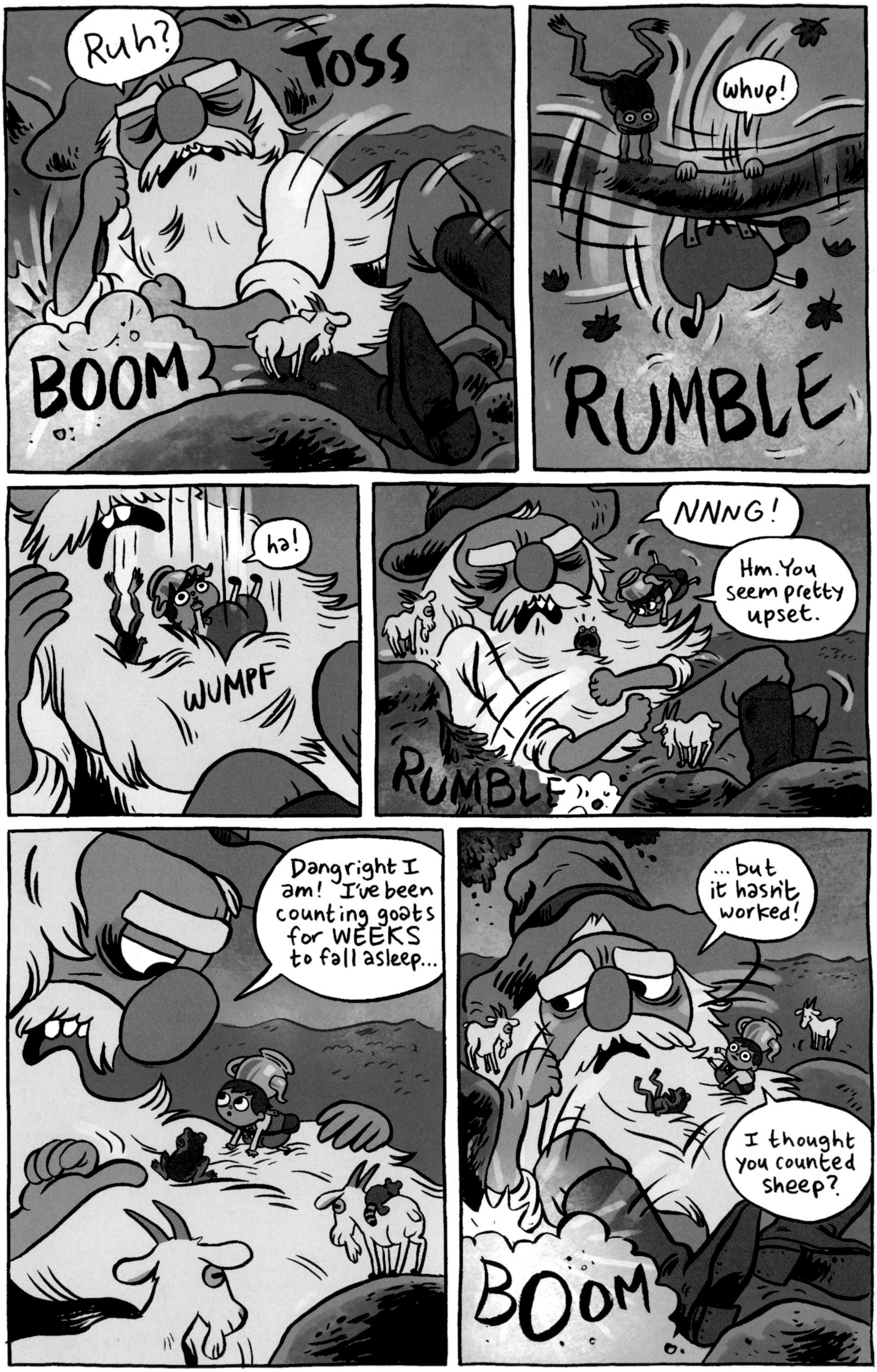
Ruh?
TOSS
BOOM
whup!
RUMBLE
ha!
WUMPF
NNNG!
Hm. You seem pretty upset.
RUMBLE
Dangright I am! I've been counting goats for WEEKS to fall asleep...
...but it hasn't worked!
I thought you counted sheep?
BOOM

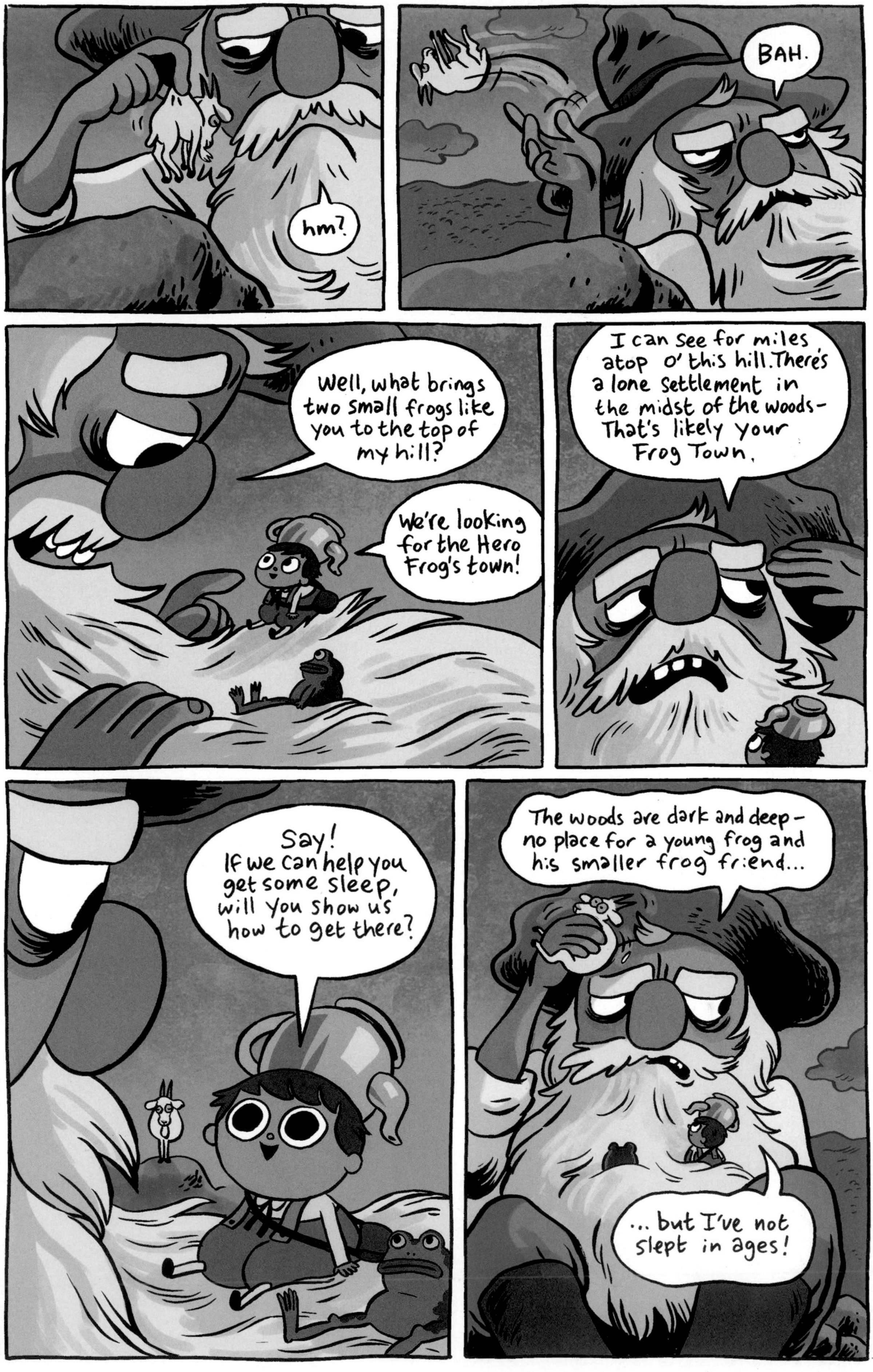
hm?
BAH.
Well, what brings two small frogs like you to the top of my hill?
We're looking for the Hero Frog's town!
I can see for miles atop o' this hill. There's a lone settlement in the midst of the woods- That's likely your Frog Town.
Say! If we can help you get some sleep, will you show us how to get there?
The woods are dark and deep- no place for a young frog and his smaller frog friend...
...but I've not slept in ages!

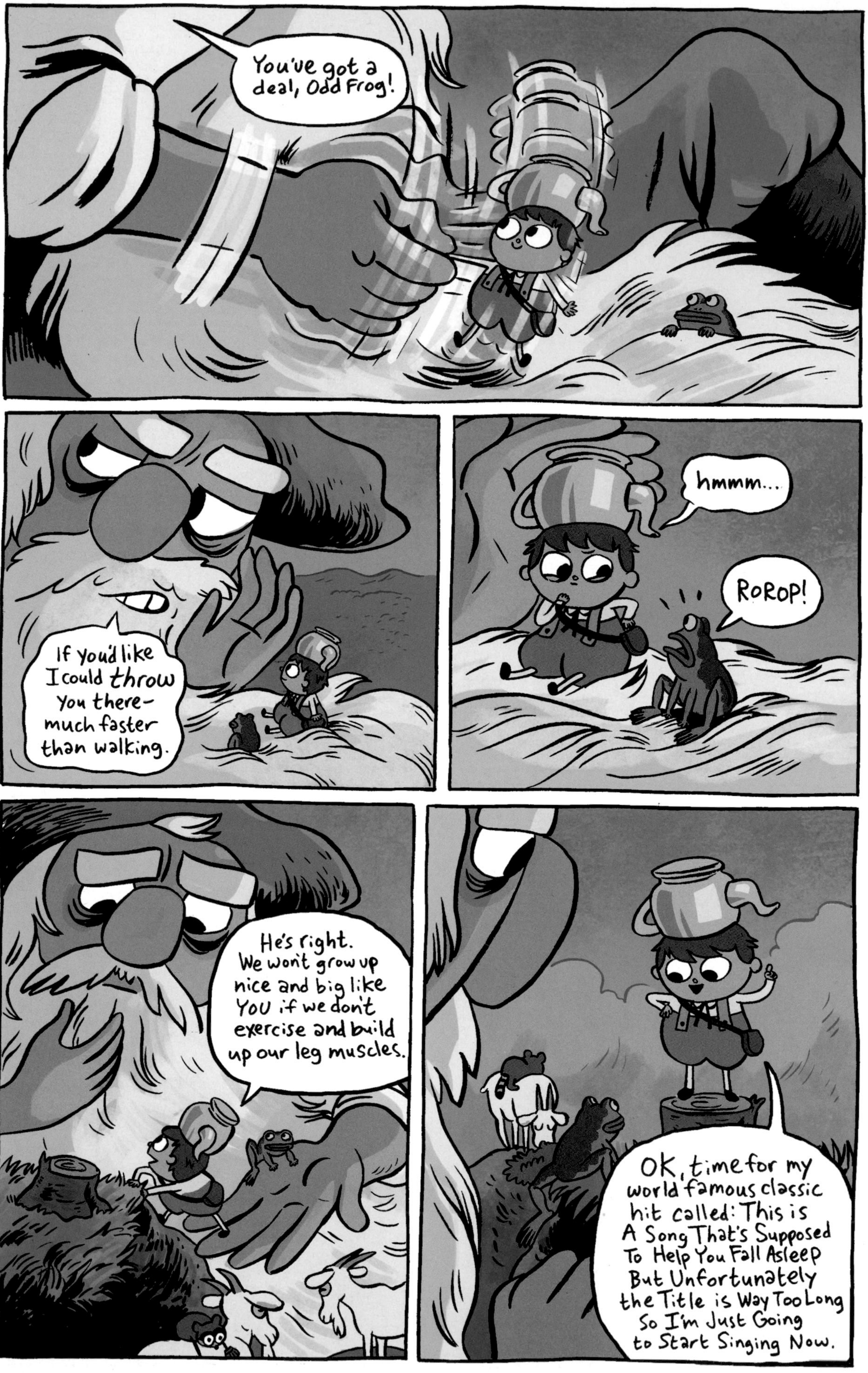
You've got a deal, Odd Frog!
If you'd like I could throw you there- much faster than walking.
hmmm...
ROROP!
He's right. We won't grow up nice and big like YOU if we don't exercise and build up our leg muscles.
OK, time for my world famous classic hit called: This is A Song That's Supposed To Help You Fall Asleep But Unfortunately the Title is Way Too Long So I'm Just Going to Start Singing Now.

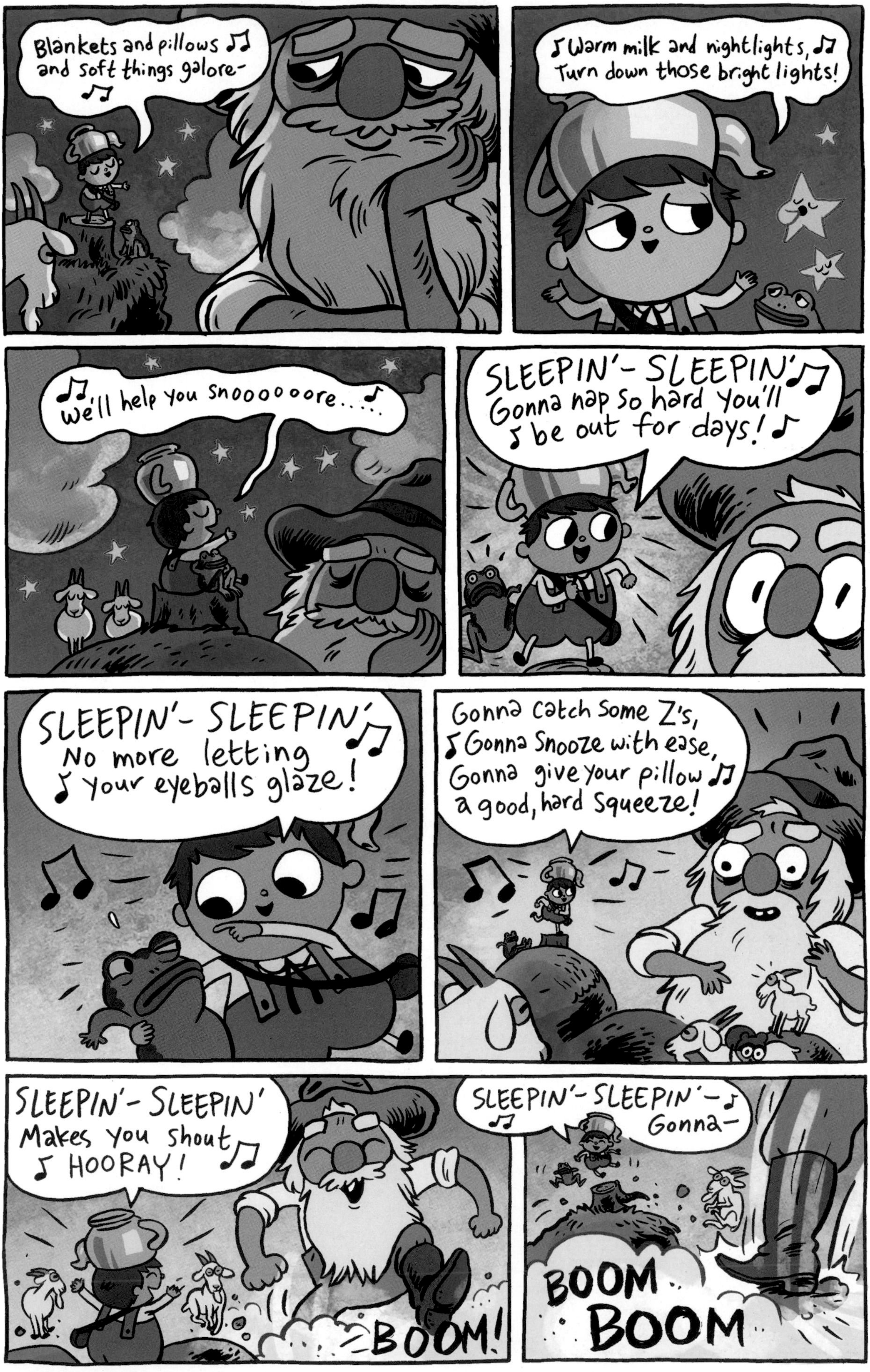
Blankets and pillows ♫ and soft things galore- ♫
♪ Warm milk and nightlights, ♫ Turn down those bright lights!
♫ We'll help you snoooooore..... ♪
SLEEPIN'- SLEEPIN' ♫ Gonna nap so hard you'll ♪ be out for days! ♪
SLEEPIN'- SLEEPIN' ♫ No more letting ♪ your eyeballs glaze!
Gonna catch some Z's, ♪ Gonna snooze with ease, Gonna give your pillow ♫ a good, hard squeeze!
SLEEPIN'- SLEEPIN' Makes you shout ♫ ♪ HOORAY!
BOOM!
SLEEPIN'- SLEEPIN'- ♪ ♫ Gonna-
BOOM
BOOM

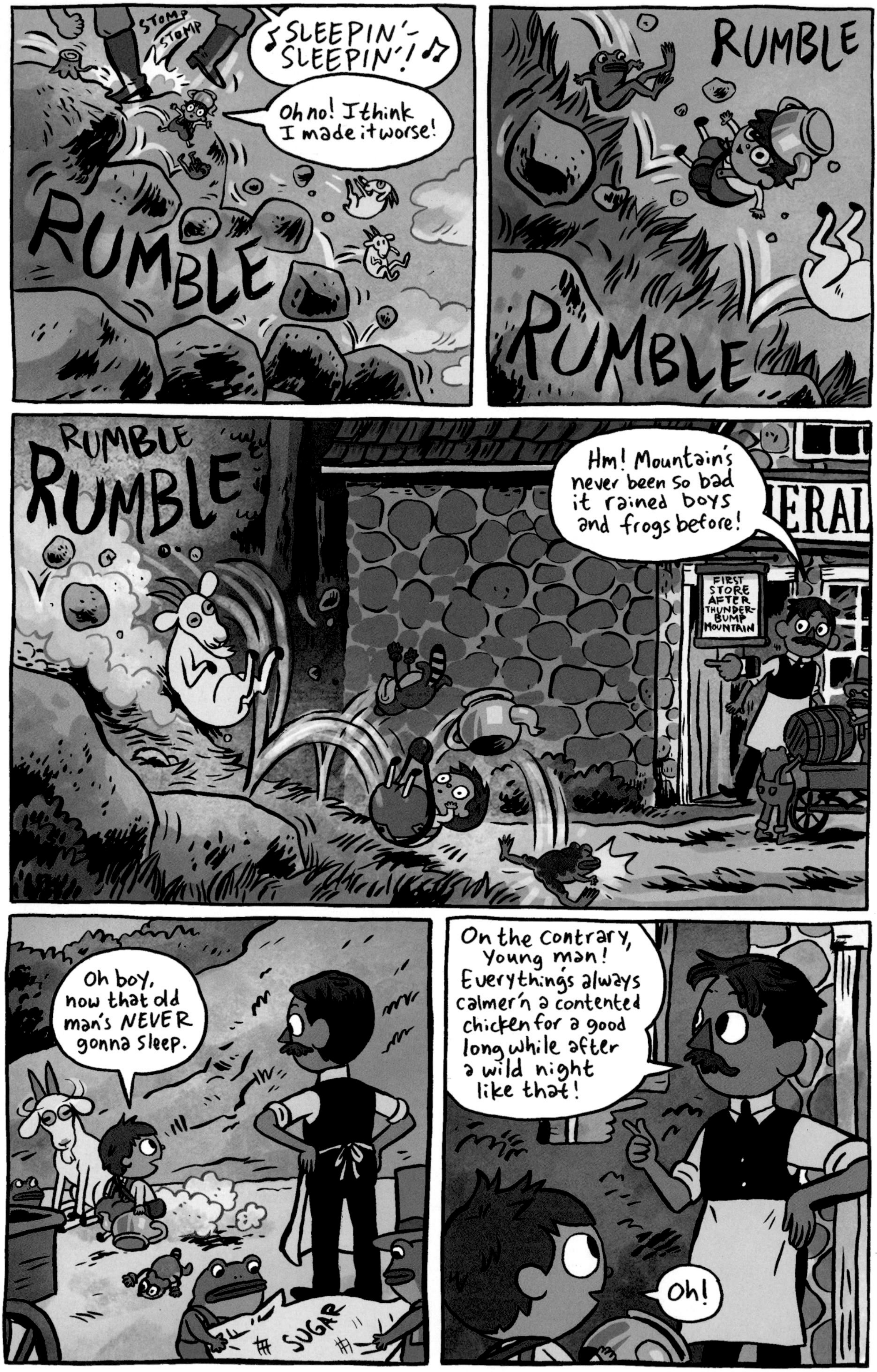
STOMP STOMP
SLEEPIN'-SLEEPIN'!
Oh no! I think I made it worse!
RUMBLE
RUMBLE
RUMBLE
RUMBLE
RUMBLE
Hm! Mountain's never been so bad it rained boys and frogs before!
FIRST STORE AFTER THUNDER-BUMP MOUNTAIN
Oh boy, now that old man's NEVER gonna sleep.
SUGAR
On the contrary, young man! Everything's always calmer'n a contented chicken for a good long while after a wild night like that!
Oh!

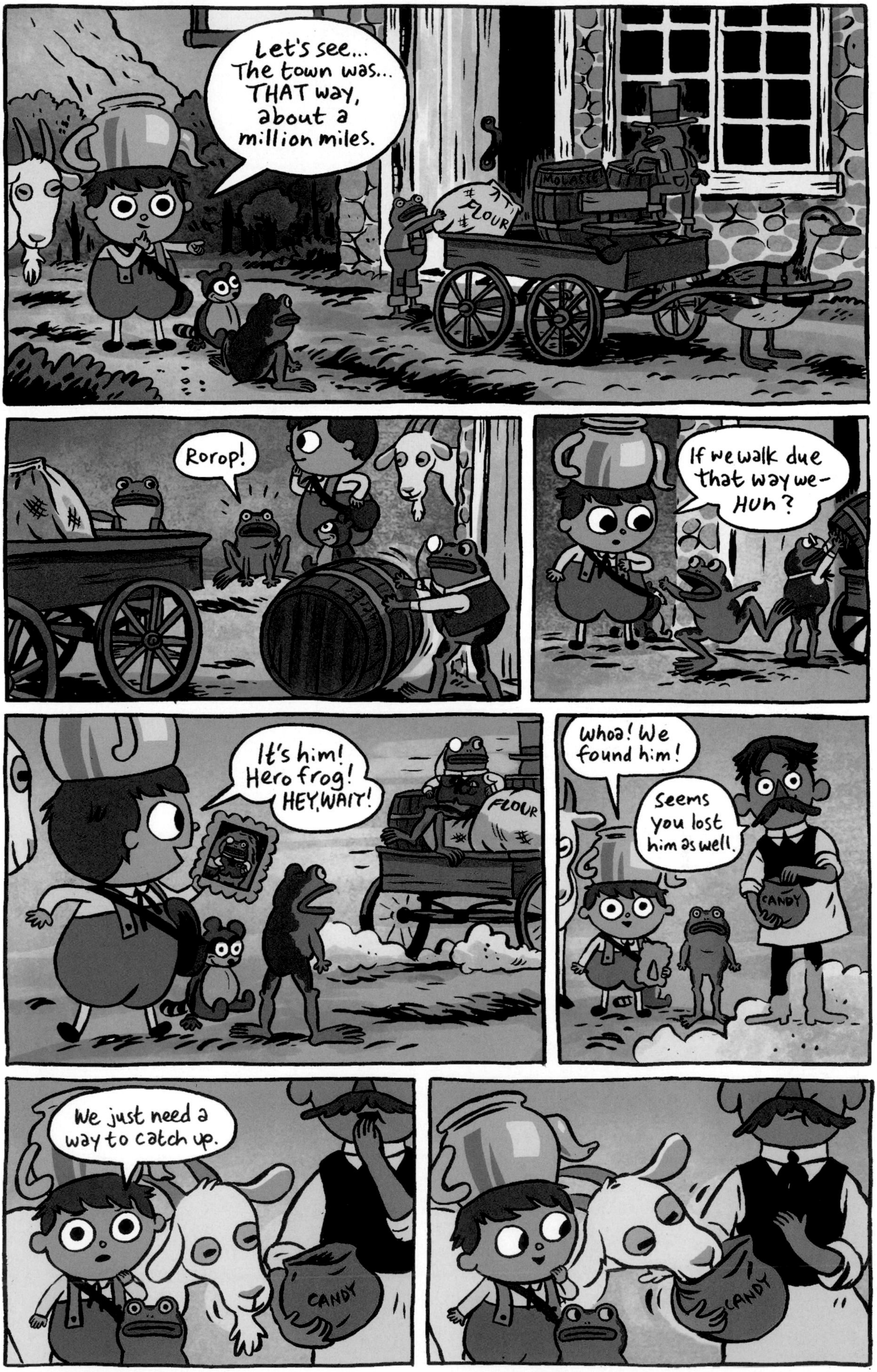

Let's see... The town was... THAT way, about a million miles.
MOLASSE
FLOUR
Rorop!
If we walk due that way we- HUH?
It's him! Hero frog! HEY, WAIT!
FLOUR
Whoa! We found him!
Seems you lost him as well.
CANDY
We just need a way to catch up.
CANDY
CANDY

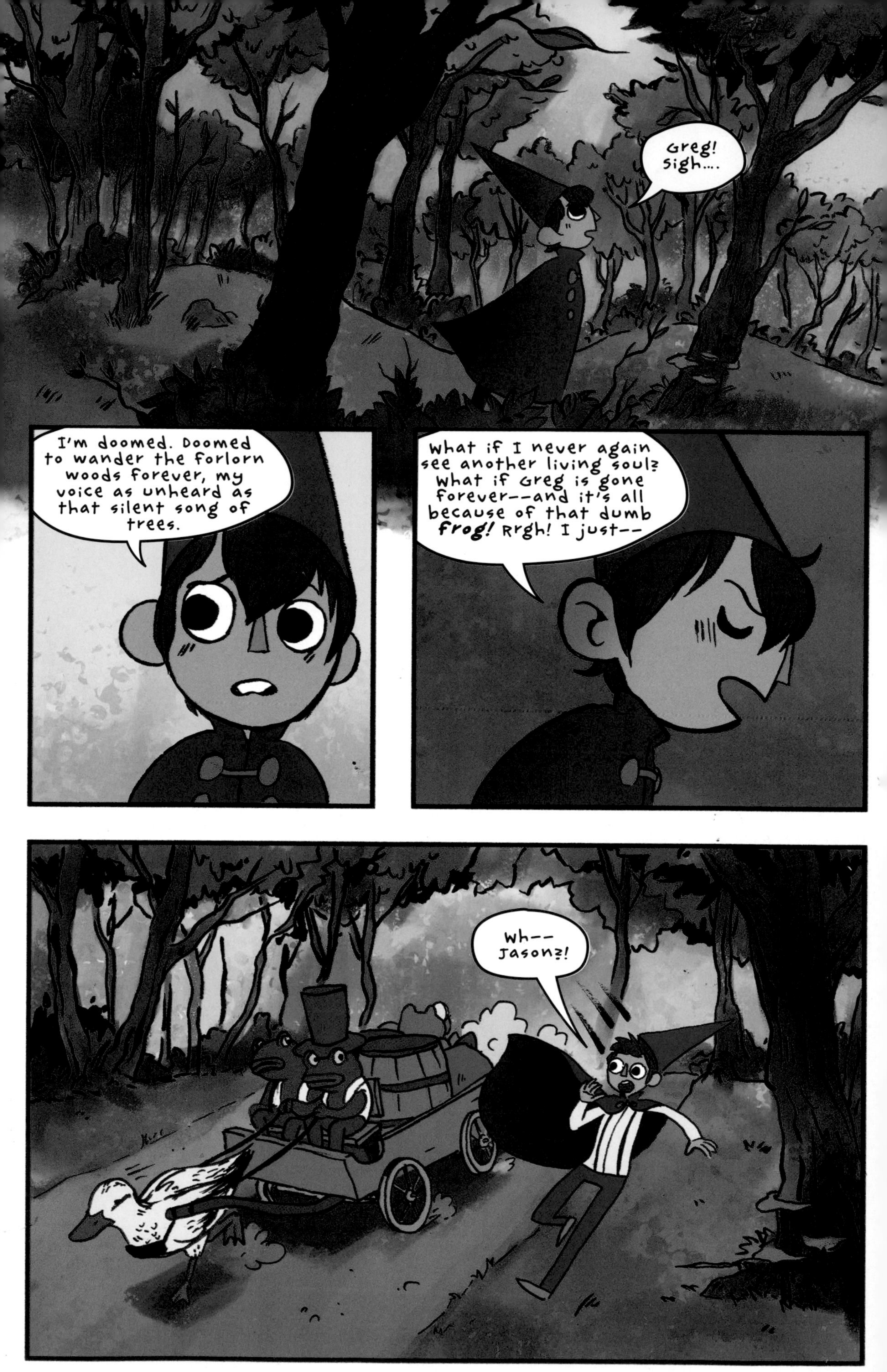
Greg! Sigh....
I'm doomed. Doomed to wander the forlorn woods forever, my voice as unheard as that silent song of trees.
What if I never again see another living soul? What if Greg is gone forever--and it's all because of that dumb **frog!** Rrgh! I just--
Wh-- Jason?!

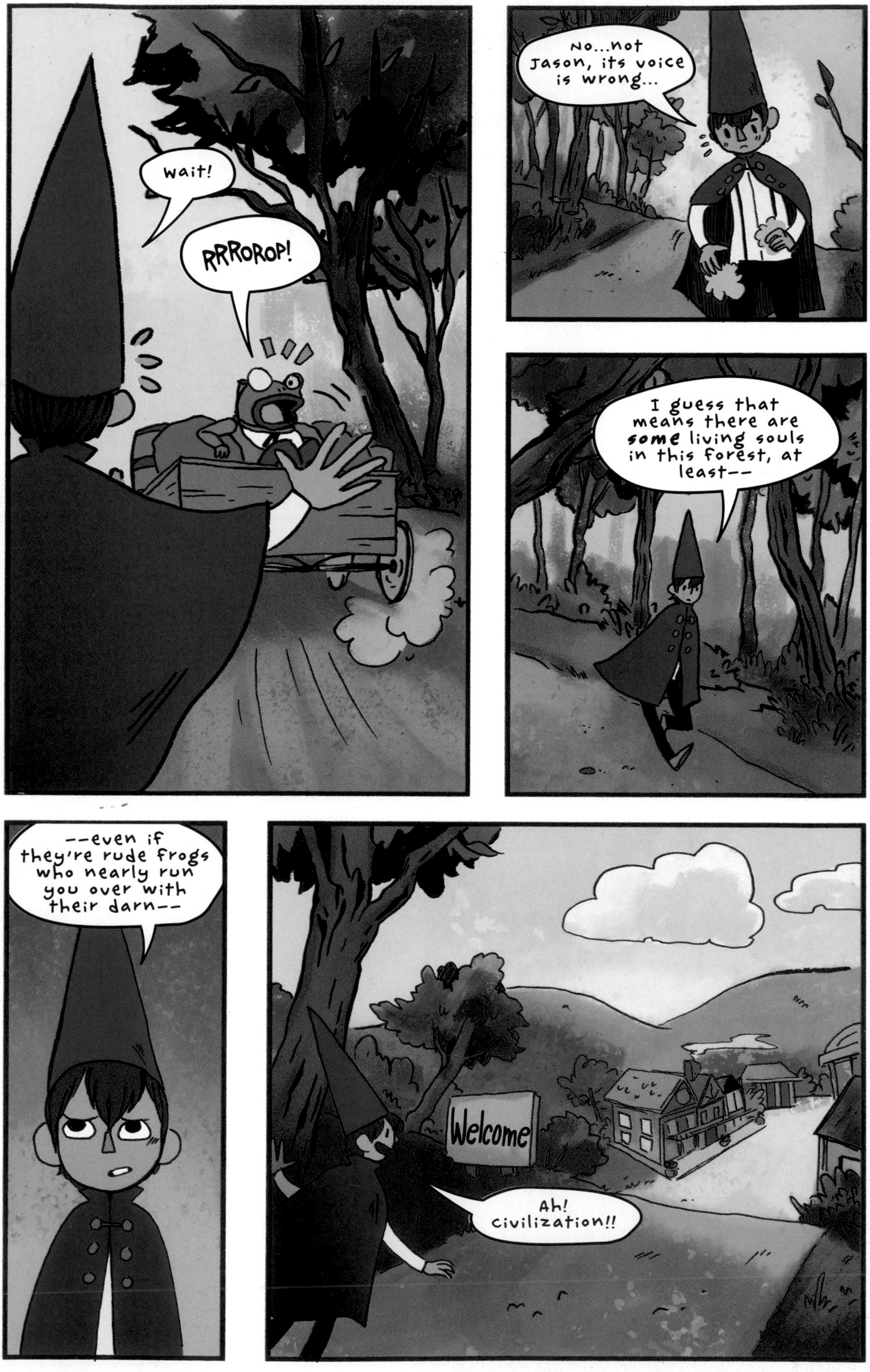
Wait!
RRROROP!
No...not Jason, its voice is wrong...
I guess that means there are **some** living souls in this forest, at least--
--even if they're rude frogs who nearly run you over with their darn--
Welcome
Ah! civilization!!

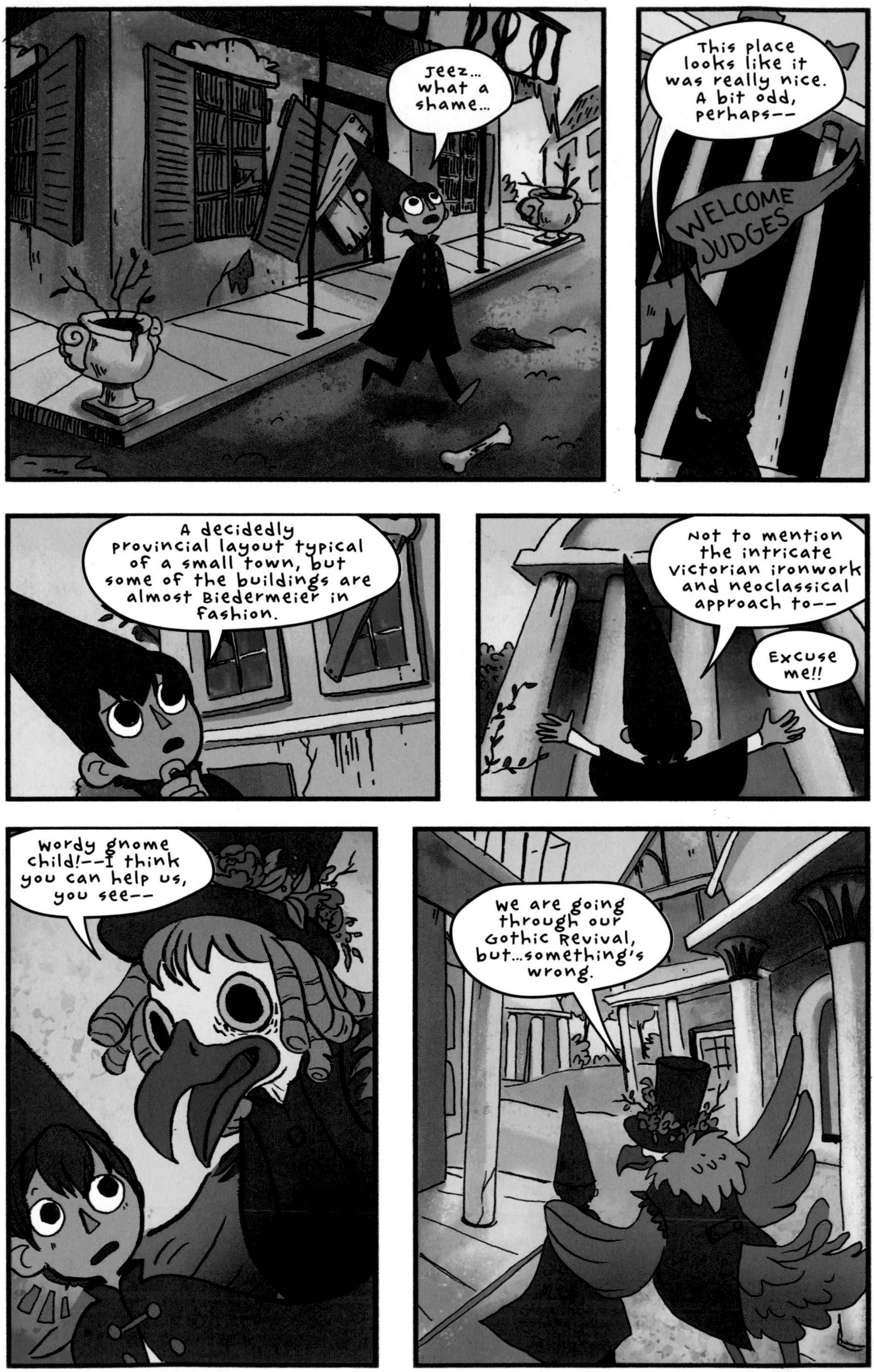
Jeez... what a shame...
This place looks like it was really nice. A bit odd, perhaps--
WELCOME JUDGES
A decidedly provincial layout typical of a small town, but some of the buildings are almost Biedermeier in fashion.
Not to mention the intricate Victorian ironwork and neoclassical approach to--
Excuse me!!
Wordy gnome child!--I think you can help us, you see--
We are going through our Gothic Revival, but...something's wrong.

Gothic Revival? There's nothing Gothic here--look--your buildings are all rounded or square-- Gothic Revival buildings are usually much taller and pointier--

Like your hat?

Uh, yeah, I guess...

Friends!!

We have a new chief of Gothic Fashion!

What! Wait--no, I can't--

YAY!

I have to find my brother, he--

Am I wearing this corset properly?

What's the proper way to wear this?

No, no, this goes under your outfit, not on your head--and *that* is a stocking, not a scarf, besides, I don't think scarves are widely worn in the Gothic Revival period--

I knew you could help us-- you must meet the Bishop Buzzard at once!

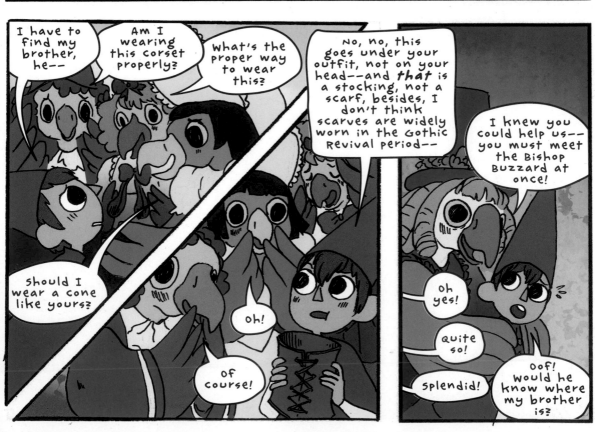

Should I wear a cone like yours?

oh!

of course!

oh yes!

Quite so!

Splendid!

Oof! Would he know where my brother is?

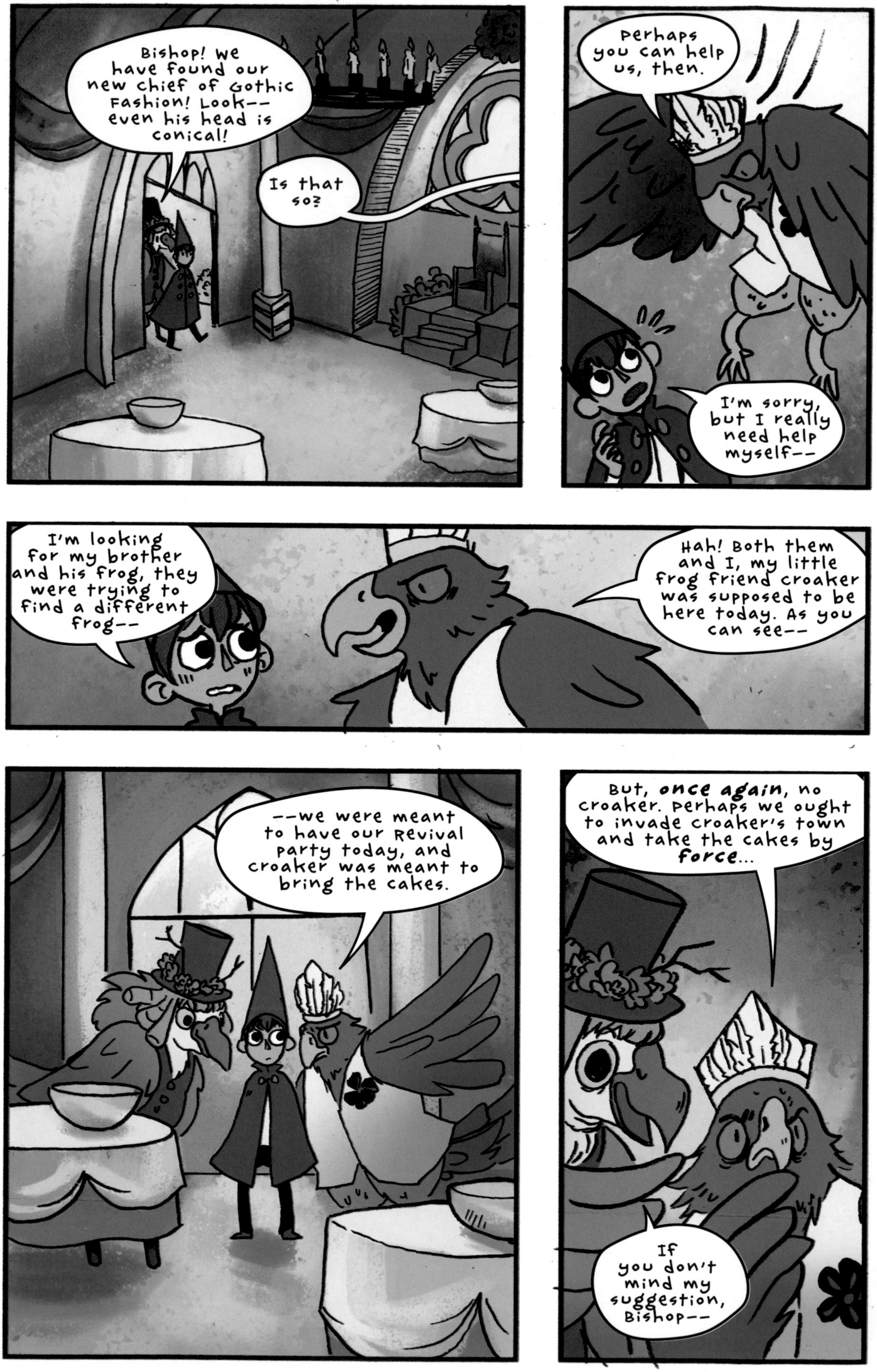
Bishop! We have found our new chief of Gothic Fashion! Look-- even his head is conical!
Is that so?
Perhaps you can help us, then.
I'm sorry, but I really need help myself--
I'm looking for my brother and his frog, they were trying to find a different frog--
Hah! Both them and I, my little frog friend Croaker was supposed to be here today. As you can see--
--we were meant to have our Revival party today, and Croaker was meant to bring the cakes.
But, **once again**, no Croaker. Perhaps we ought to invade Croaker's town and take the cakes by **force**...
If you don't mind my suggestion, Bishop--

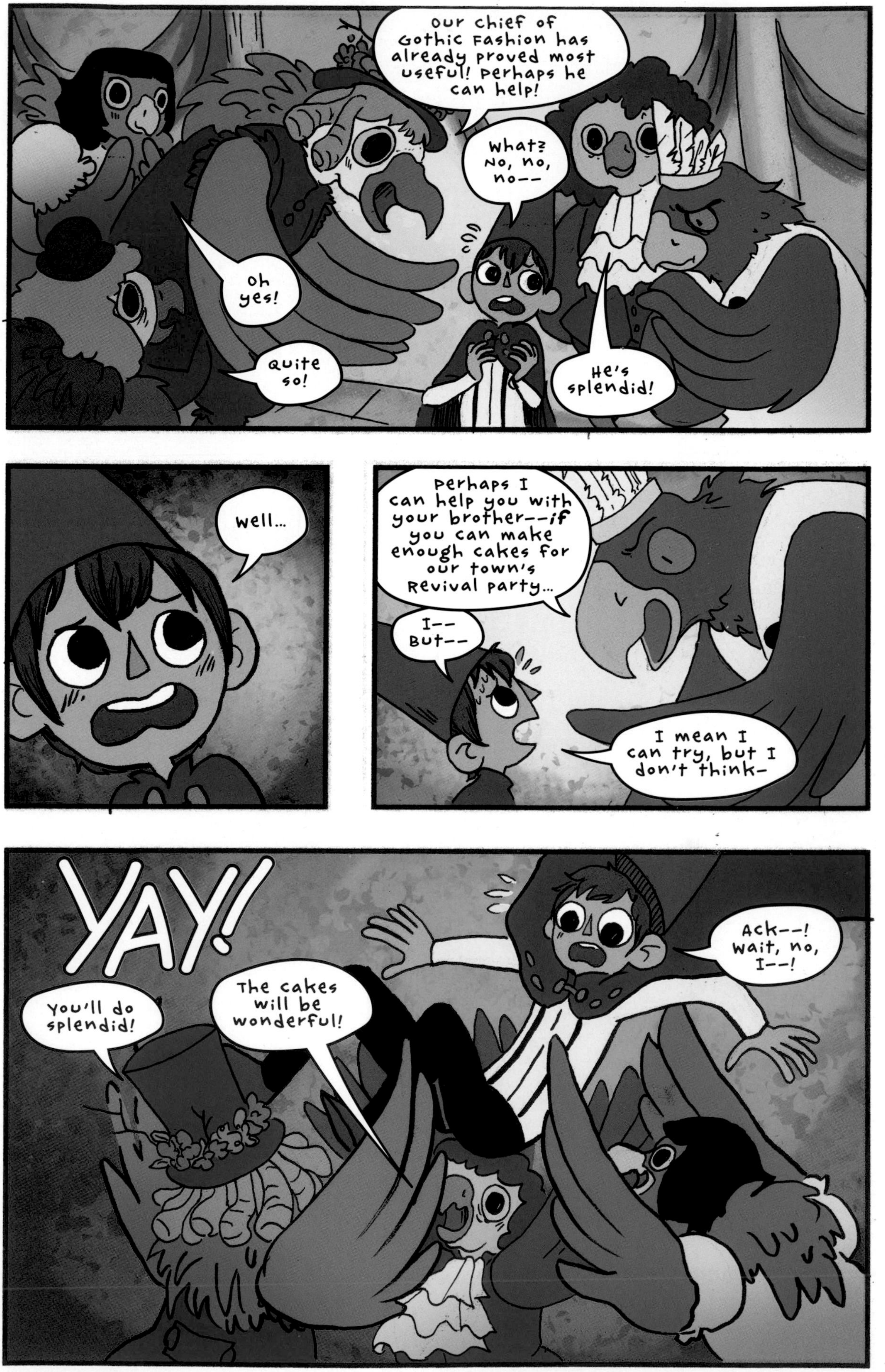

Our chief of Gothic Fashion has already proved most useful! Perhaps he can help!
What? No, no, no--
Oh yes!
Quite so!
He's splendid!
Well...
Perhaps I can help you with your brother--*if* you can make enough cakes for our town's Revival party...
I-- But--
I mean I can try, but I don't think-
YAY!
Ack--! Wait, no, I--!
You'll do splendid!
The cakes will be wonderful!

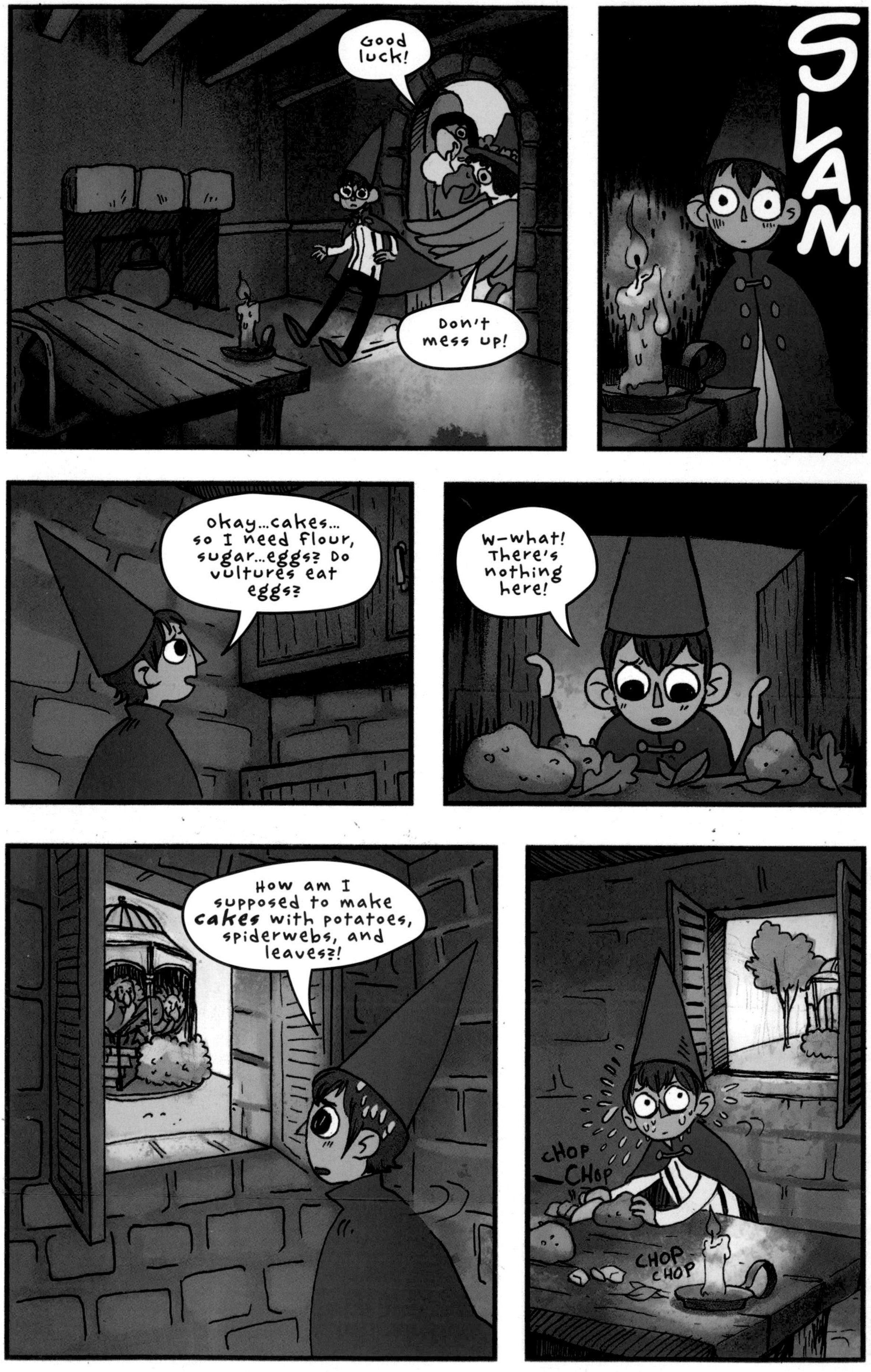
Good luck!
Don't mess up!
SLAM
Okay...cakes... so I need flour, sugar...eggs? Do vultures eat eggs?
W-what! There's nothing here!
How am I supposed to make cakes with potatoes, spiderwebs, and leaves?!
CHOP CHOP
CHOP CHOP

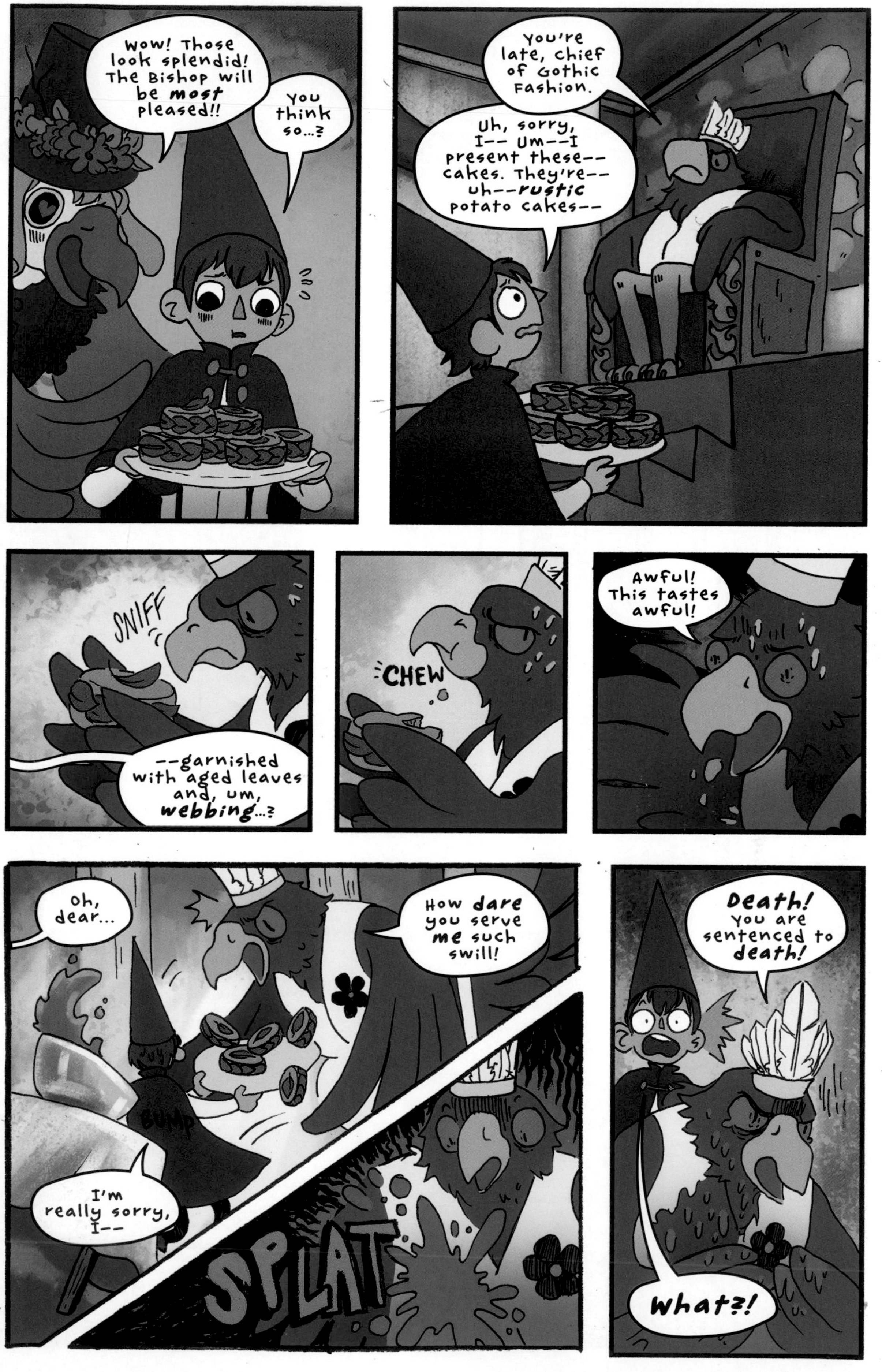
Wow! Those look splendid! The Bishop will be **most** pleased!!
You think so...?
You're late, chief of Gothic Fashion.
Uh, sorry, I-- Um--I present these--cakes. They're--uh--**rustic** potato cakes--
SNIFF
--garnished with aged leaves and, um, **webbing**...?
CHEW
Awful! This tastes awful!
Oh, dear...
BUMP
How **dare** you serve **me** such swill!
I'm really sorry, I--
SPLAT
Death! You are sentenced to **death!**
What?!

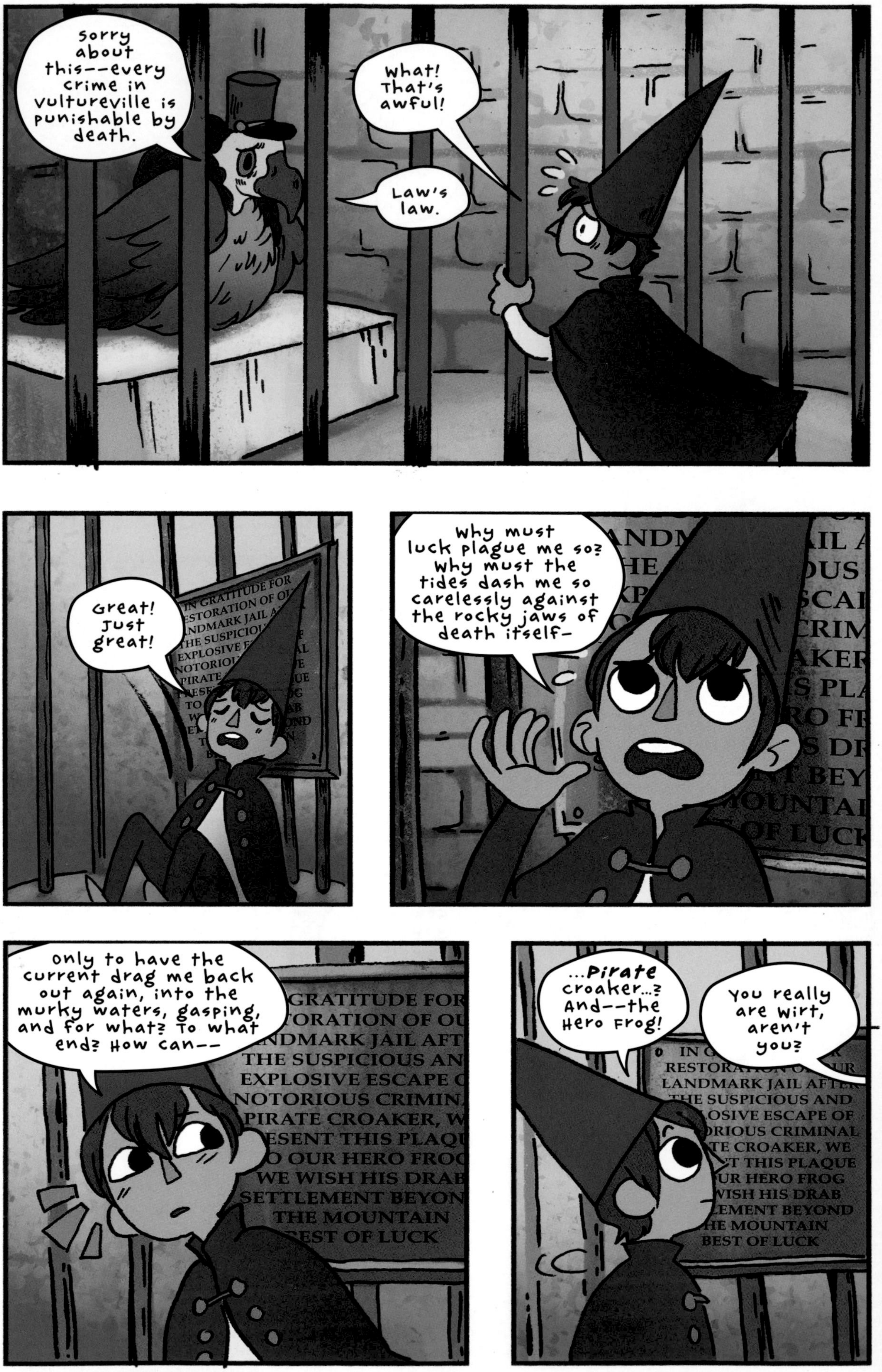

sorry about this--every crime in vultureville is punishable by death.
What! That's awful!
Law's law.
Great! Just great!
Why must luck plague me so? Why must the tides dash me so carelessly against the rocky jaws of death itself—
only to have the current drag me back out again, into the murky waters, gasping, and for what? To what end? How can--
...Pirate croaker...? And--the Hero Frog!
You really are Wirt, aren't you?

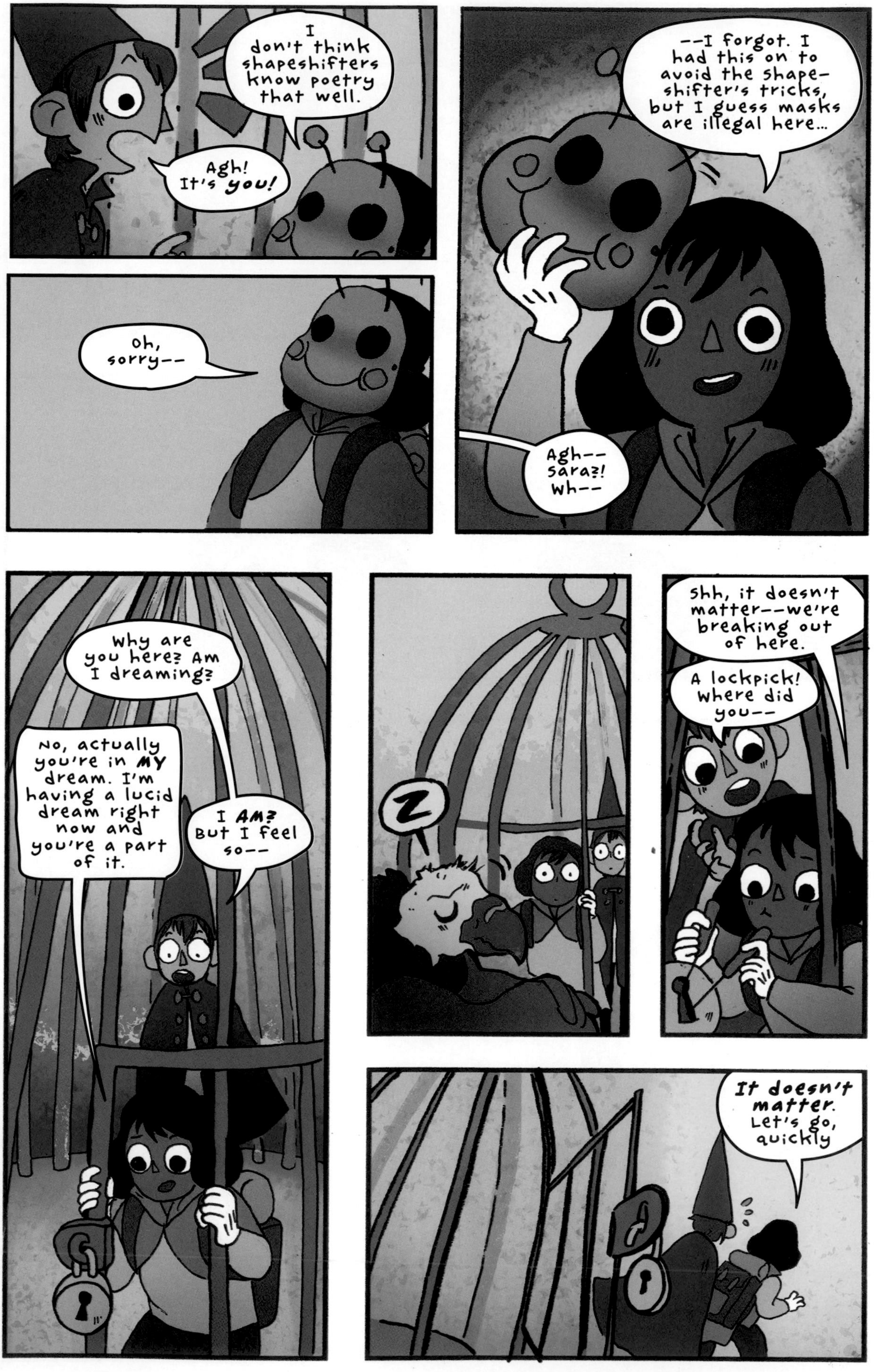
I don't think shapeshifters know poetry that well.
Agh! It's you!
Oh, sorry--
--I forgot. I had this on to avoid the shape-shifter's tricks, but I guess masks are illegal here...
Agh-- Sara?! Wh--
Why are you here? Am I dreaming?
No, actually you're in MY dream. I'm having a lucid dream right now and you're a part of it.
I AM? But I feel so--
Z
Shh, it doesn't matter--we're breaking out of here.
A lockpick! Where did you--
It doesn't matter. Let's go, quickly

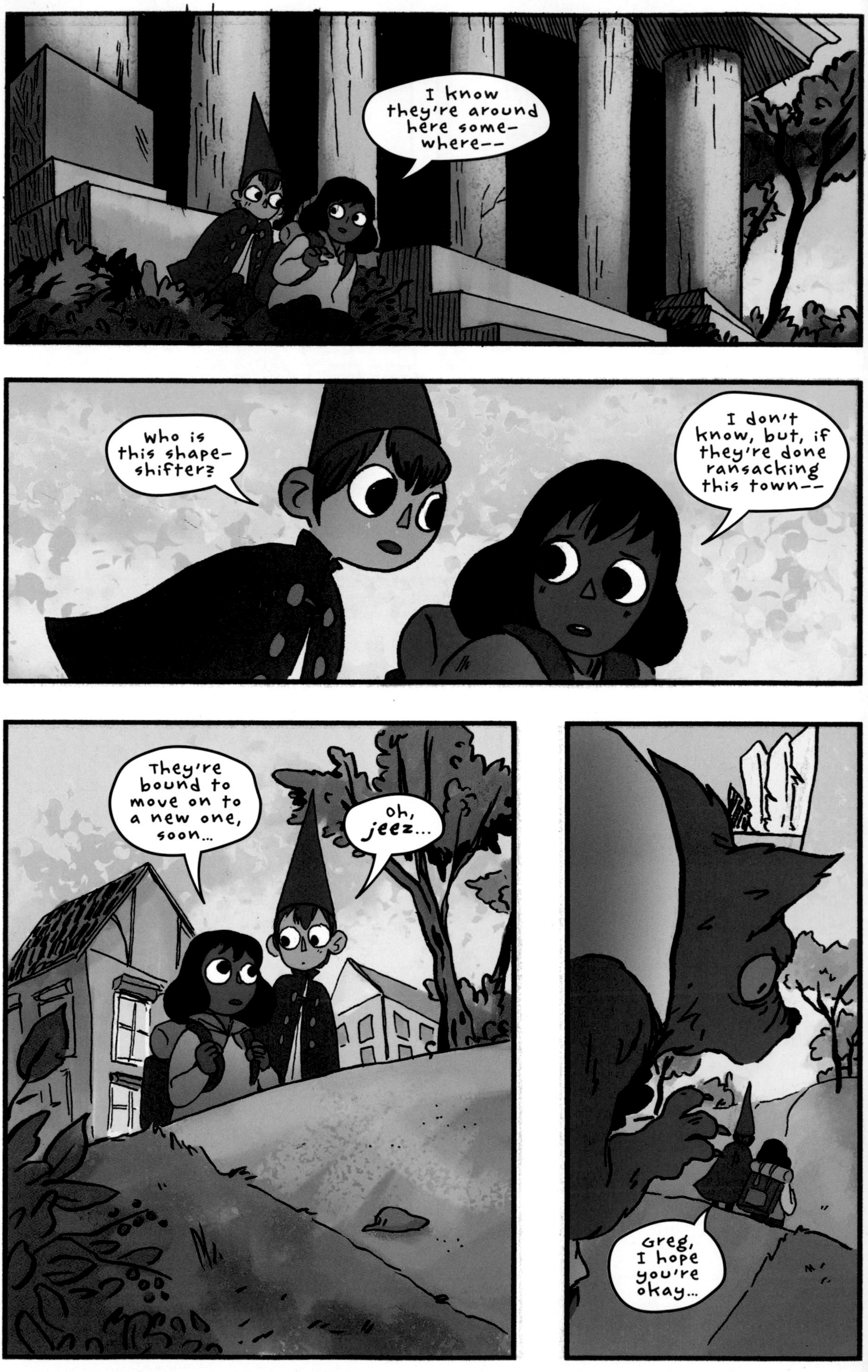
I know they're around here some-where--
Who is this shape-shifter?
I don't know, but, if they're done ransacking this town--
They're bound to move on to a new one, soon...
oh, jeez...
Greg, I hope you're okay...

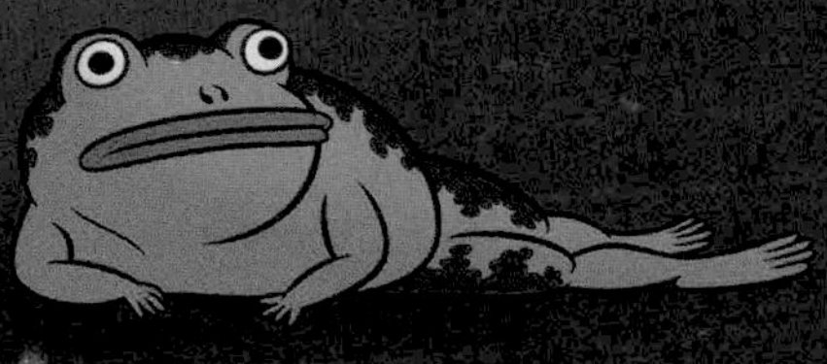

OOF!

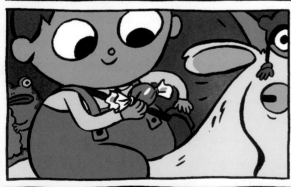

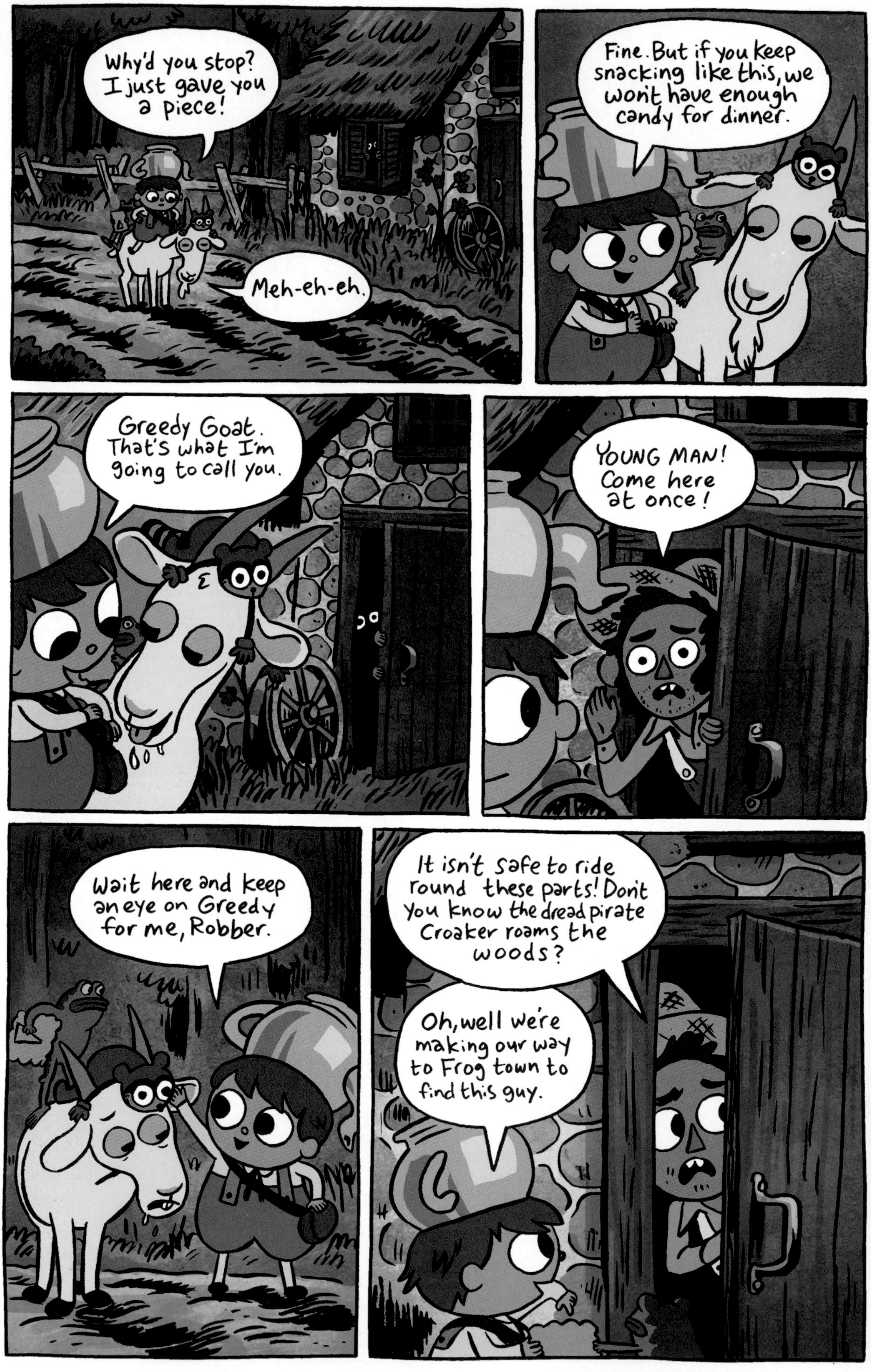
Why'd you stop? I just gave you a piece!
Meh-eh-eh.
Fine. But if you keep snacking like this, we won't have enough candy for dinner.
Greedy Goat. That's what I'm going to call you.
YOUNG MAN! Come here at once!
Wait here and keep an eye on Greedy for me, Robber.
It isn't safe to ride round these parts! Don't you know the dread pirate Croaker roams the woods?
Oh, well we're making our way to Frog town to find this guy.

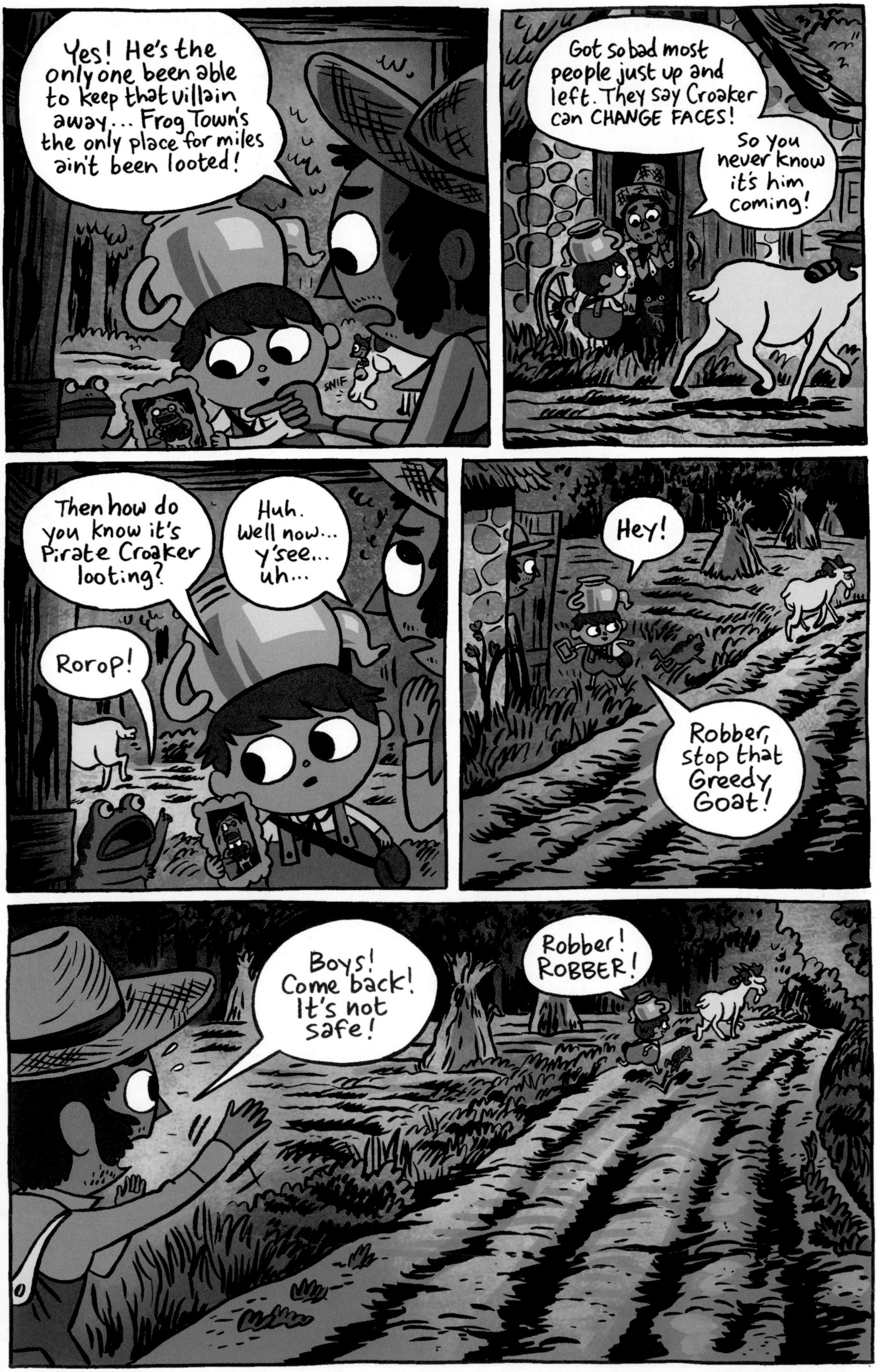

Yes! He's the only one been able to keep that villain away... Frog Town's the only place for miles ain't been looted!
SNIF
Got so bad most people just up and left. They say Croaker can CHANGE FACES!
So you never know it's him coming!
Then how do you know it's Pirate Croaker looting?
Huh. Well now... y'see... uh...
Rorop!
Hey!
Robber, stop that Greedy Goat!
Boys! Come back! It's not safe!
Robber! ROBBER!

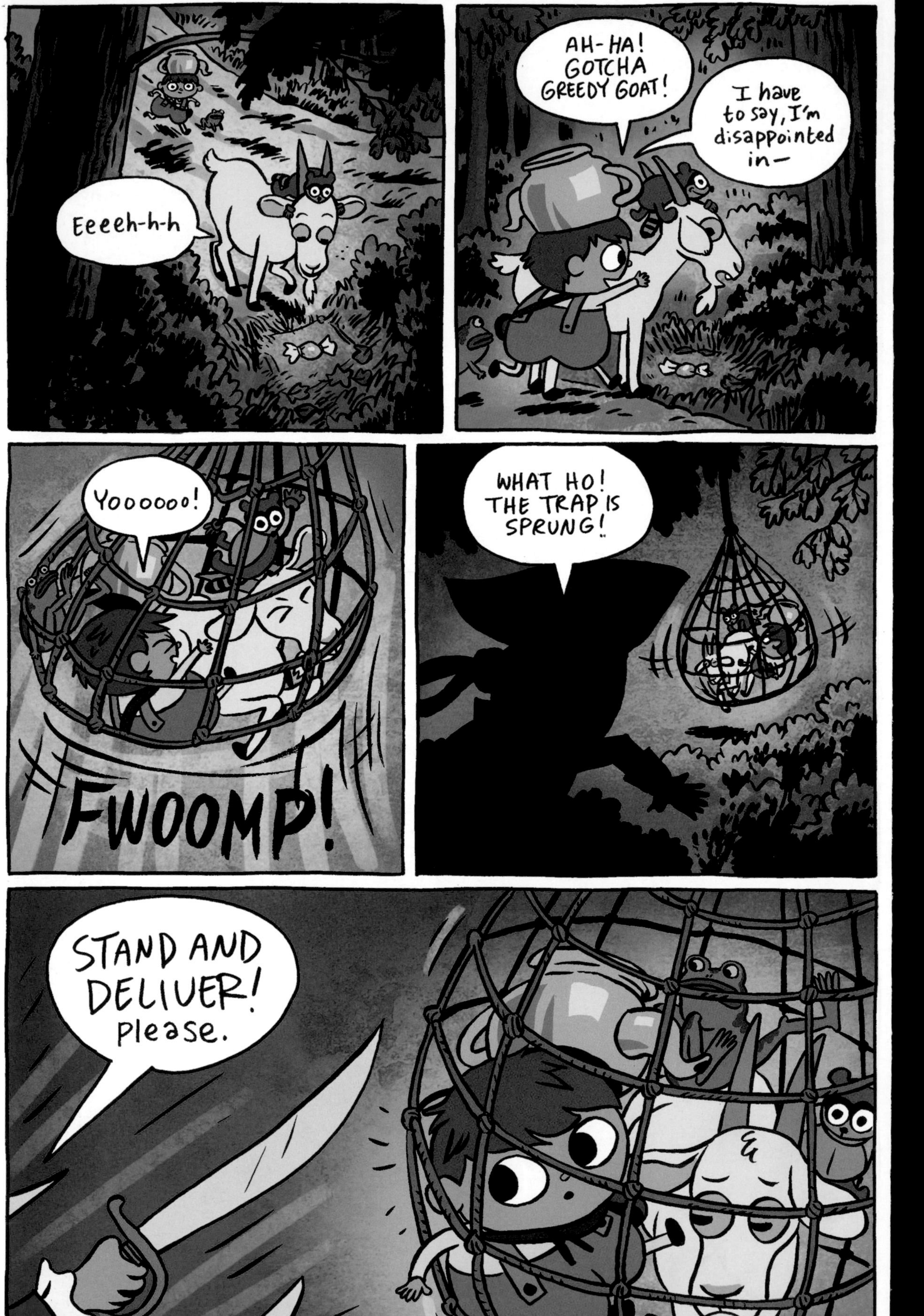
Eeeeh-h-h
AH-HA! GOTCHA GREEDY GOAT!
I have to say, I'm disappointed in—
Yoooooo!
FWOOMP!
WHAT HO! THE TRAP IS SPRUNG!
STAND AND DELIVER! please.

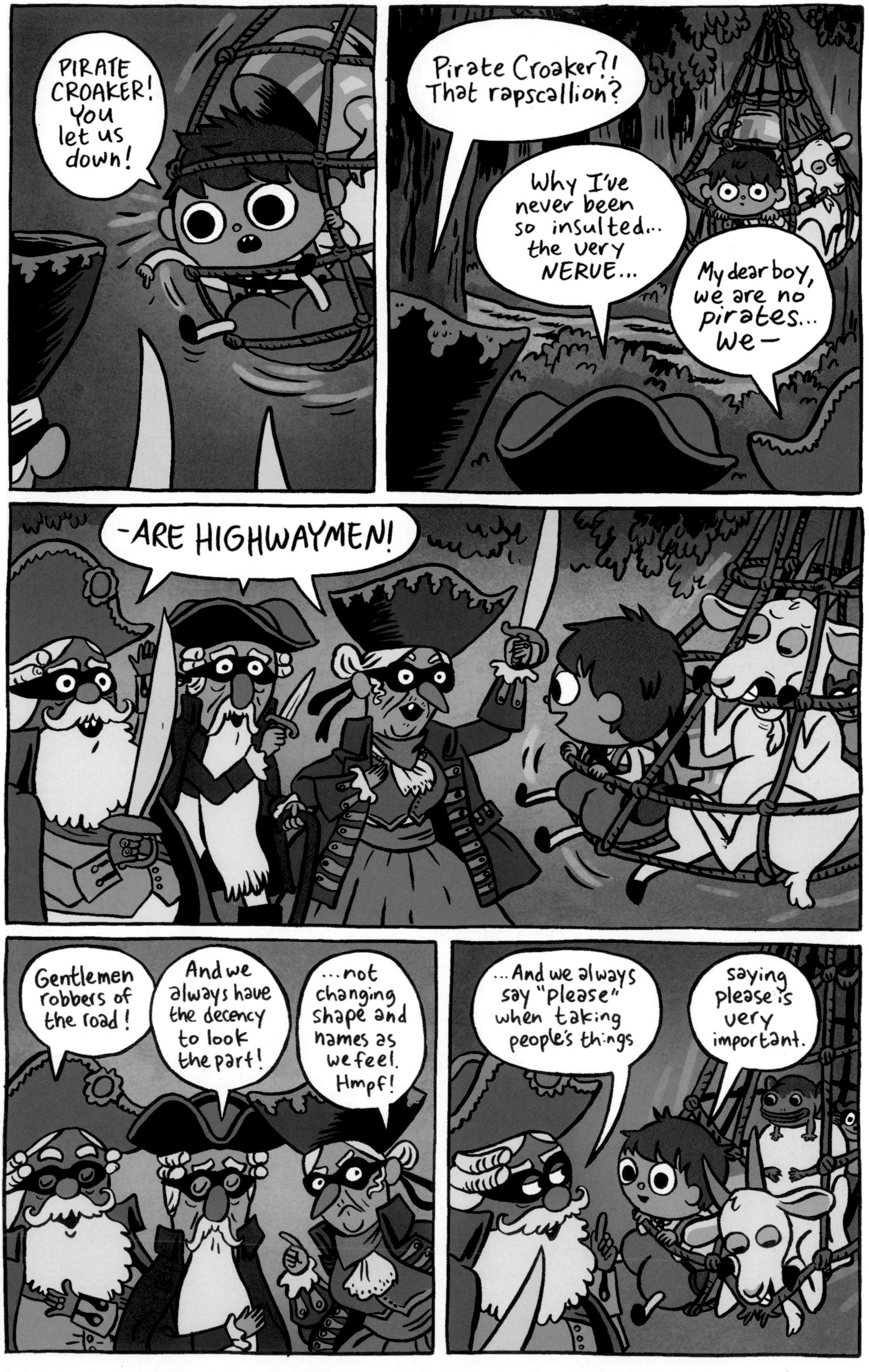
PIRATE CROAKER! You let us down!
Pirate Croaker?! That rapscallion?
Why I've never been so insulted... the very NERVE...
My dear boy, we are no pirates... We—
-ARE HIGHWAYMEN!
Gentlemen robbers of the road!
And we always have the decency to look the part!
...not changing shape and names as we feel. Hmpf!
...And we always say "please" when taking people's things
saying please is very important.

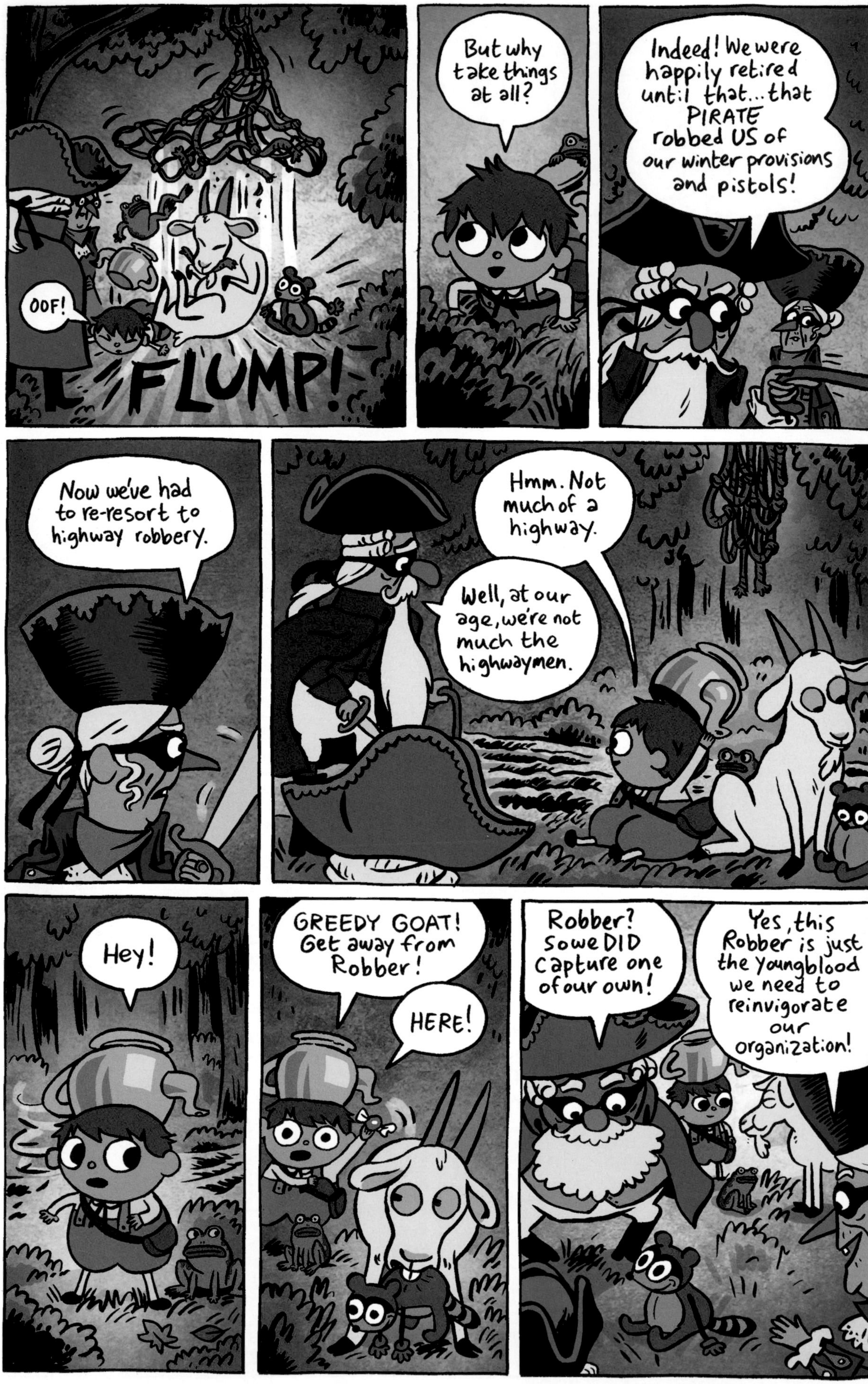
OOF!
FLUMP!
But why take things at all?
Indeed! We were happily retired until that...that PIRATE robbed US of our winter provisions and pistols!
Now we've had to re-resort to highway robbery.
Hmm. Not much of a highway.
Well, at our age, we're not much the highwaymen.
Hey!
GREEDY GOAT! Get away from Robber!
HERE!
Robber? So we DID capture one of our own!
Yes, this Robber is just the youngblood we need to reinvigorate our organization!

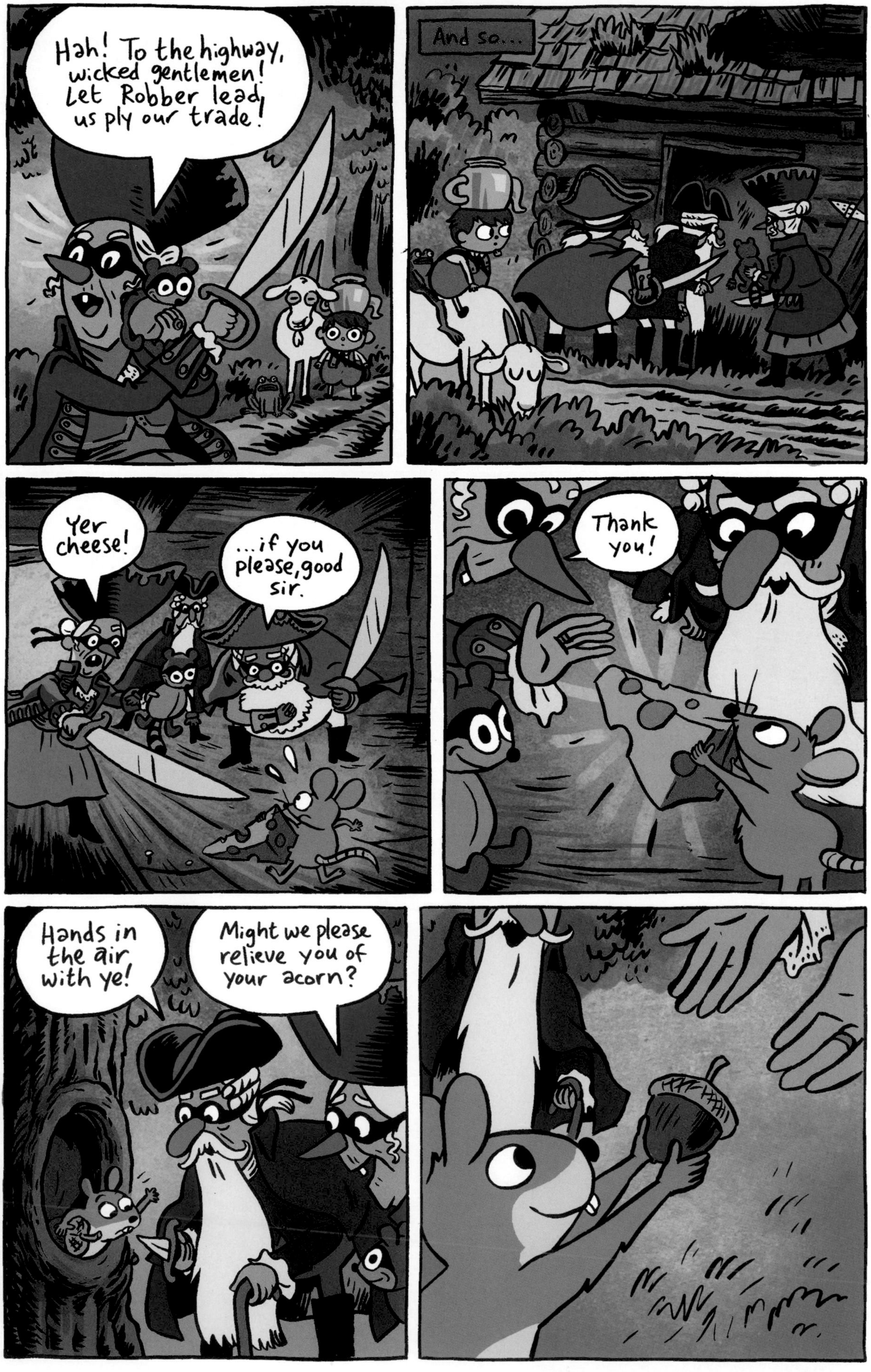
Hah! To the highway, wicked gentlemen! Let Robber lead us ply our trade!
And so...
Yer cheese!
...if you please, good sir.
Thank you!
Hands in the air with ye!
Might we please relieve you of your acorn?

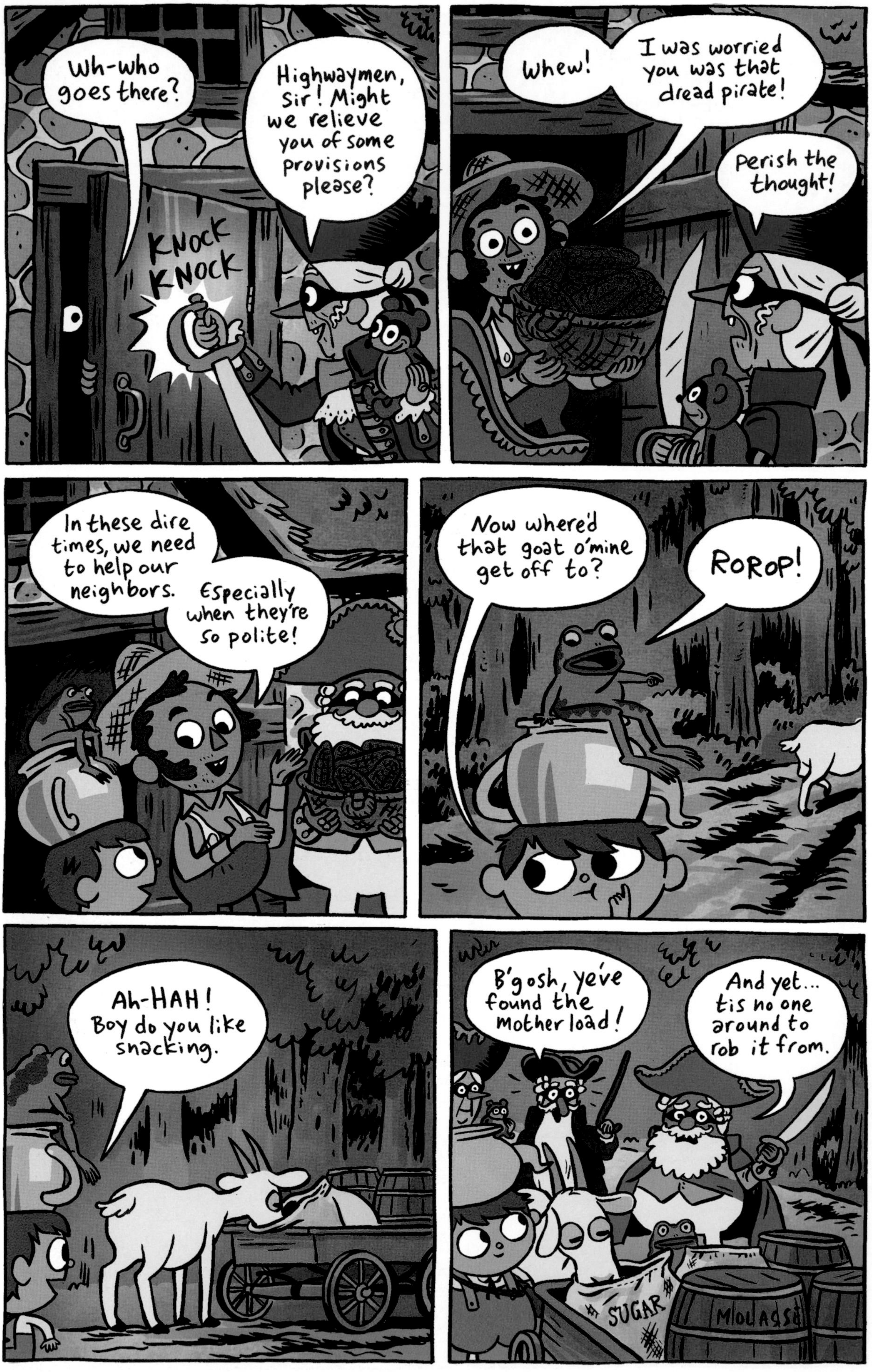
Wh-who goes there?
KNOCK KNOCK
Highwaymen, Sir! Might we relieve you of some provisions please?
Whew!
I was worried you was that dread pirate!
Perish the thought!
In these dire times, we need to help our neighbors.
Especially when they're so polite!
Now where'd that goat o'mine get off to?
ROROP!
Ah-HAH! Boy do you like snacking.
B'gosh, ye've found the mother load!
And yet... tis no one around to rob it from.
SUGAR
MOLASSE

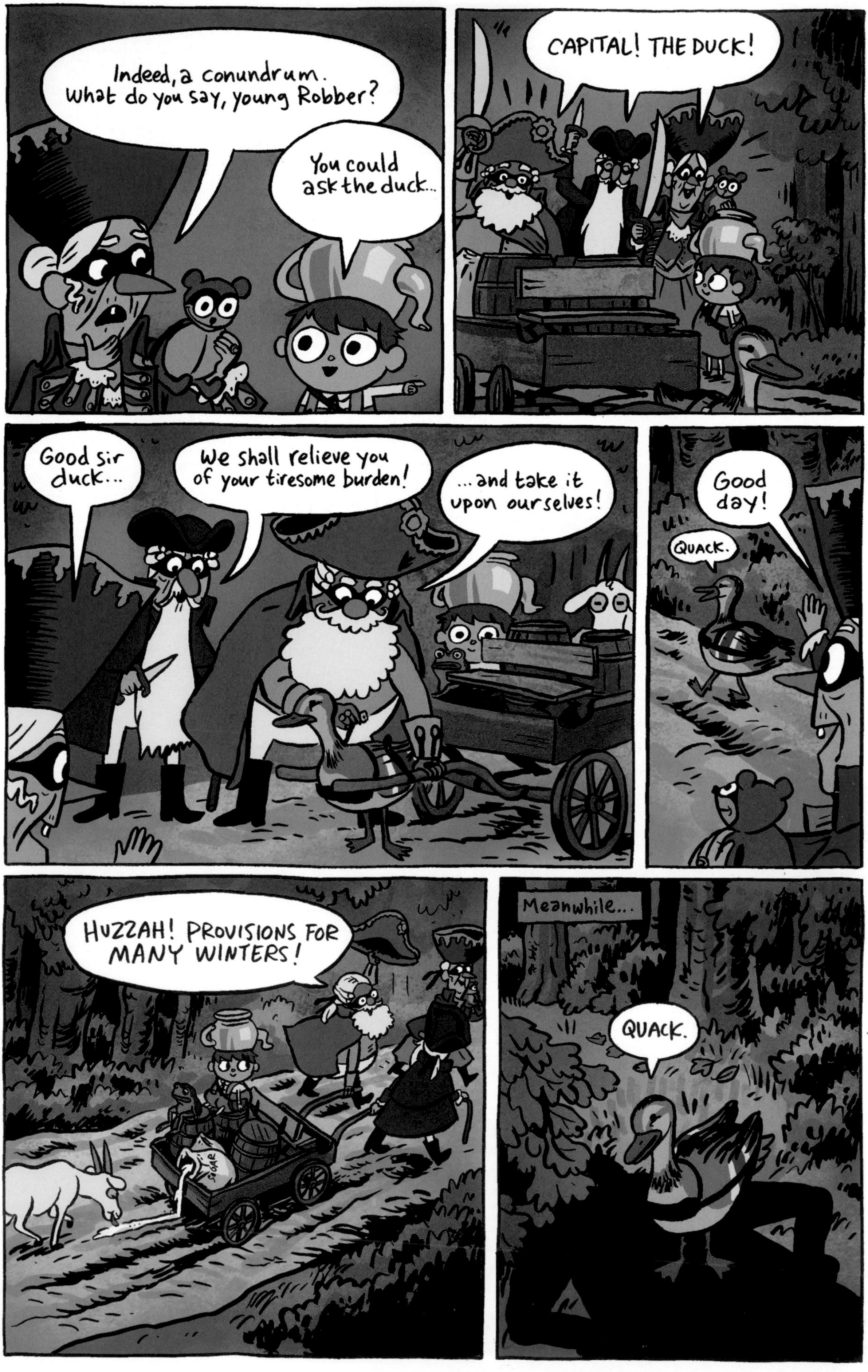
Indeed, a conundrum. What do you say, young Robber?
You could ask the duck...
CAPITAL! THE DUCK!
Good sir duck...
We shall relieve you of your tiresome burden!
...and take it upon ourselves!
Good day!
QUACK.
HUZZAH! PROVISIONS FOR MANY WINTERS!
SUGAR
Meanwhile...
QUACK.

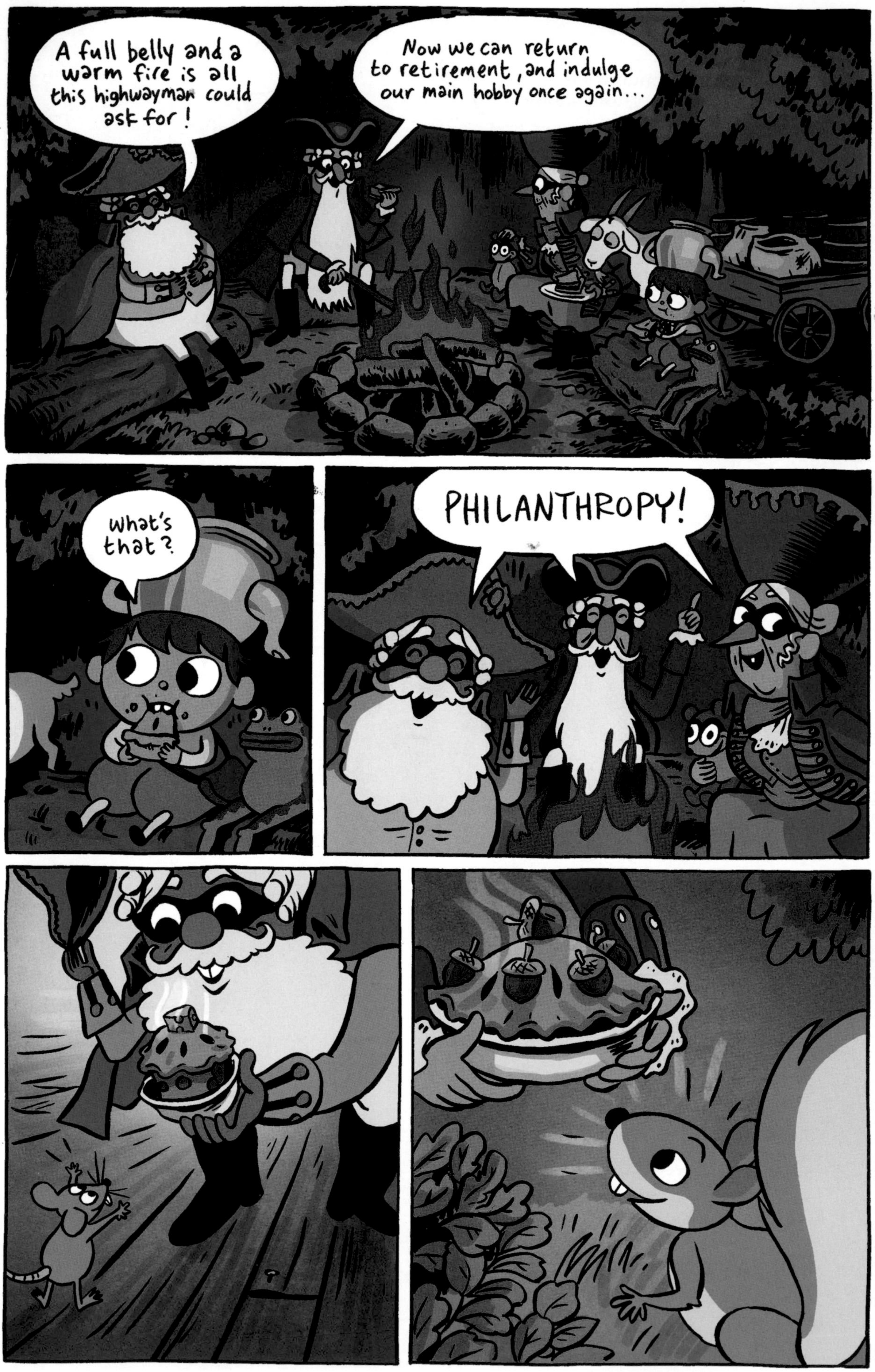
A full belly and a warm fire is all this highwayman could ask for!
Now we can return to retirement, and indulge our main hobby once again...
What's that?
PHILANTHROPY!

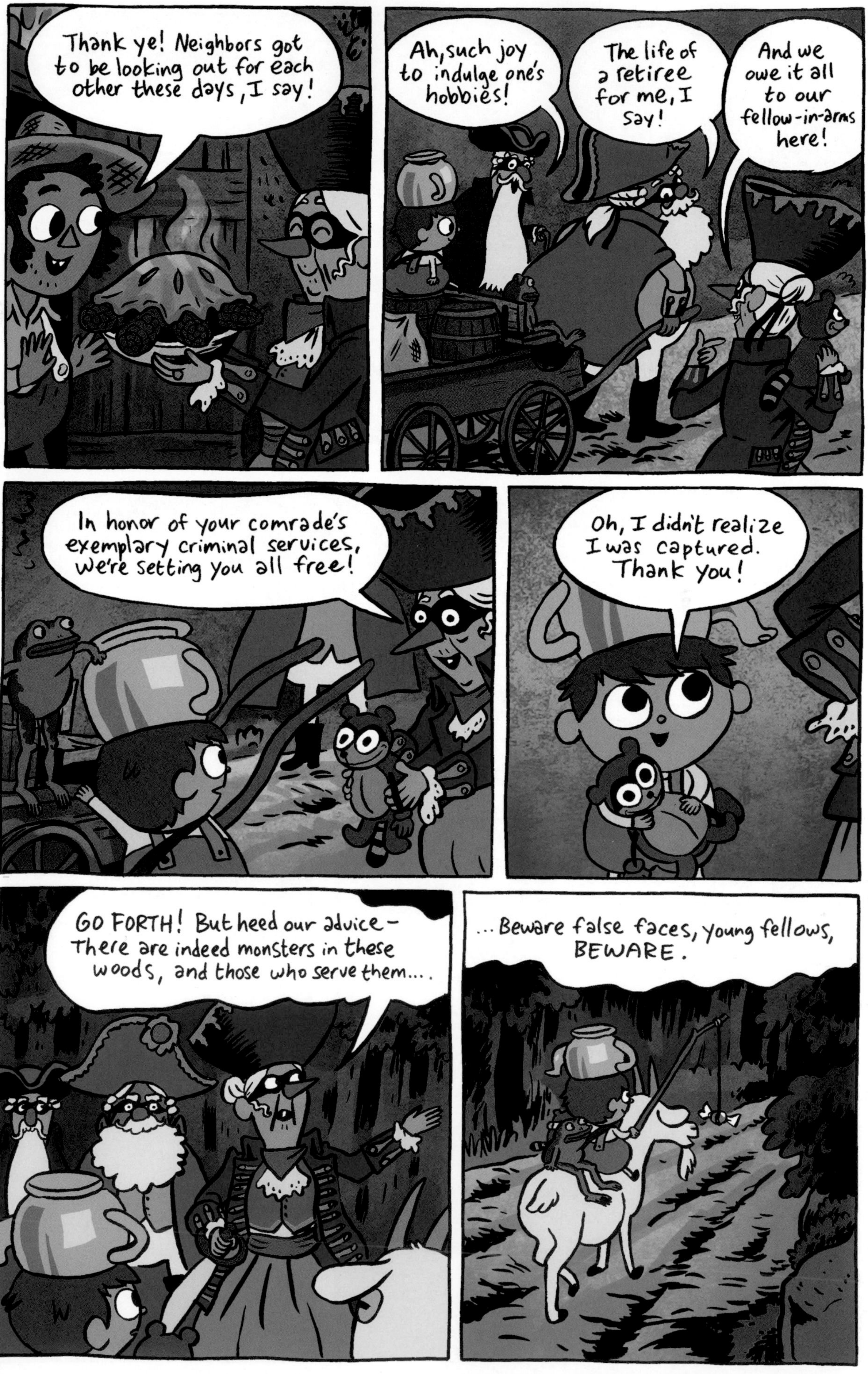
Thank ye! Neighbors got to be looking out for each other these days, I say!
Ah, such joy to indulge one's hobbies!
The life of a retiree for me, I say!
And we owe it all to our fellow-in-arms here!
In honor of your comrade's exemplary criminal services, we're setting you all free!
Oh, I didn't realize I was captured. Thank you!
GO FORTH! But heed our advice - There are indeed monsters in these woods, and those who serve them....
... Beware false faces, young fellows, BEWARE.

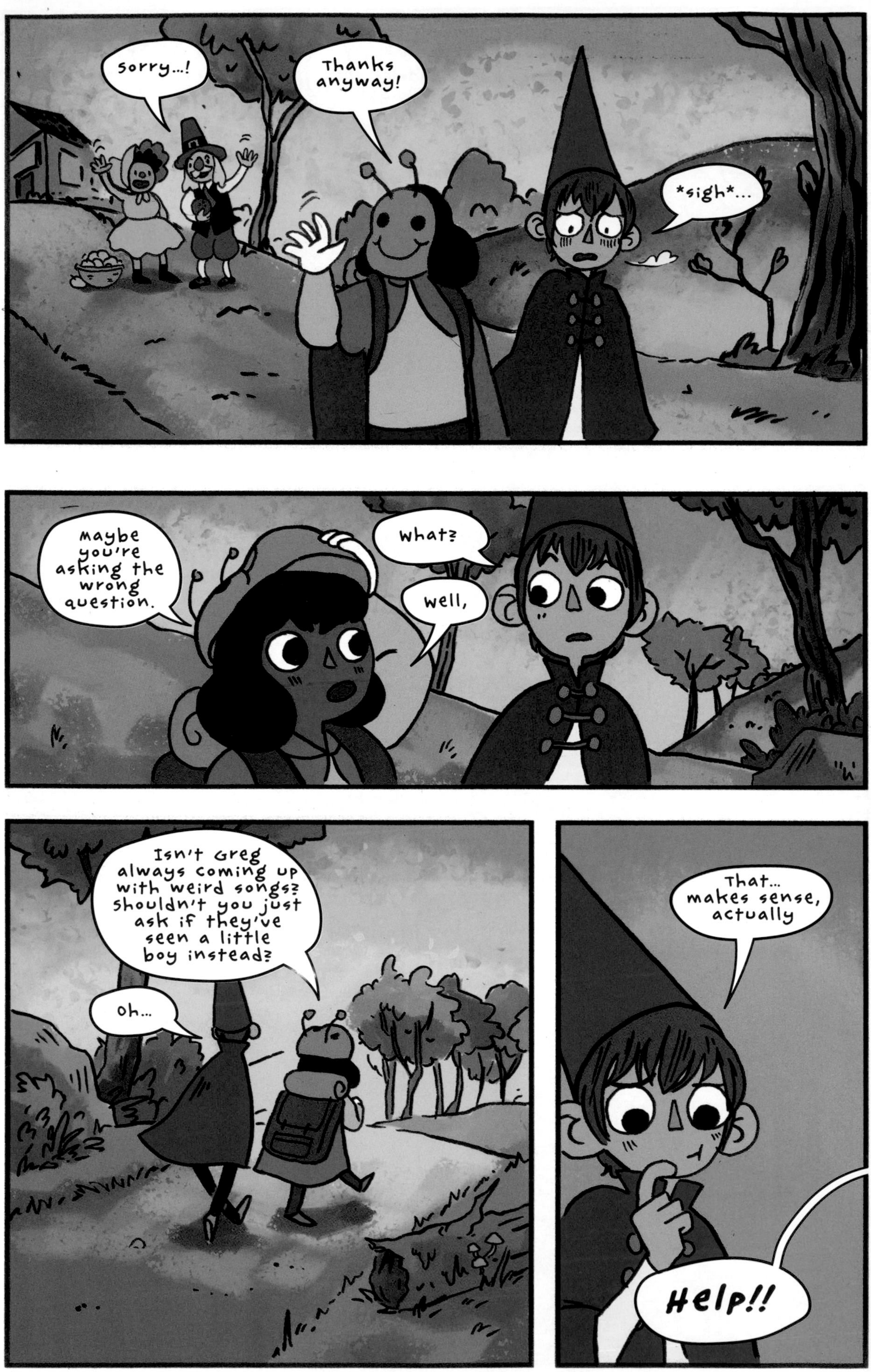
Sorry...!
Thanks anyway!
sigh...
Maybe you're asking the wrong question.
What?
Well,
Isn't Greg always coming up with weird songs? Shouldn't you just ask if they've seen a little boy instead?
Oh...
That... makes sense, actually
Help!!

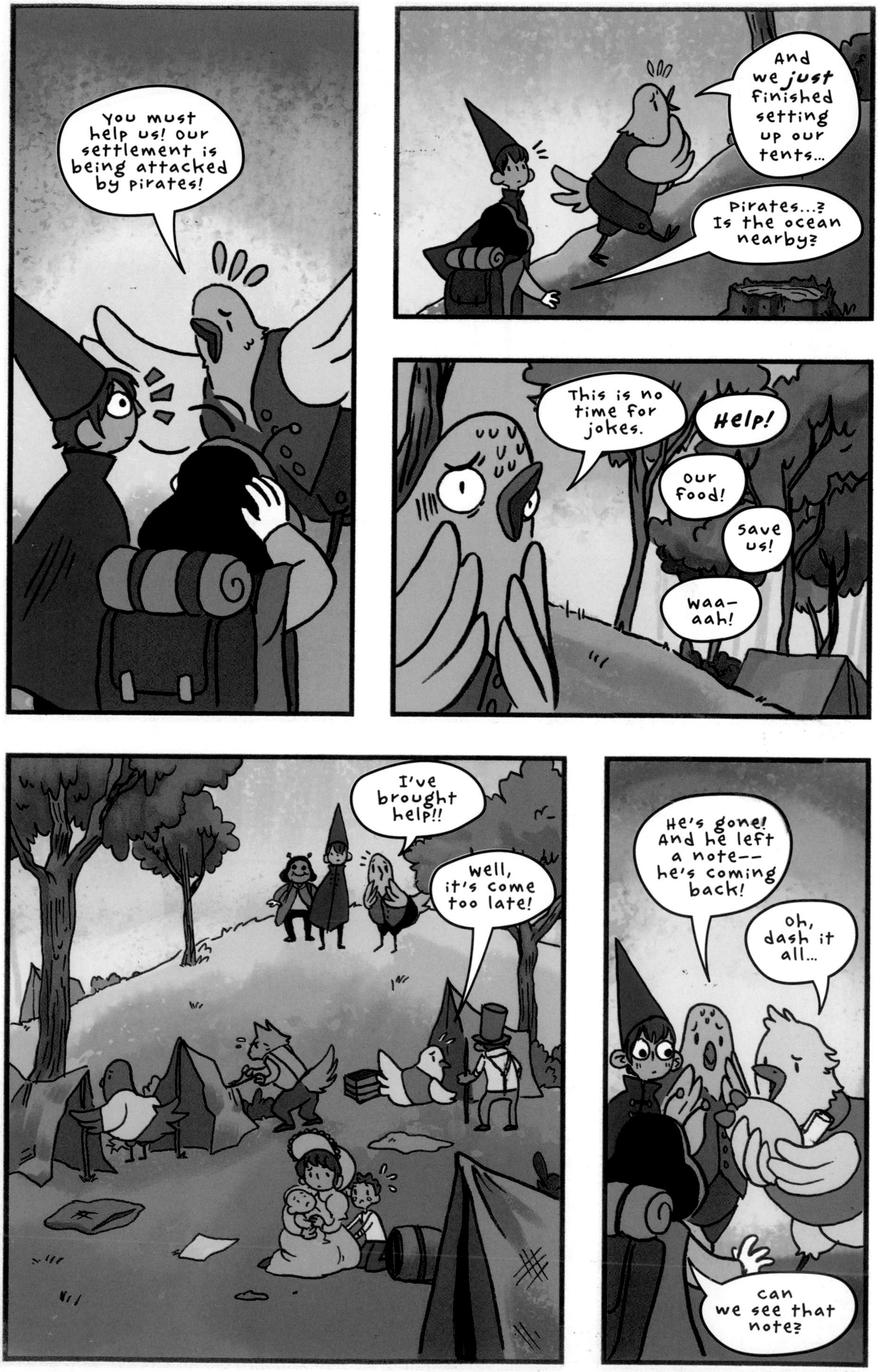
You must help us! Our settlement is being attacked by pirates!
And we *just* finished setting up our tents...
Pirates...? Is the ocean nearby?
This is no time for jokes.
Help!
Our food!
Save us!
Waa-aah!
I've brought help!!
Well, it's come too late!
He's gone! And he left a note-- he's coming back!
Oh, dash it all...
Can we see that note?

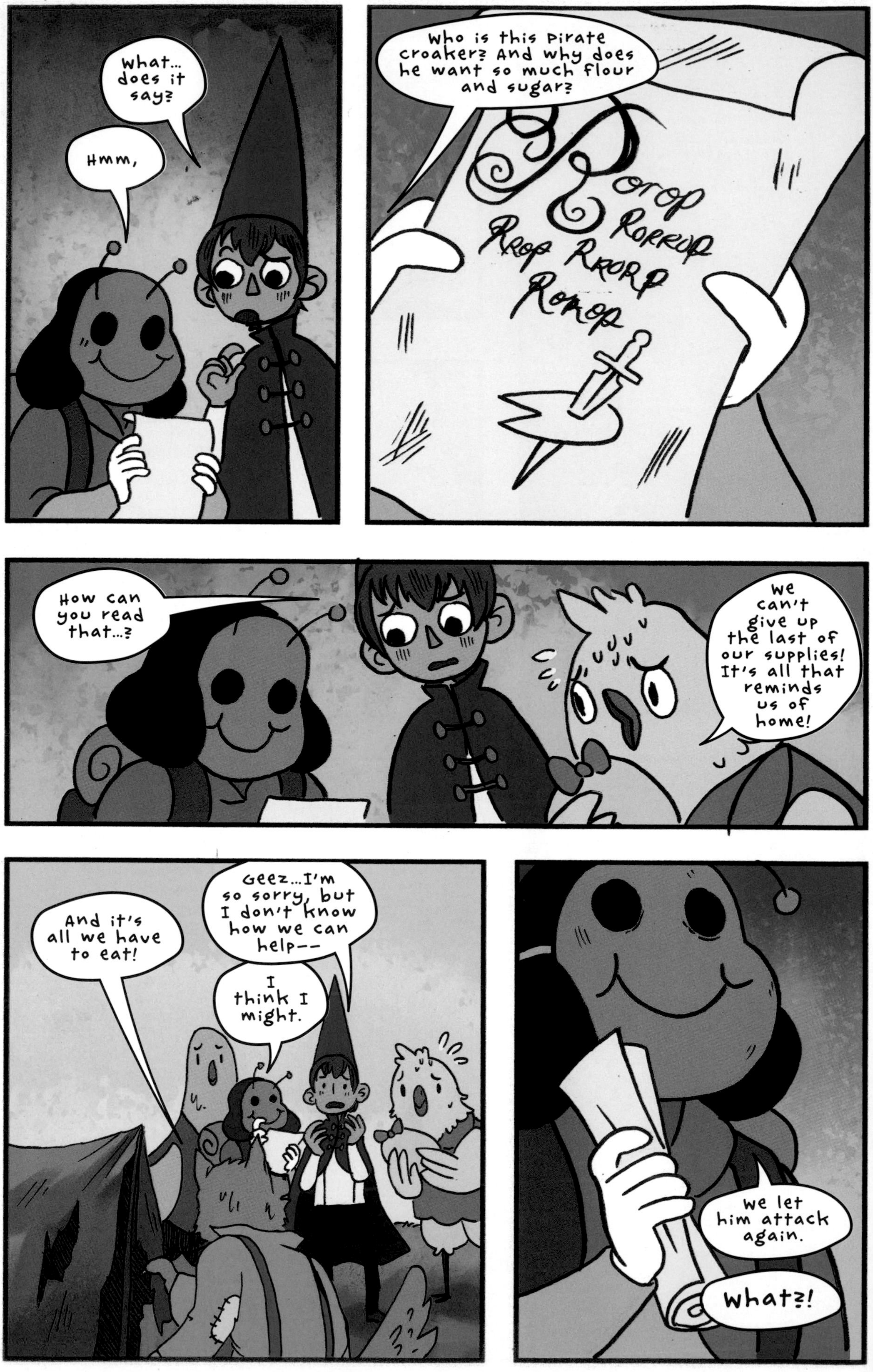
What... does it say?
Hmm,
Who is this pirate croaker? And why does he want so much flour and sugar?
How can you read that...?
We can't give up the last of our supplies! It's all that reminds us of home!
And it's all we have to eat!
Geez...I'm so sorry, but I don't know how we can help--
I think I might.
We let him attack again.
What?!

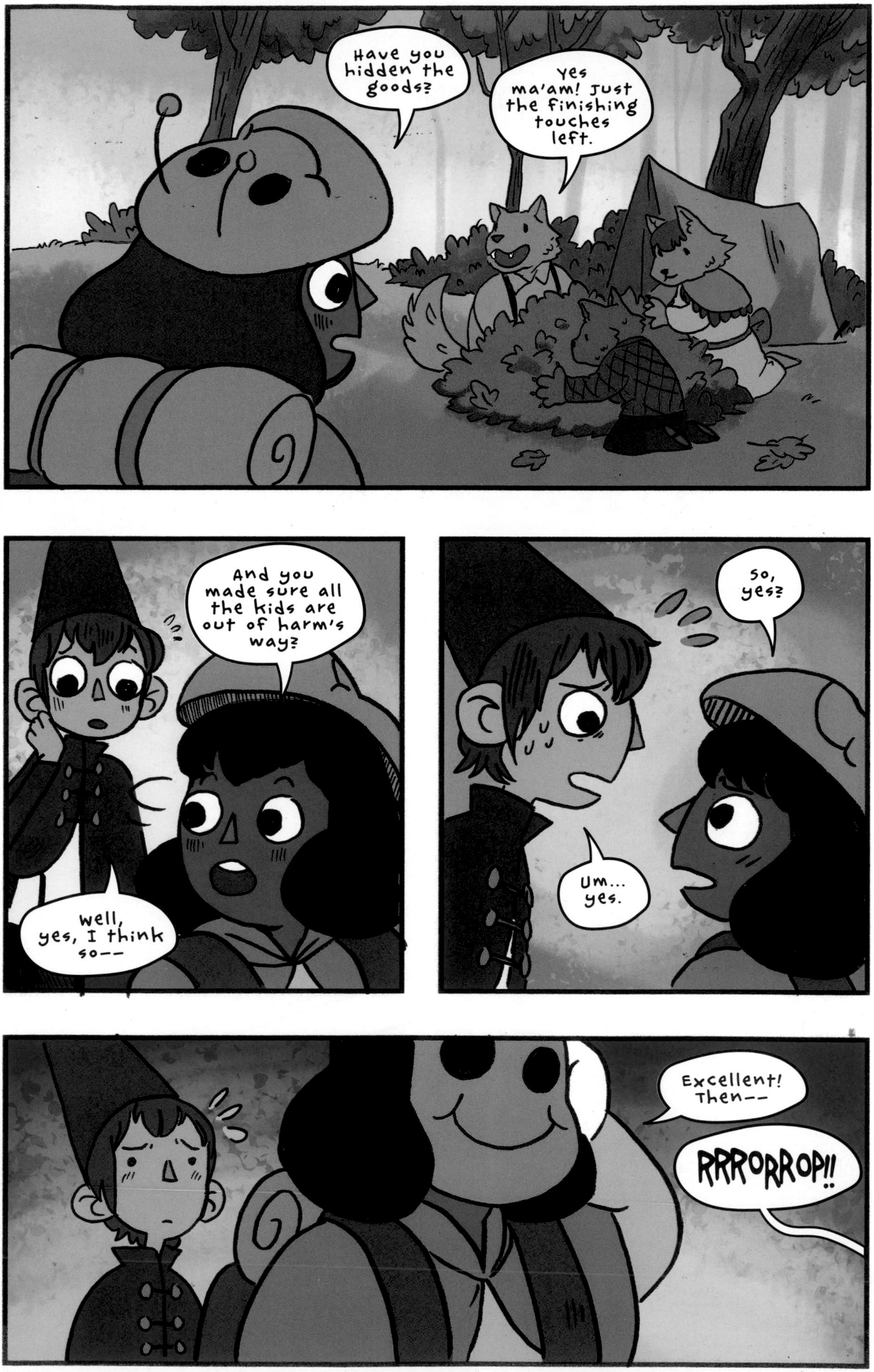
Have you hidden the goods?
Yes ma'am! Just the finishing touches left.
And you made sure all the kids are out of harm's way?
Well, yes, I think so--
So, yes?
Um... yes.
Excellent! Then--
RRRORROP!!

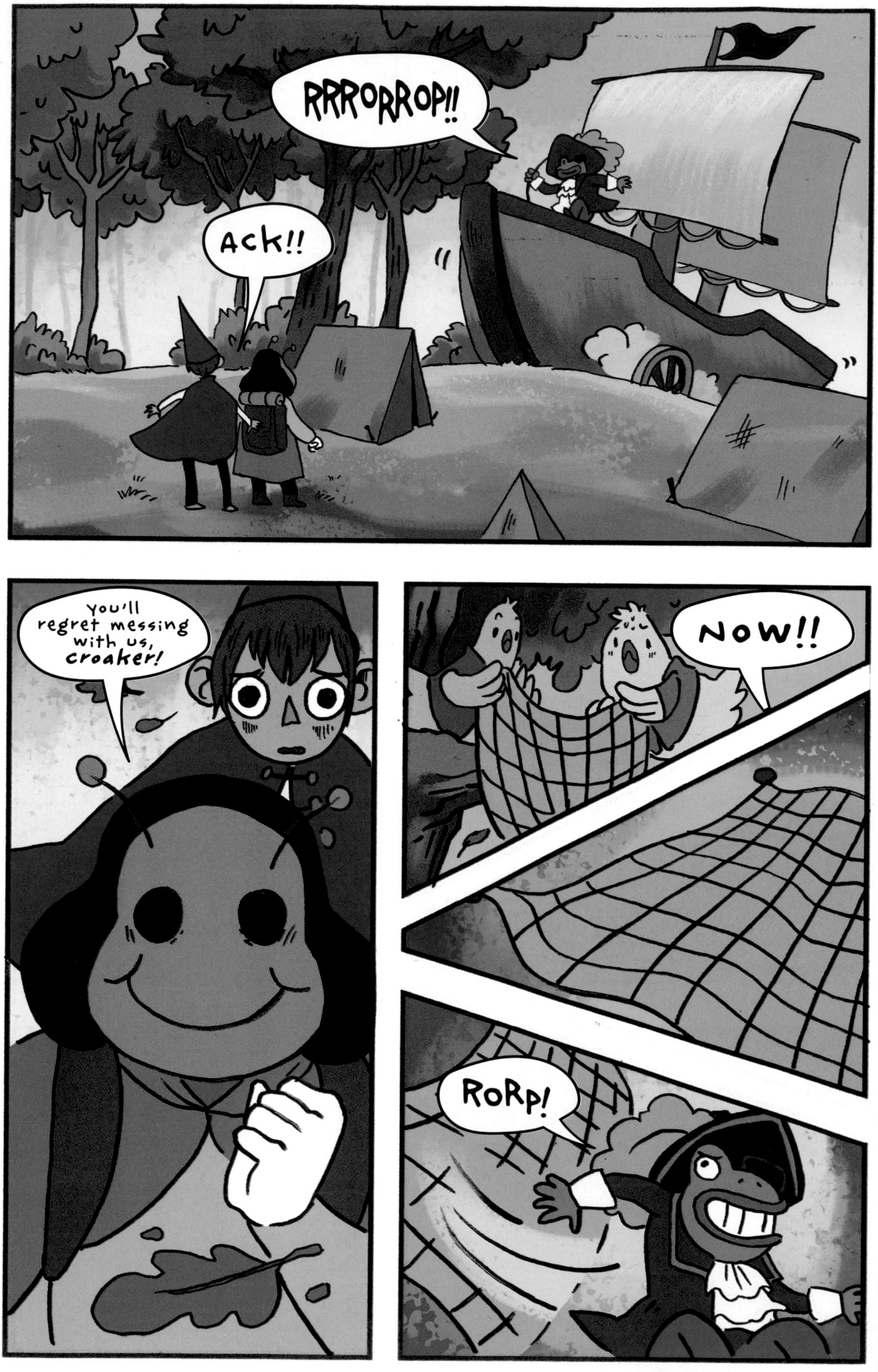
RRRORRROP!!
ACK!!
You'll regret messing with us, croaker!
NOW!!
RORP!

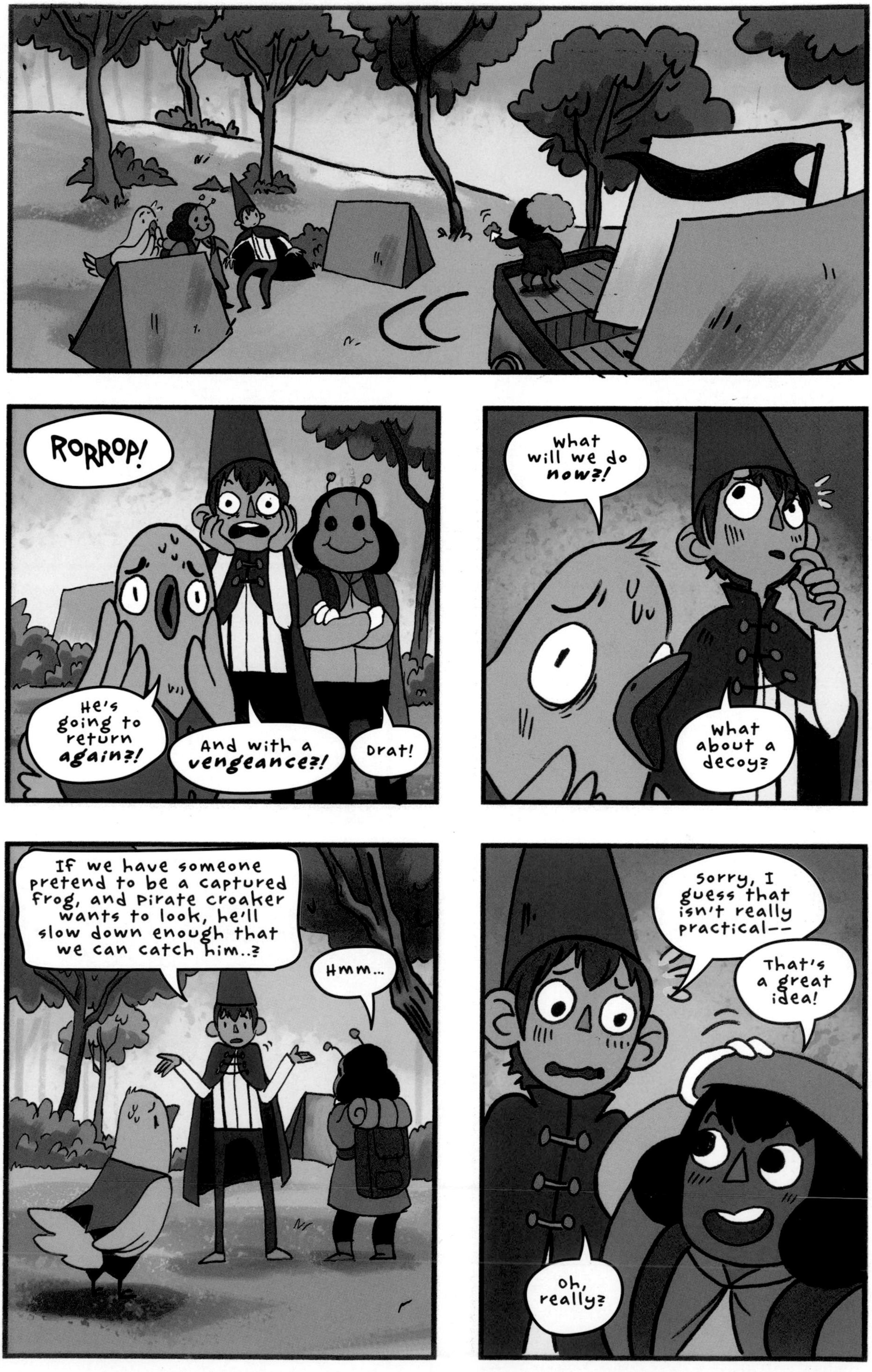
RORROP!
He's going to return again?!
And with a vengeance?!
Drat!
What will we do now?!
What about a decoy?
If we have someone pretend to be a captured frog, and Pirate Croaker wants to look, he'll slow down enough that we can catch him..?
Hmm...
Sorry, I guess that isn't really practical--
That's a great idea!
Oh, really?

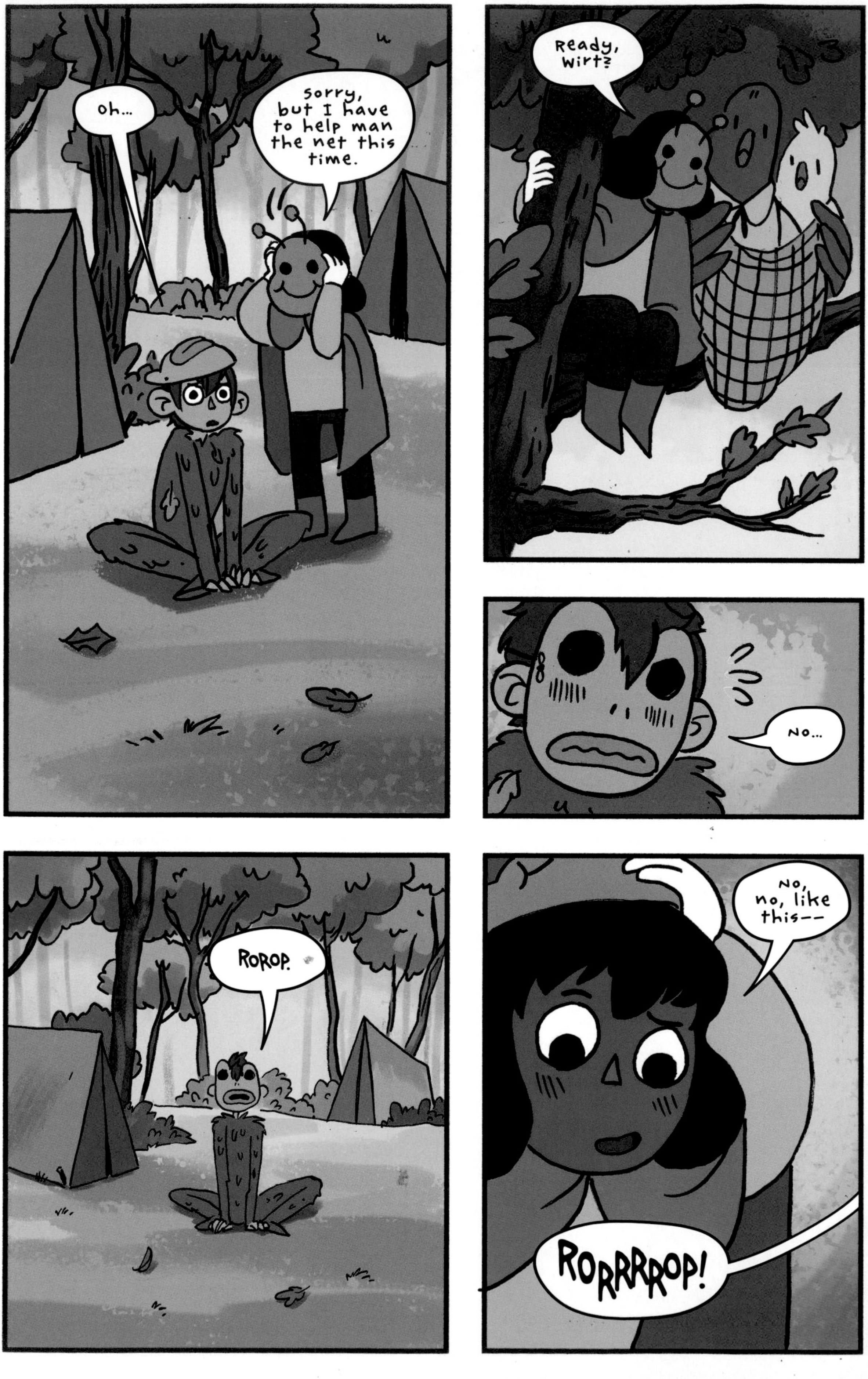
oh...
sorry, but I have to help man the net this time.
Ready, Wirt?
No...
ROROP.
No, no, like this--
RORRRROP!

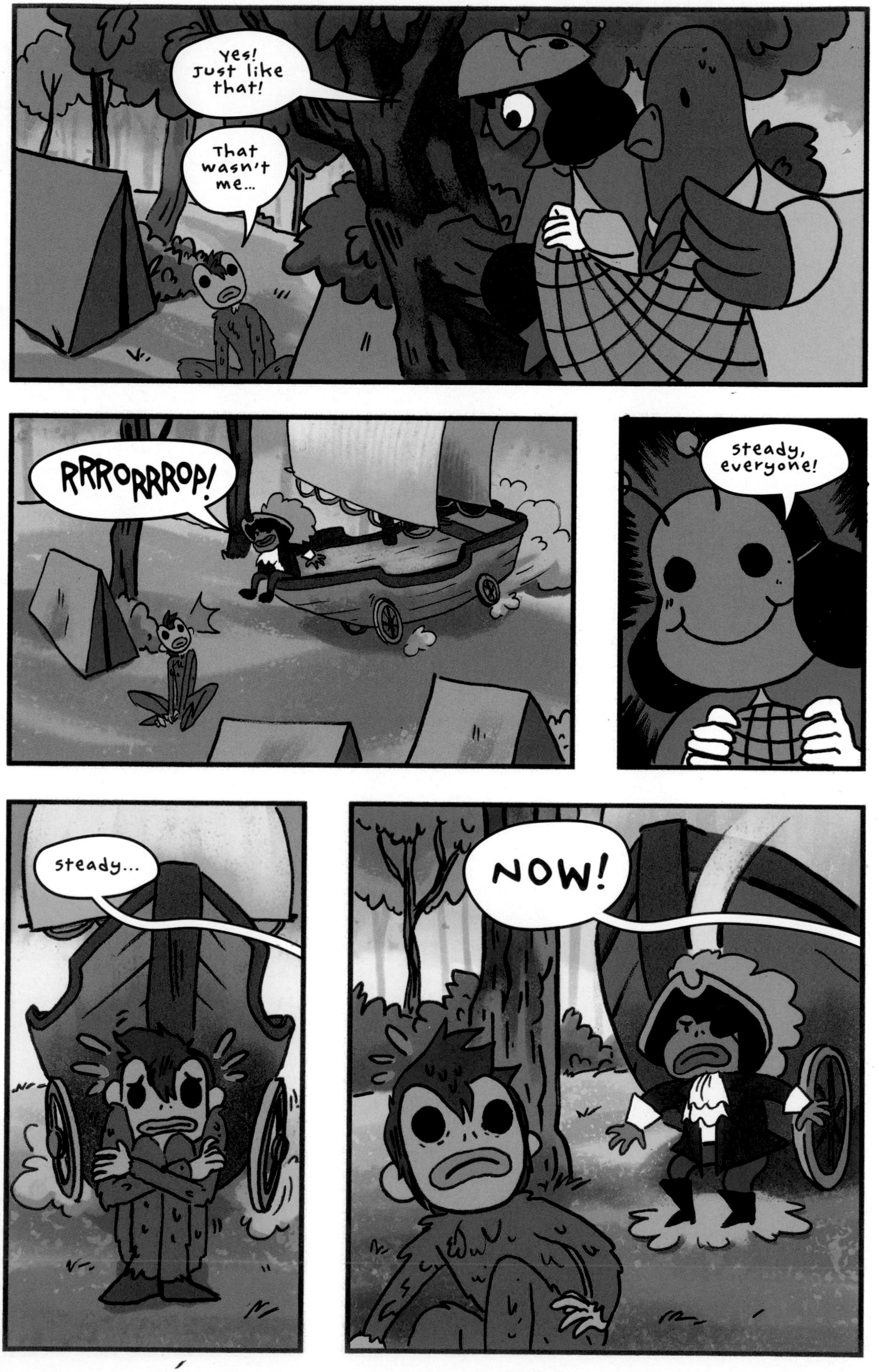
Yes! Just like that!
That wasn't me...
RRRORRROP!
steady, everyone!
steady...
NOW!

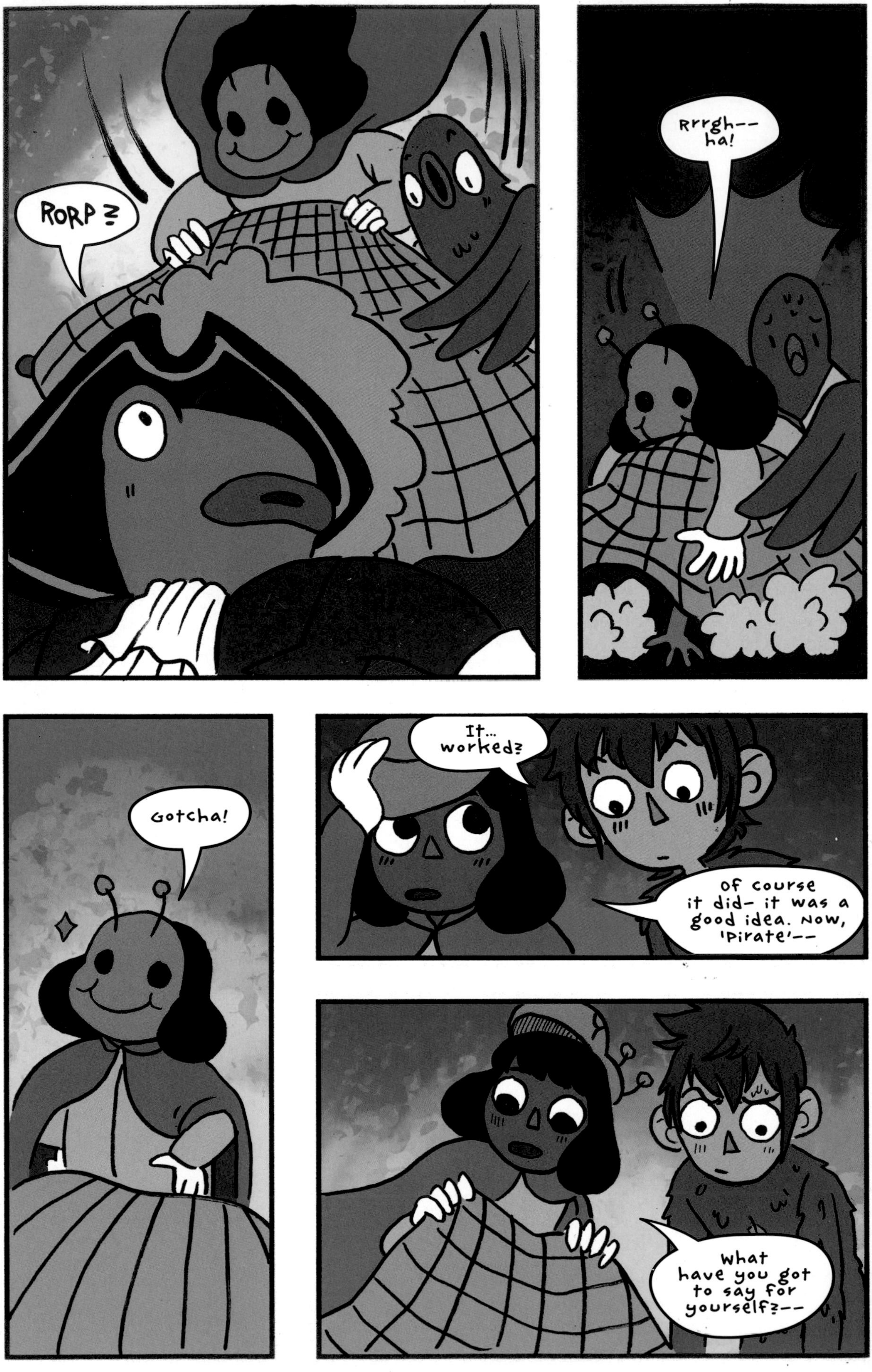
RORP?
Rrrgh-- ha!
Gotcha!
It... worked?
Of course it did- it was a good idea. Now, 'pirate'--
What have you got to say for yourself?--

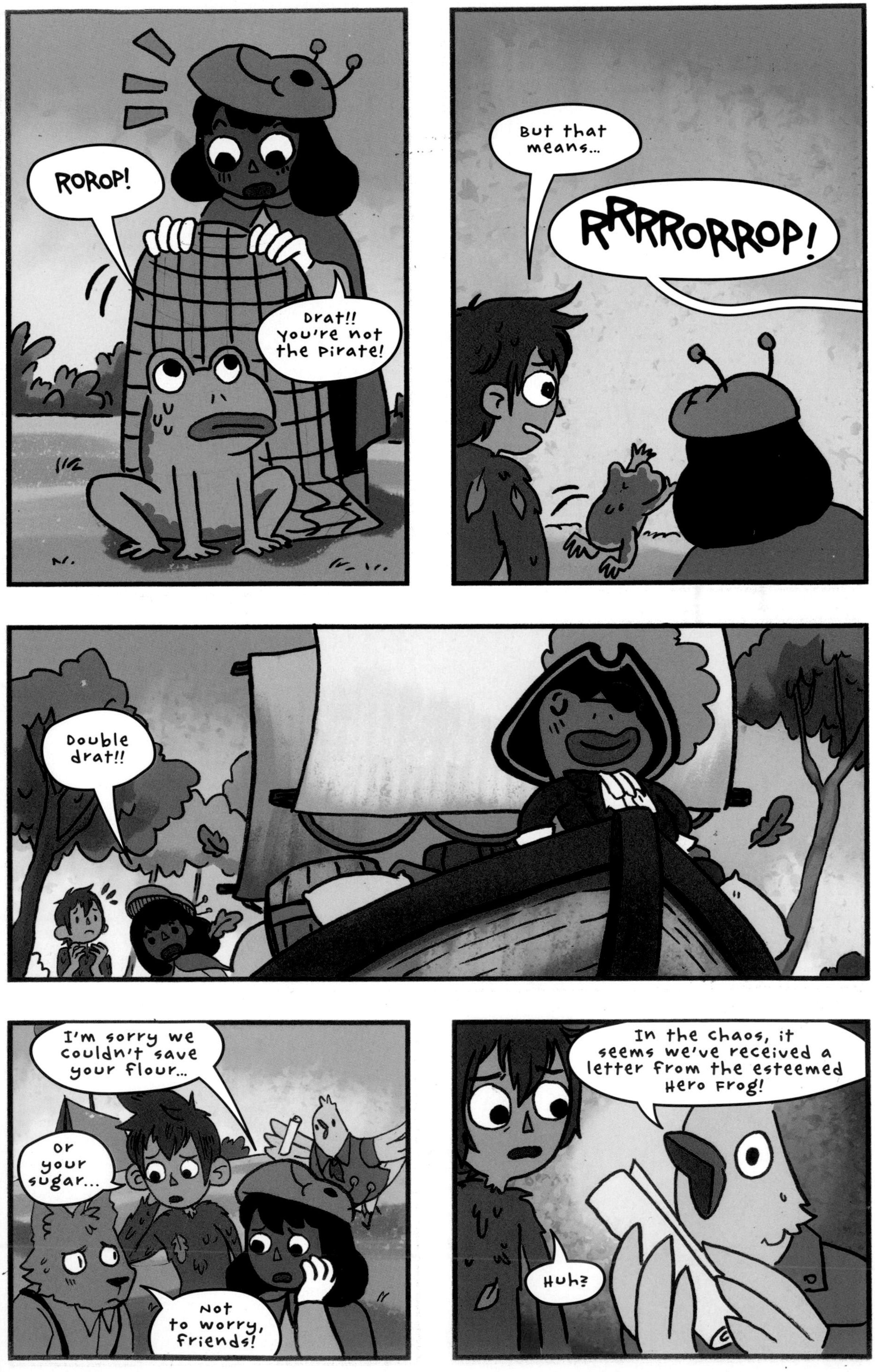
RoRop!
Drat!! You're not the Pirate!
But that means...
RRRRORROP!
Double drat!!
I'm sorry we couldn't save your flour...
or your sugar...
Not to worry, friends!
In the chaos, it seems we've received a letter from the esteemed Hero Frog!
Huh?

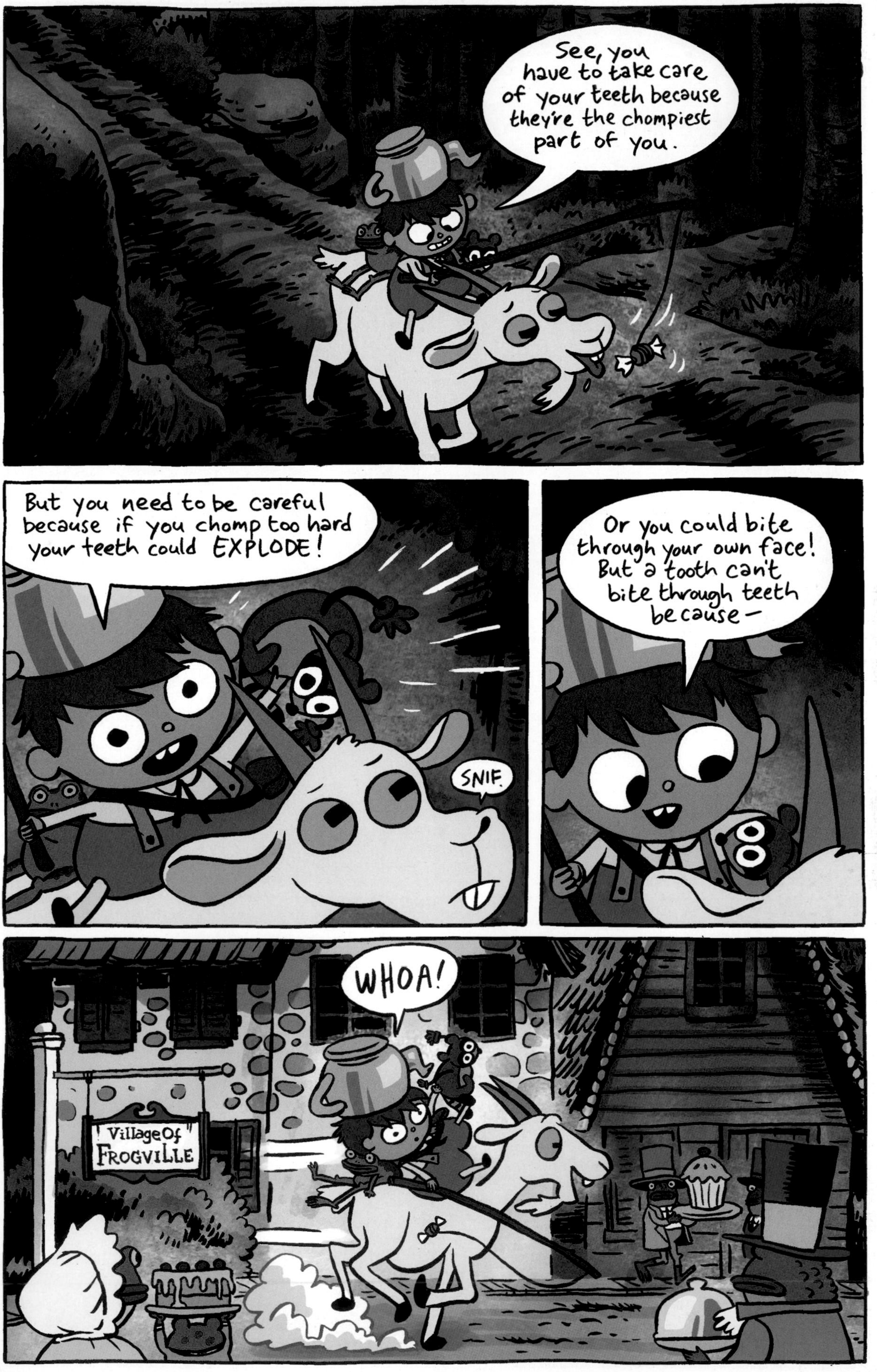
See, you have to take care of your teeth because they're the chompiest part of you.
But you need to be careful because if you chomp too hard your teeth could EXPLODE!
SNIF.
Or you could bite through your own face! But a tooth can't bite through teeth because—
WHOA!
Village Of FROGVILLE

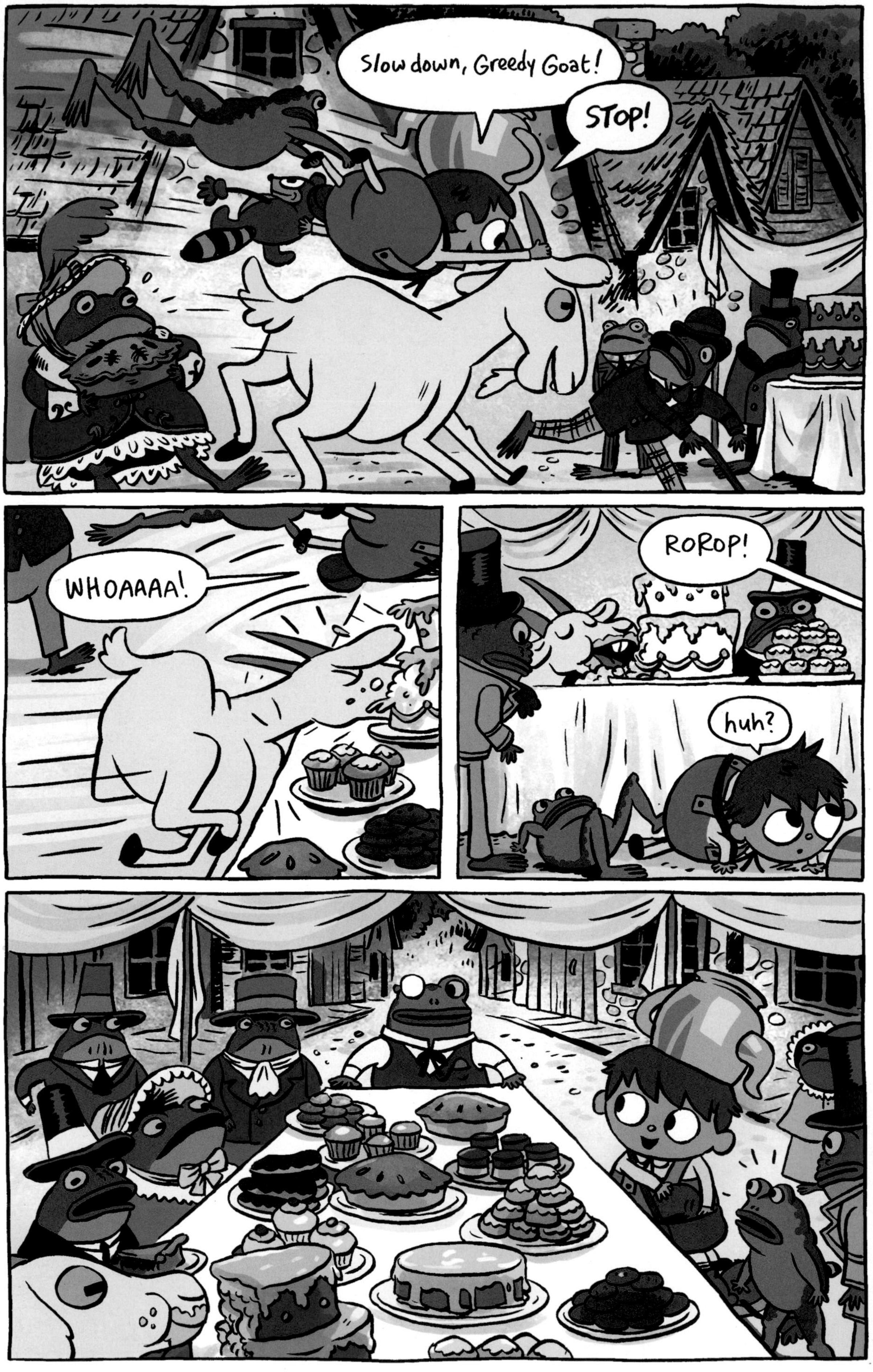
Slow down, Greedy Goat!
STOP!
WHOAAAA!
ROROP!
huh?

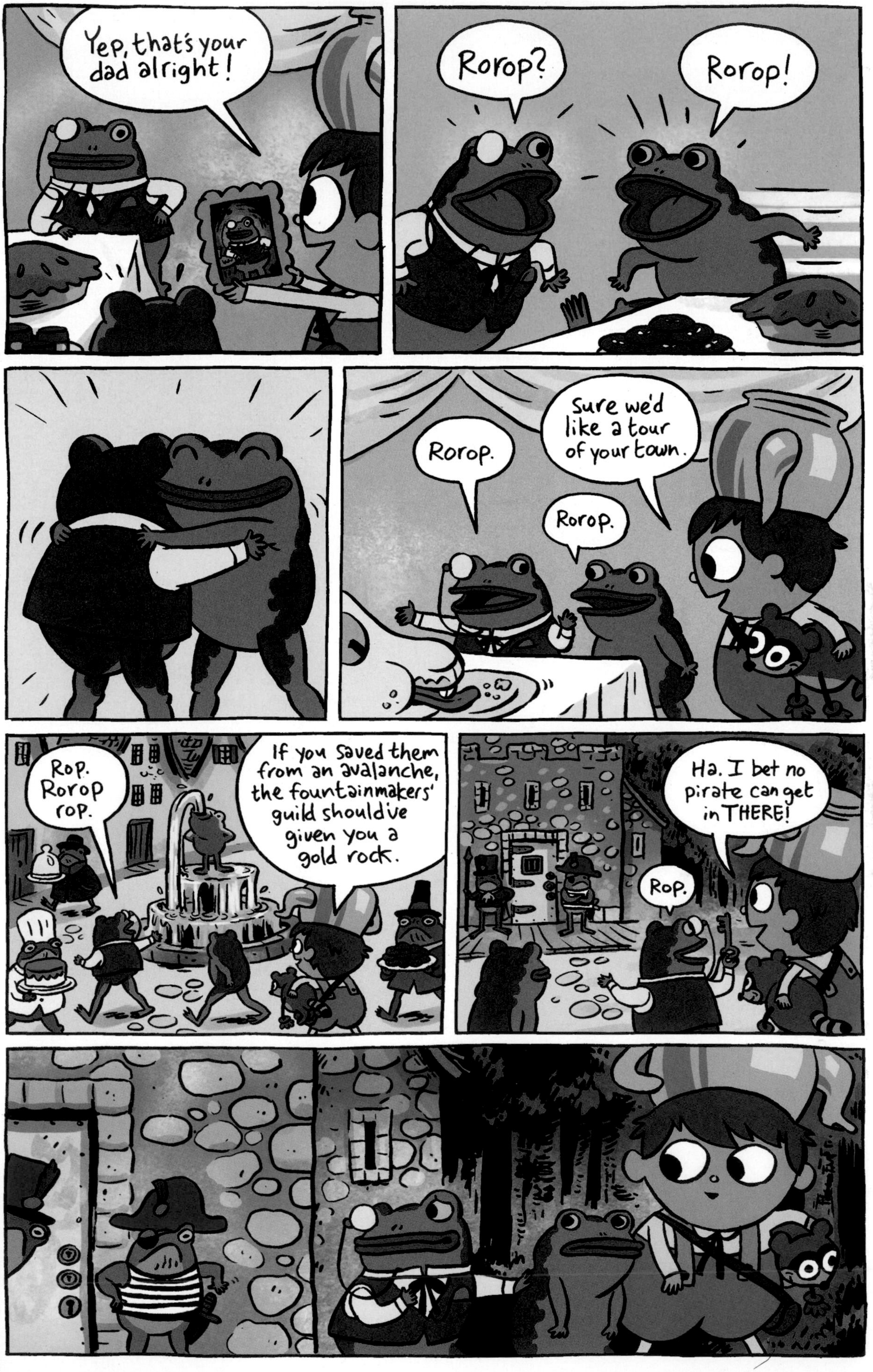
Yep, that's your dad alright!
Rorop?
Rorop!
Rorop.
Sure we'd like a tour of your town.
Rorop.
Rop. Rorop rop.
If you saved them from an avalanche, the fountainmakers' guild should've given you a gold rock.
Ha. I bet no pirate can get in THERE!
Rop.

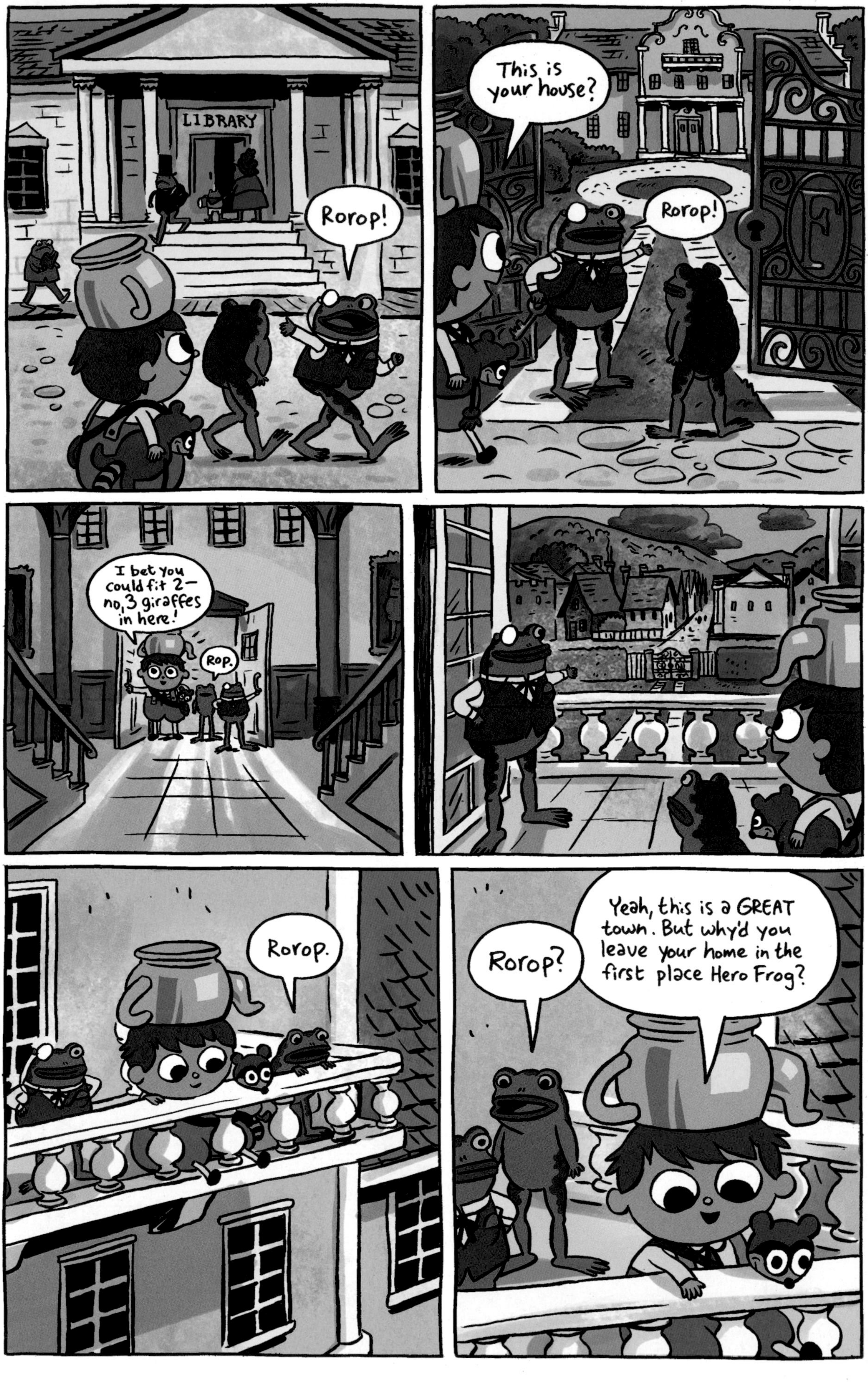
LIBRARY
Rorop!
This is your house?
Rorop!
I bet you could fit 2— no, 3 giraffes in here!
Rop.
Rorop.
Rorop?
Yeah, this is a GREAT town. But why'd you leave your home in the first place Hero Frog?

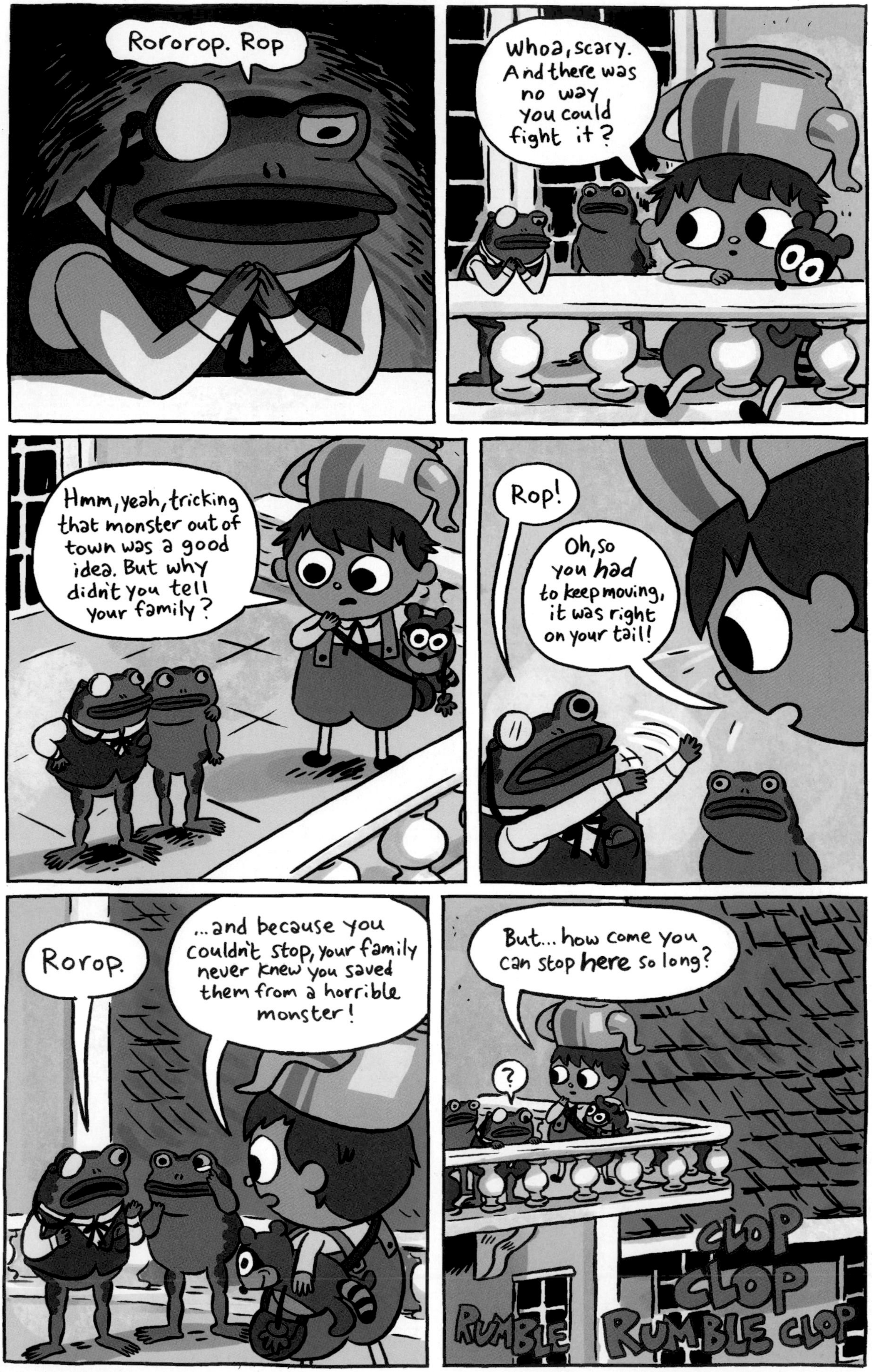
Rororop. Rop
Whoa, scary. And there was no way you could fight it?
Hmm, yeah, tricking that monster out of town was a good idea. But why didn't you tell your family?
Rop!
Oh, so you *had* to keep moving, it was right on your tail!
Rorop.
...and because you couldn't stop, your family never knew you saved them from a horrible monster!
But... how come you can stop **here** so long?
?
CLOP
CLOP
RUMBLE
RUMBLE CLOP

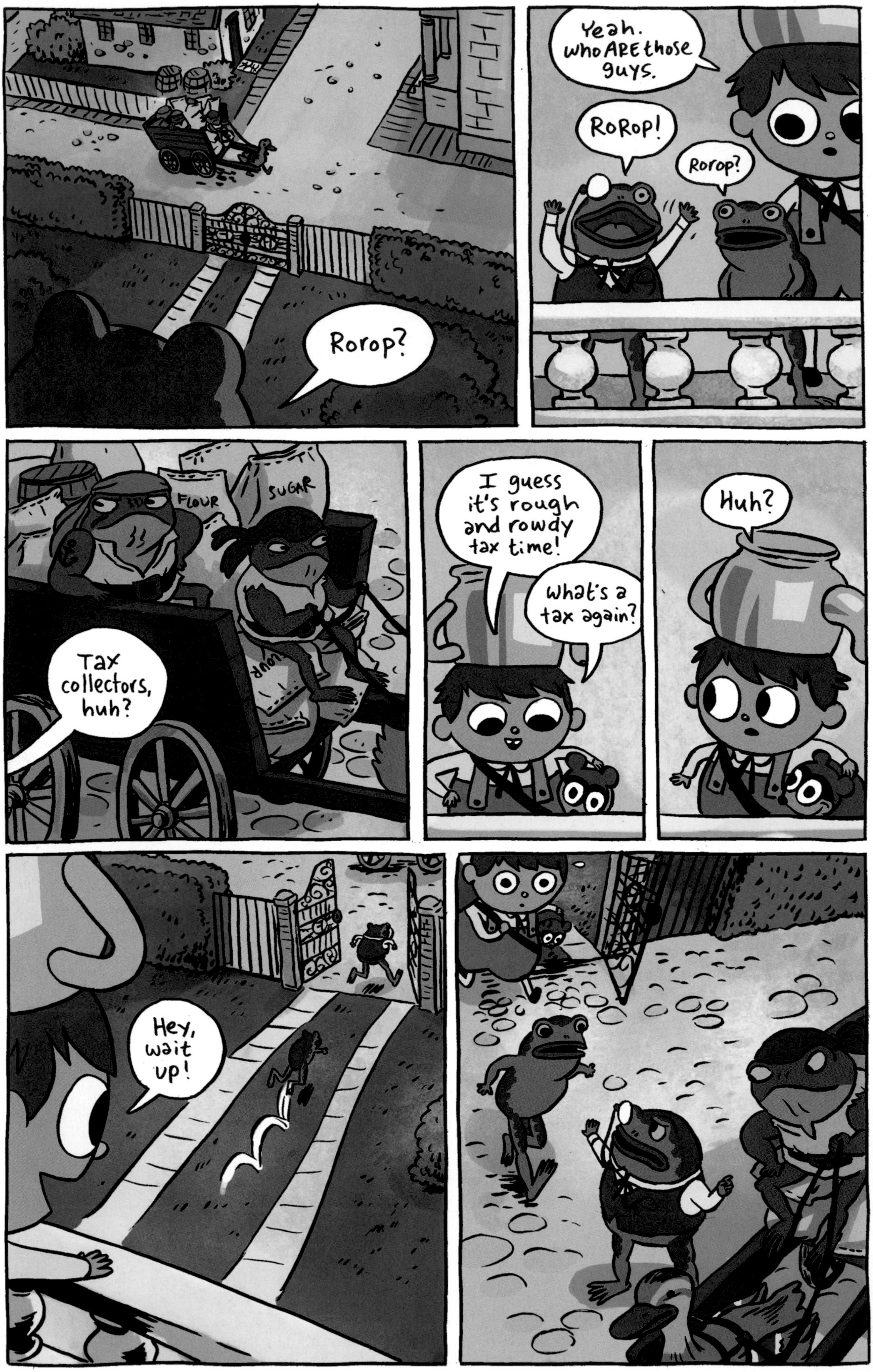
Rorop?
Yeah. who ARE those guys.
RoRop!
Rorop?
FLOUR
SUGAR
Tax collectors, huh?
I guess it's rough and rowdy tax time!
what's a tax again?
Huh?
Hey, wait up!

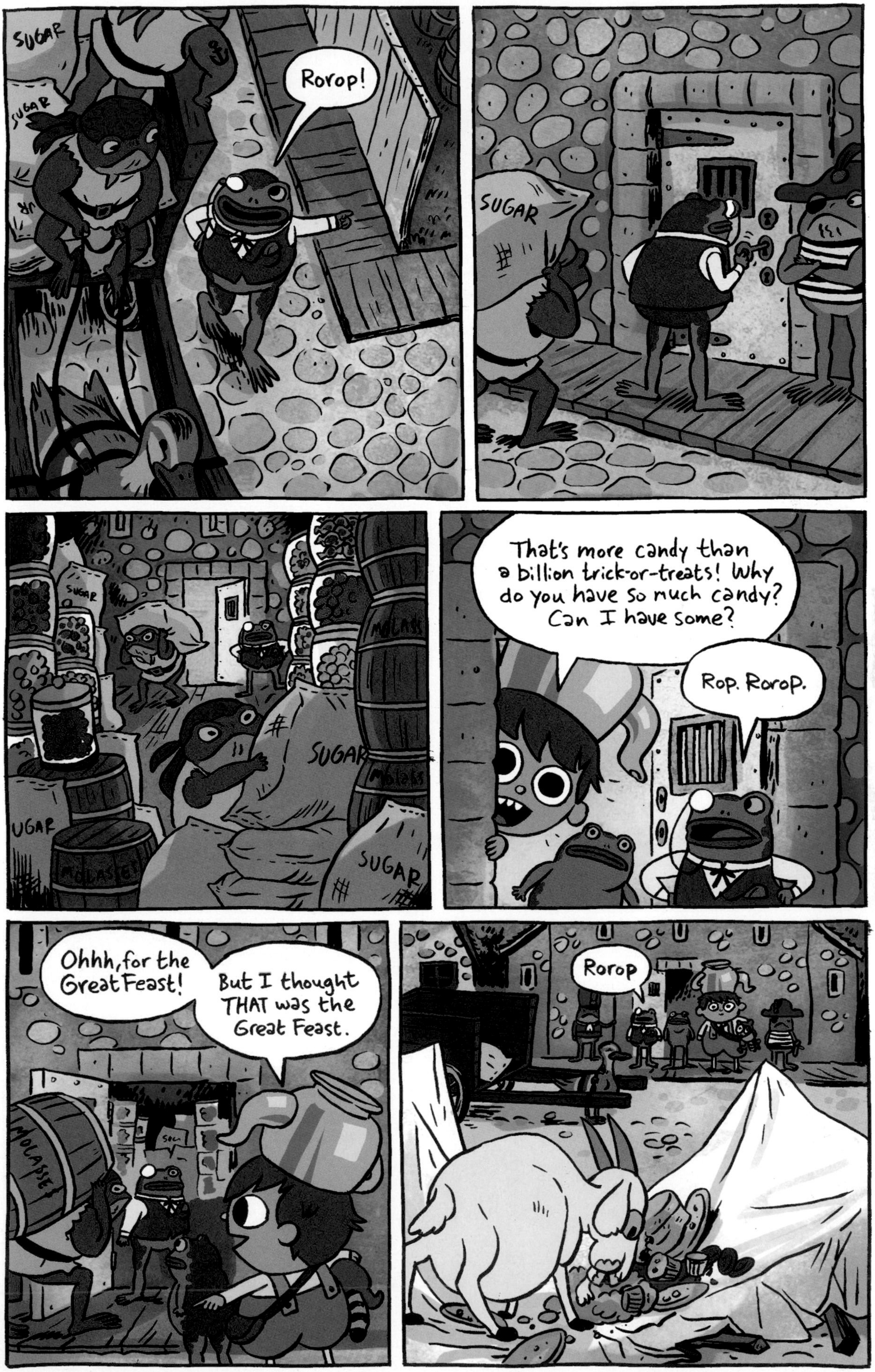
SUGAR
Rorop!
SUGAR
That's more candy than a billion trick-or-treats! Why do you have so much candy? Can I have some?
Rop. Rorop.
Ohhh, for the Great Feast!
But I thought THAT was the Great Feast.
Rorop

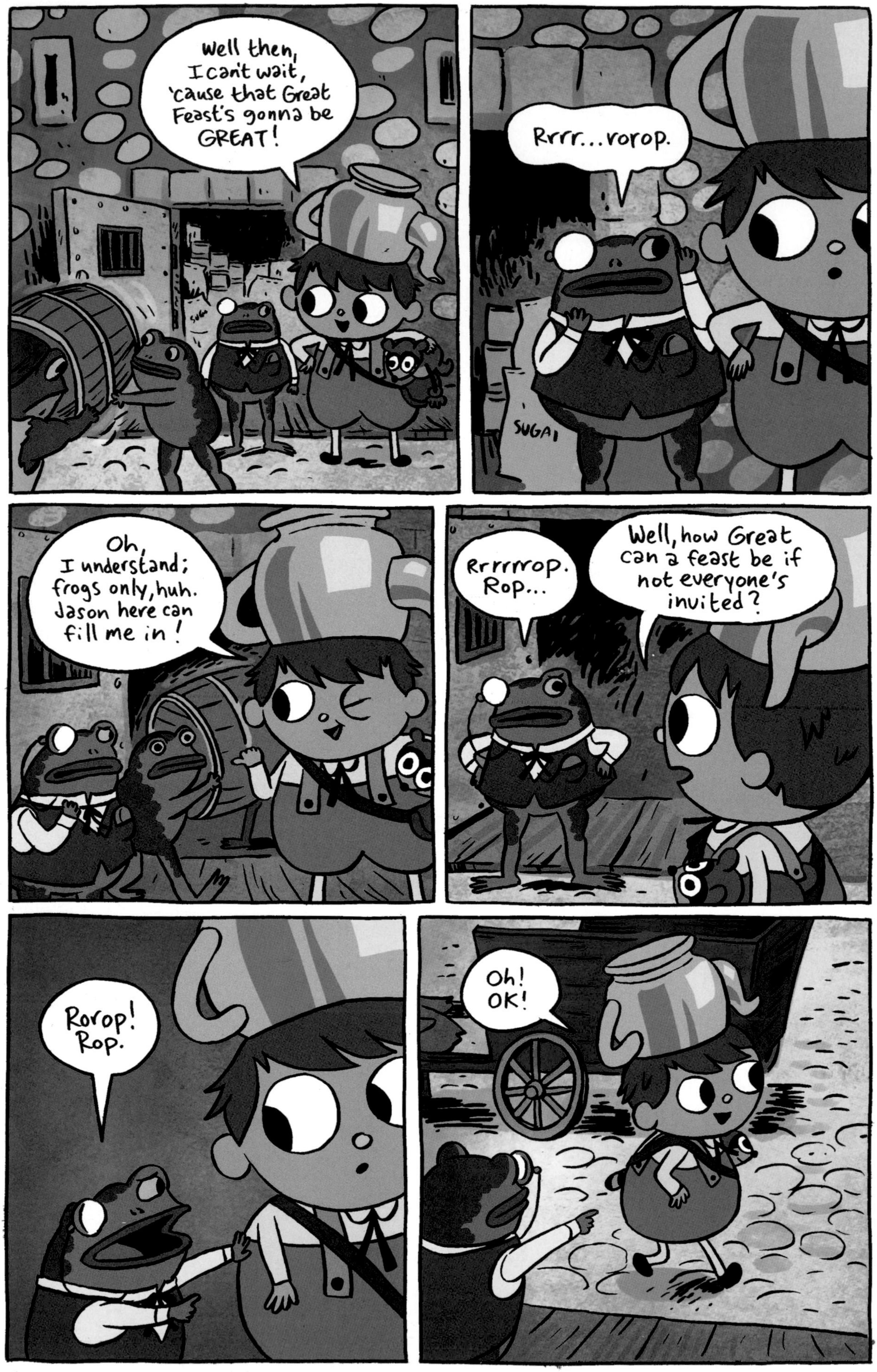
Well then, I can't wait, 'cause that Great Feast's gonna be GREAT!
SUGA
Rrrr...rorop.
SUGA
Oh, I understand; frogs only, huh. Jason here can fill me in!
Rrrrrrop. Rop...
Well, how Great can a feast be if not everyone's invited?
Rorop! Rop.
Oh! OK!

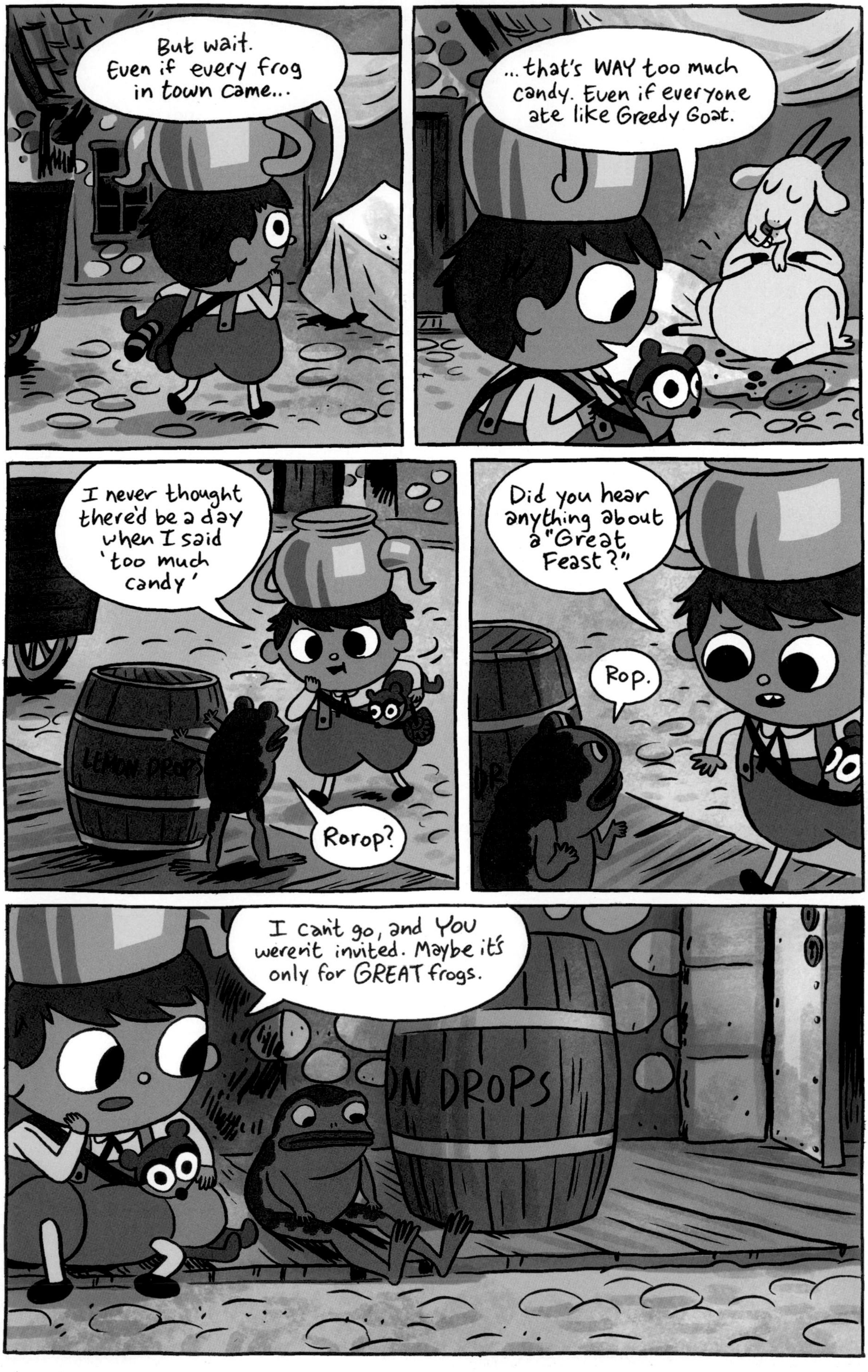
But wait. Even if every frog in town came...
...that's WAY too much candy. Even if everyone ate like Greedy Goat.
I never thought there'd be a day when I said 'too much candy'
LEMON DROP
Rorop?
Did you hear anything about a "Great Feast?"
Rop.
I can't go, and YOU weren't invited. Maybe it's only for GREAT frogs.
ON DROPS

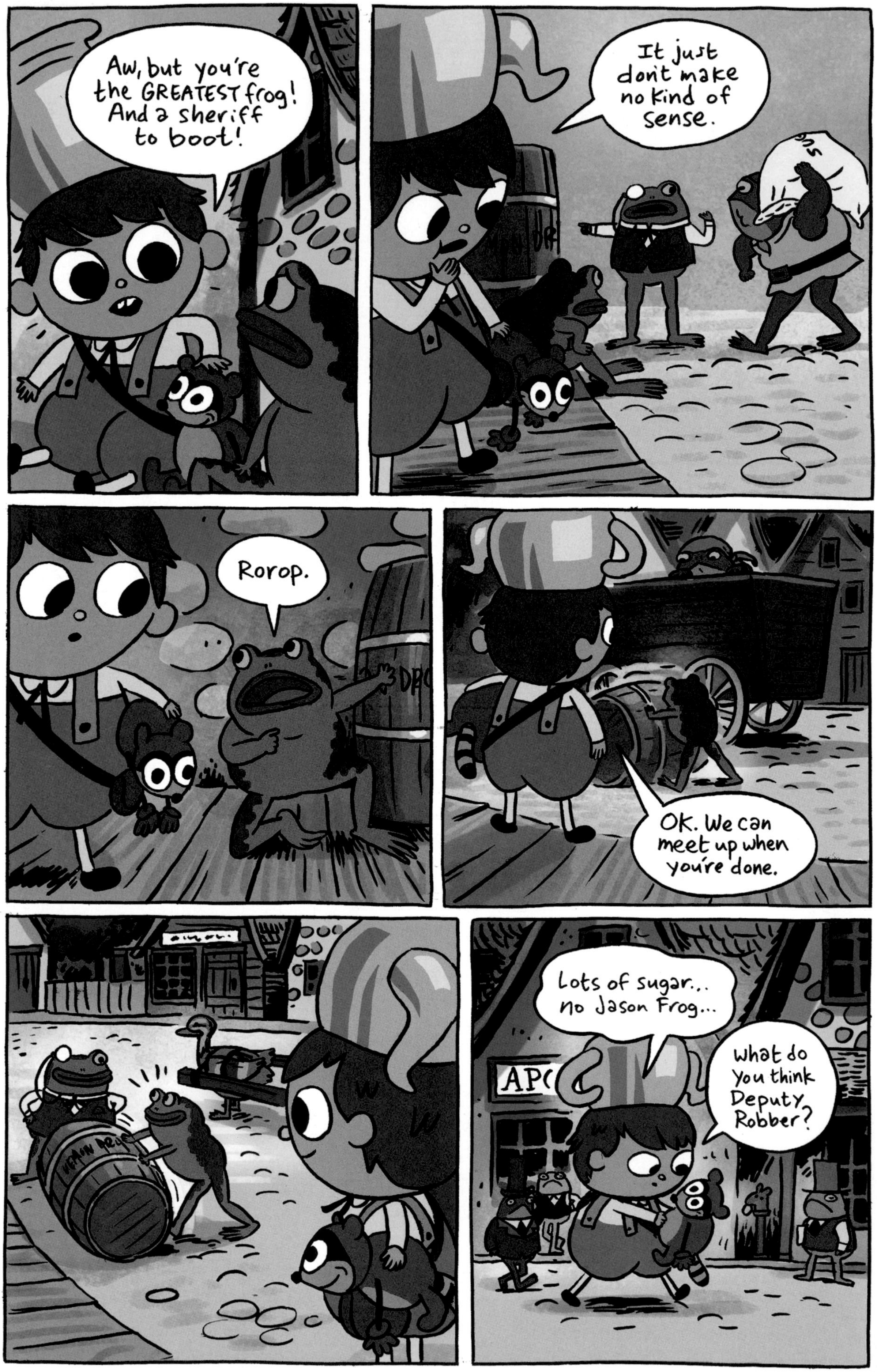
Aw, but you're the GREATEST frog! And a sheriff to boot!
It just don't make no kind of sense.
Rorop.
OK. We can meet up when you're done.
Lots of sugar.. no Jason Frog...
What do you think Deputy Robber?

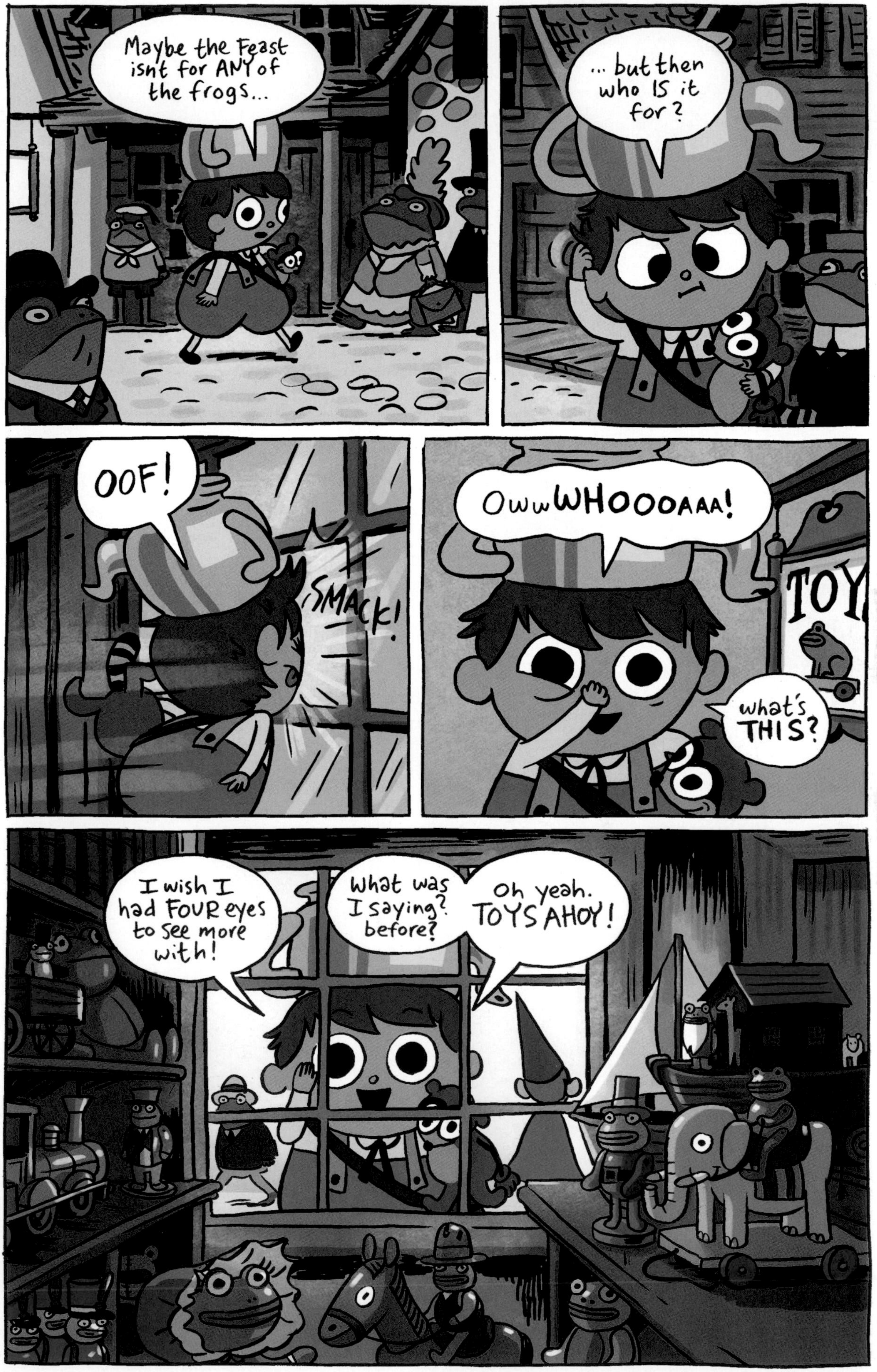
Maybe the Feast isn't for ANY of the frogs...
... but then who IS it for?
OOF!
SMACK!
OwwWHOOOAAA!
TOY
what's THIS?
I wish I had FOUR eyes to see more with!
What was I saying? before?
Oh yeah. TOYS AHOY!

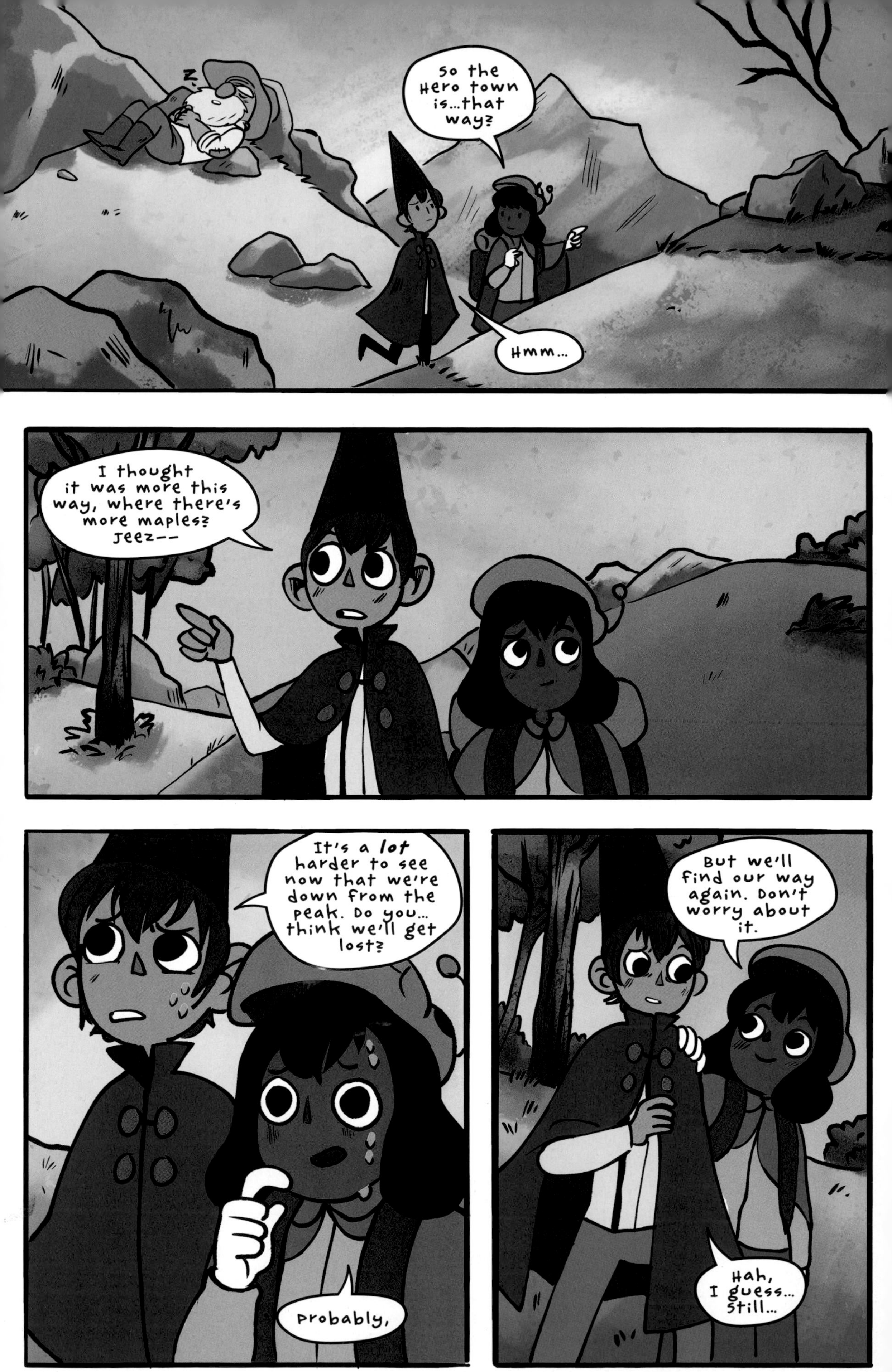
Z
So the Hero town is...that way?
Hmm...
I thought it was more this way, where there's more maples? Jeez--
It's a *lot* harder to see now that we're down from the peak. Do you... think we'll get lost?
Probably,
But we'll find our way again. Don't worry about it.
Hah, I guess... Still...

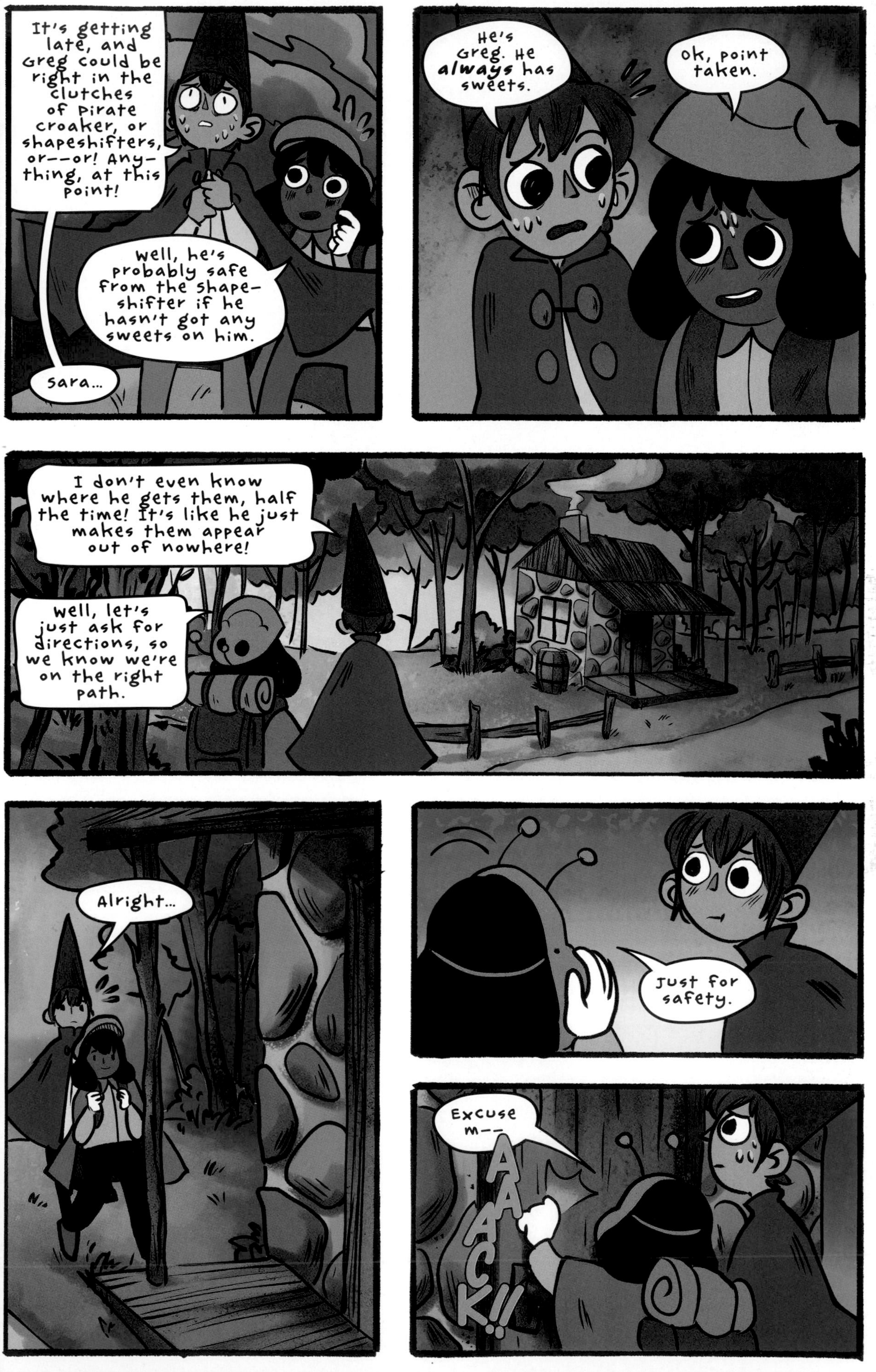
It's getting late, and Greg could be right in the clutches of Pirate Croaker, or shapeshifters, or--or! Anything, at this point!
Well, he's probably safe from the shapeshifter if he hasn't got any sweets on him.
Sara...
He's Greg. He **always** has sweets.
Ok, point taken.
I don't even know where he gets them, half the time! It's like he just makes them appear out of nowhere!
Well, let's just ask for directions, so we know we're on the right path.
Alright...
Just for safety.
Excuse m--
AAACK!!

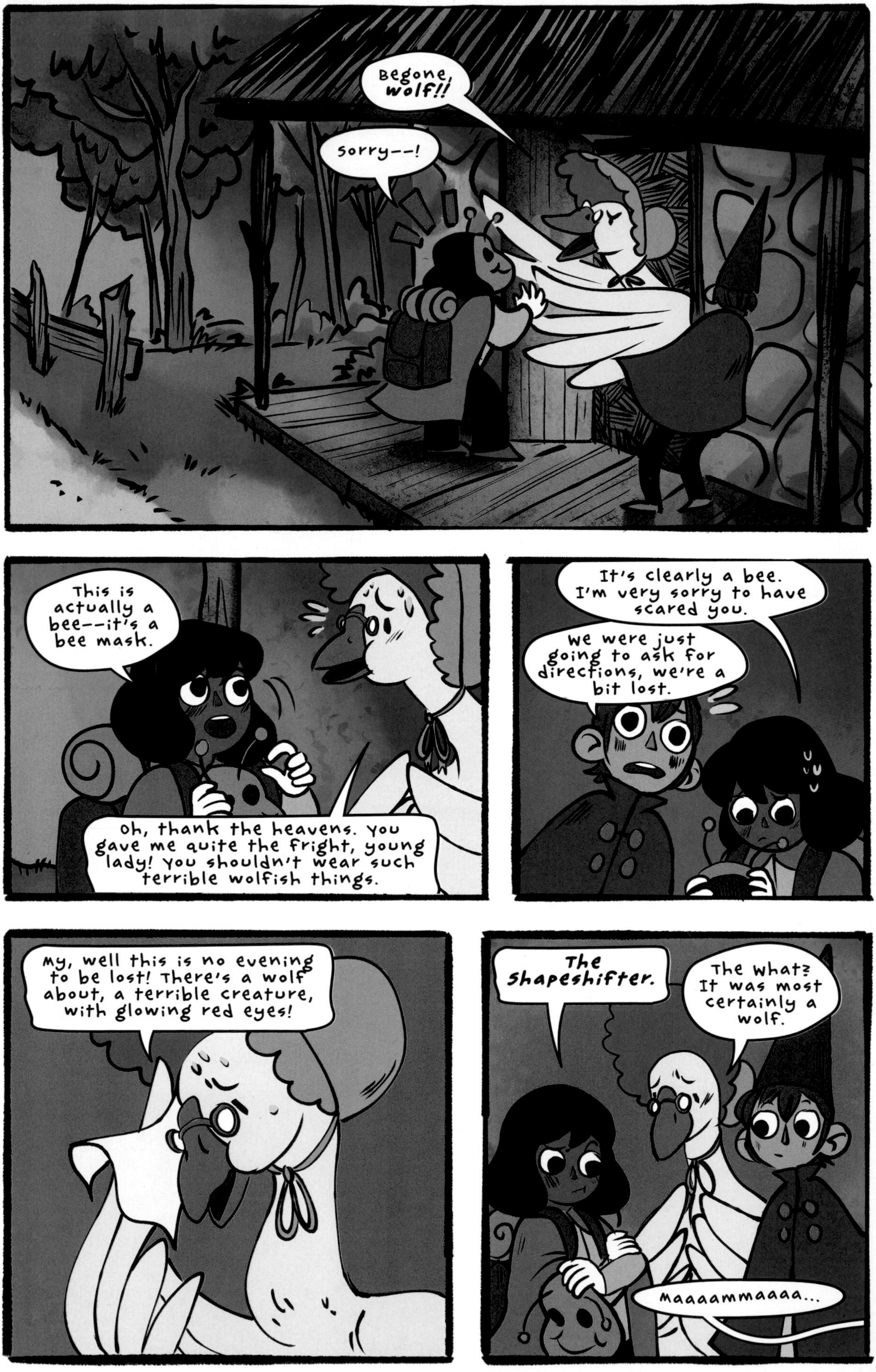
Begone, wolf!!
Sorry--!
This is actually a bee--it's a bee mask.
Oh, thank the heavens. You gave me quite the fright, young lady! You shouldn't wear such terrible wolfish things.
It's clearly a bee. I'm very sorry to have scared you.
We were just going to ask for directions, we're a bit lost.
My, well this is no evening to be lost! There's a wolf about, a terrible creature, with glowing red eyes!
The Shapeshifter.
The what? It was most certainly a wolf.
Maaaammaaaa...

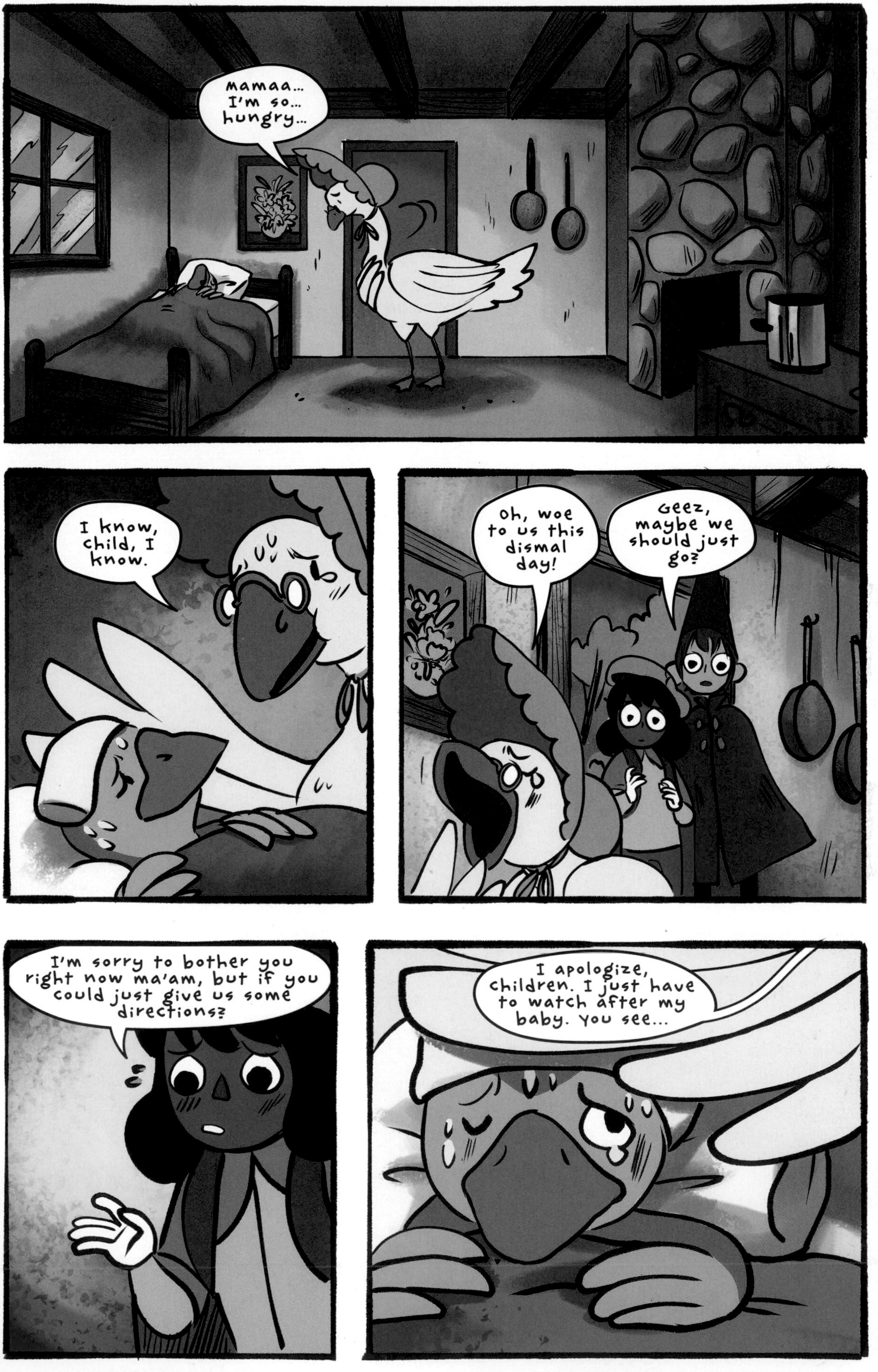
mamaa... I'm so... hungry...
I know, child, I know.
Oh, woe to us this dismal day!
Geez, maybe we should just go?
I'm sorry to bother you right now ma'am, but if you could just give us some directions?
I apologize, children. I just have to watch after my baby. You see...

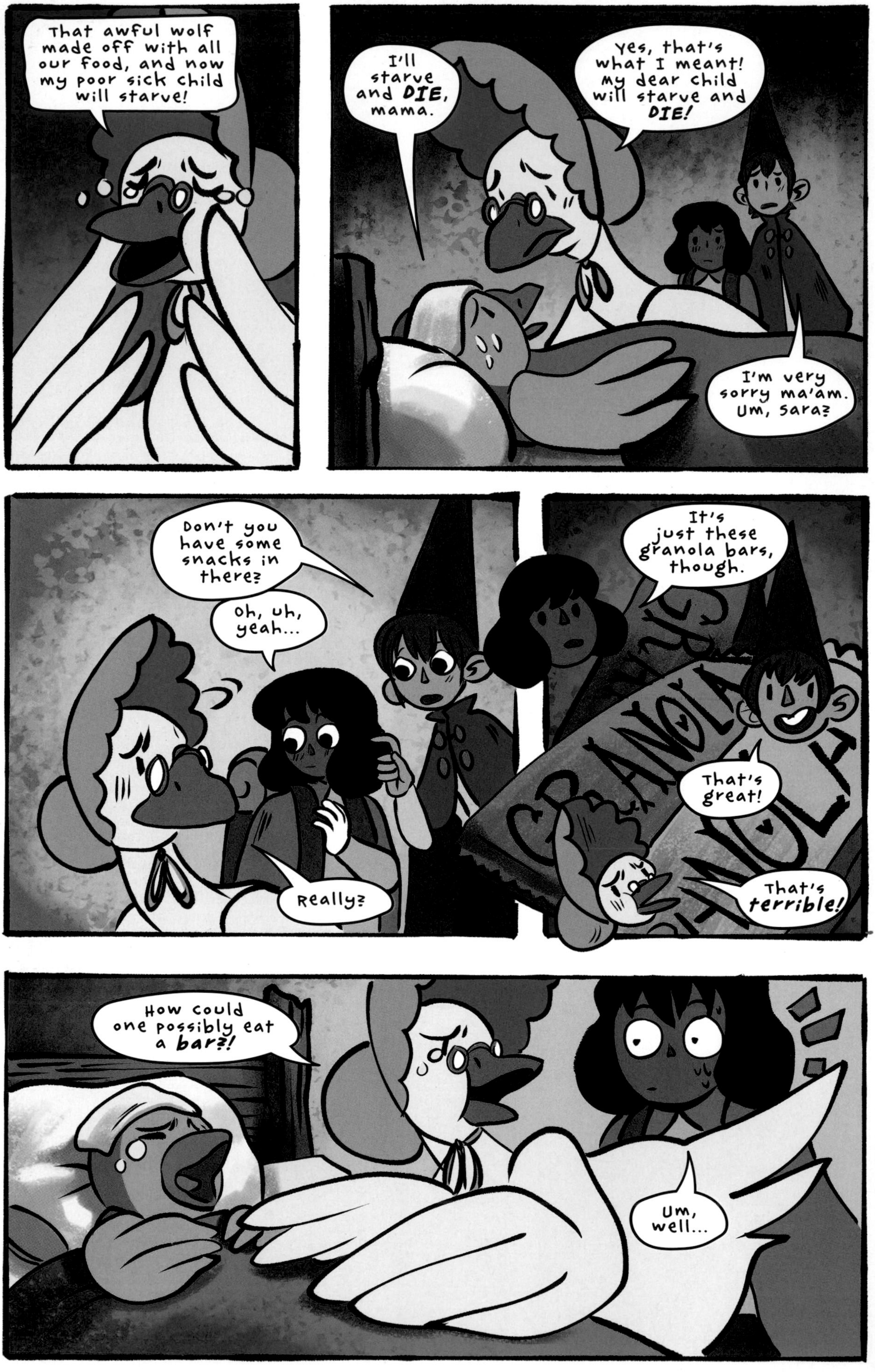
That awful wolf made off with all our food, and now my poor sick child will starve!
I'll starve and DIE, mama.
Yes, that's what I meant! My dear child will starve and DIE!
I'm very sorry ma'am. Um, Sara?
Don't you have some snacks in there?
Oh, uh, yeah...
Really?
It's just these granola bars, though.
GRANOLA
That's great!
That's terrible!
How could one possibly eat a bar?!
Um, well...

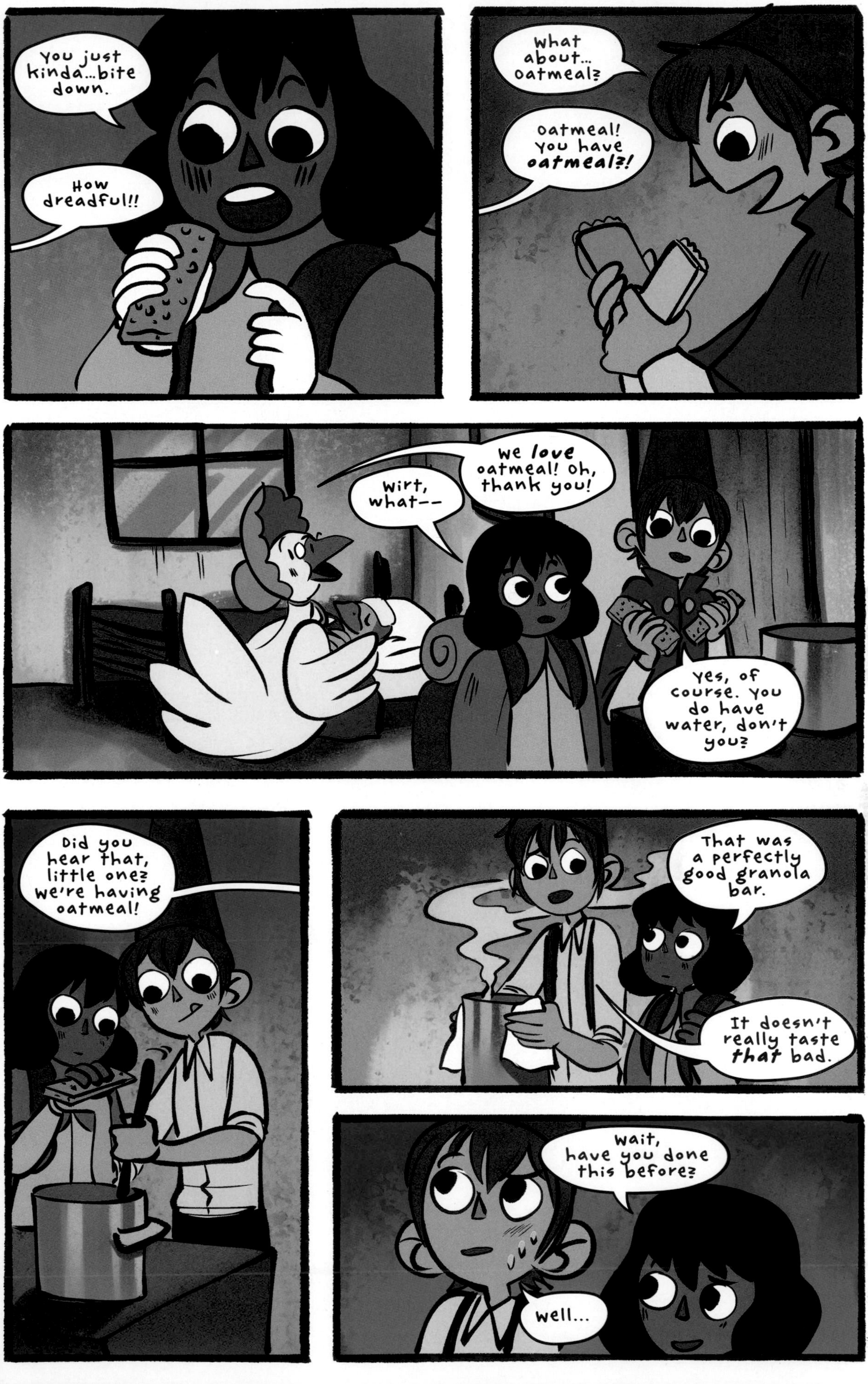
You just kinda...bite down.
How dreadful!!
What about... oatmeal?
Oatmeal! You have *oatmeal?!*
Wirt, what--
We *love* oatmeal! Oh, thank you!
Yes, of course. You do have water, don't you?
Did you hear that, little one? We're having oatmeal!
That was a perfectly good granola bar.
It doesn't really taste *that* bad.
Wait, have you done this before?
Well...

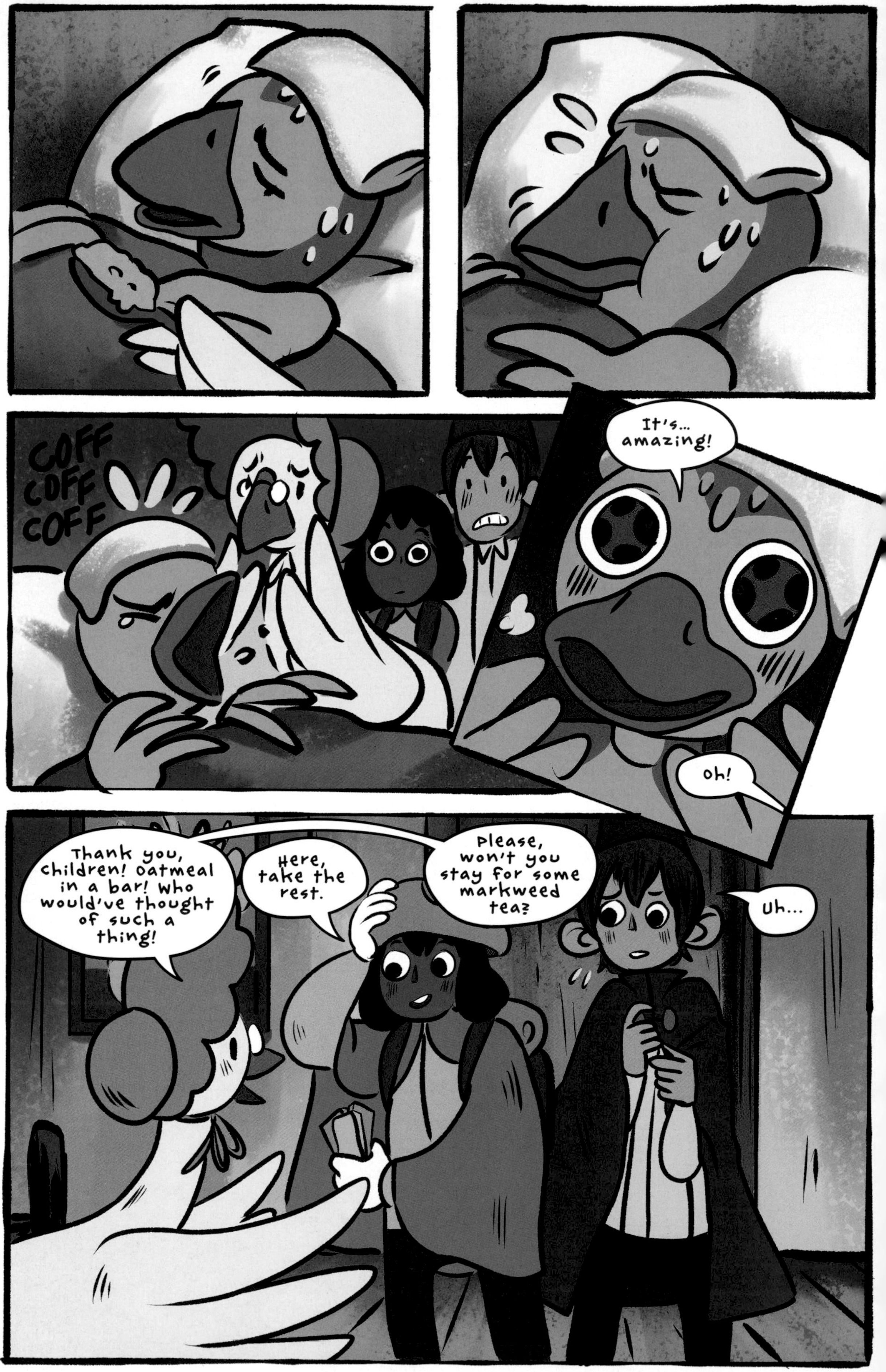
COFF COFF COFF
It's... amazing!
Oh!
Thank you, children! Oatmeal in a bar! Who would've thought of such a thing!
Please, won't you stay for some markweed tea?
Here, take the rest.
Uh...

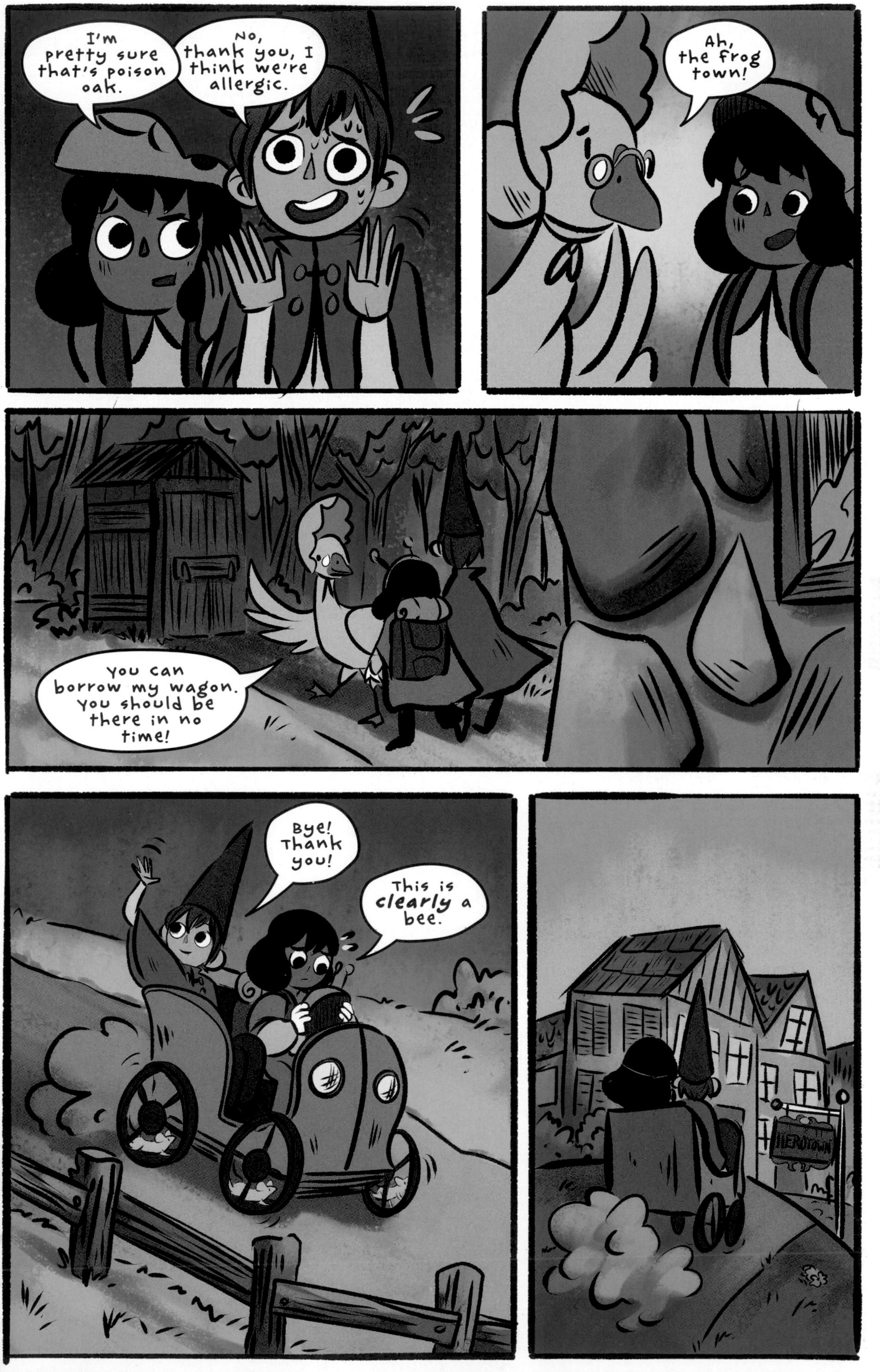
I'm pretty sure that's poison oak.
No, thank you, I think we're allergic.
Ah, the frog town!
You can borrow my wagon. You should be there in no time!
Bye! Thank you!
This is *clearly* a bee.

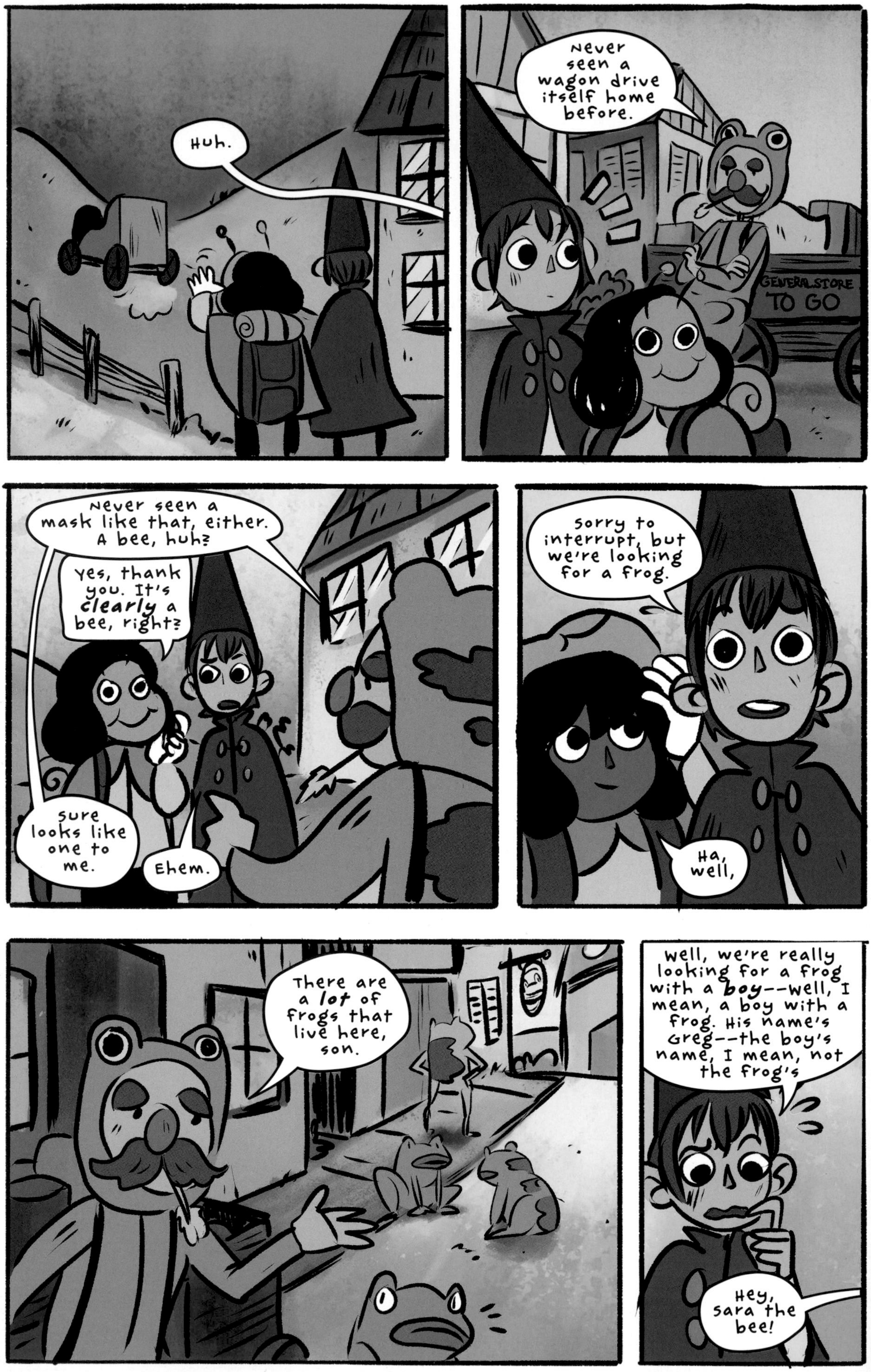
Huh.
Never seen a wagon drive itself home before.
GENERAL STORE TO GO
Never seen a mask like that, either. A bee, huh?
Yes, thank you. It's *clearly* a bee, right?
Sure looks like one to me.
Ehem.
Sorry to interrupt, but we're looking for a frog.
Ha, well,
There are a *lot* of frogs that live here, son.
Well, we're really looking for a frog with a *boy*--well, I mean, a boy with a frog. His name's Greg--the boy's name, I mean, not the frog's
Hey, Sara the bee!

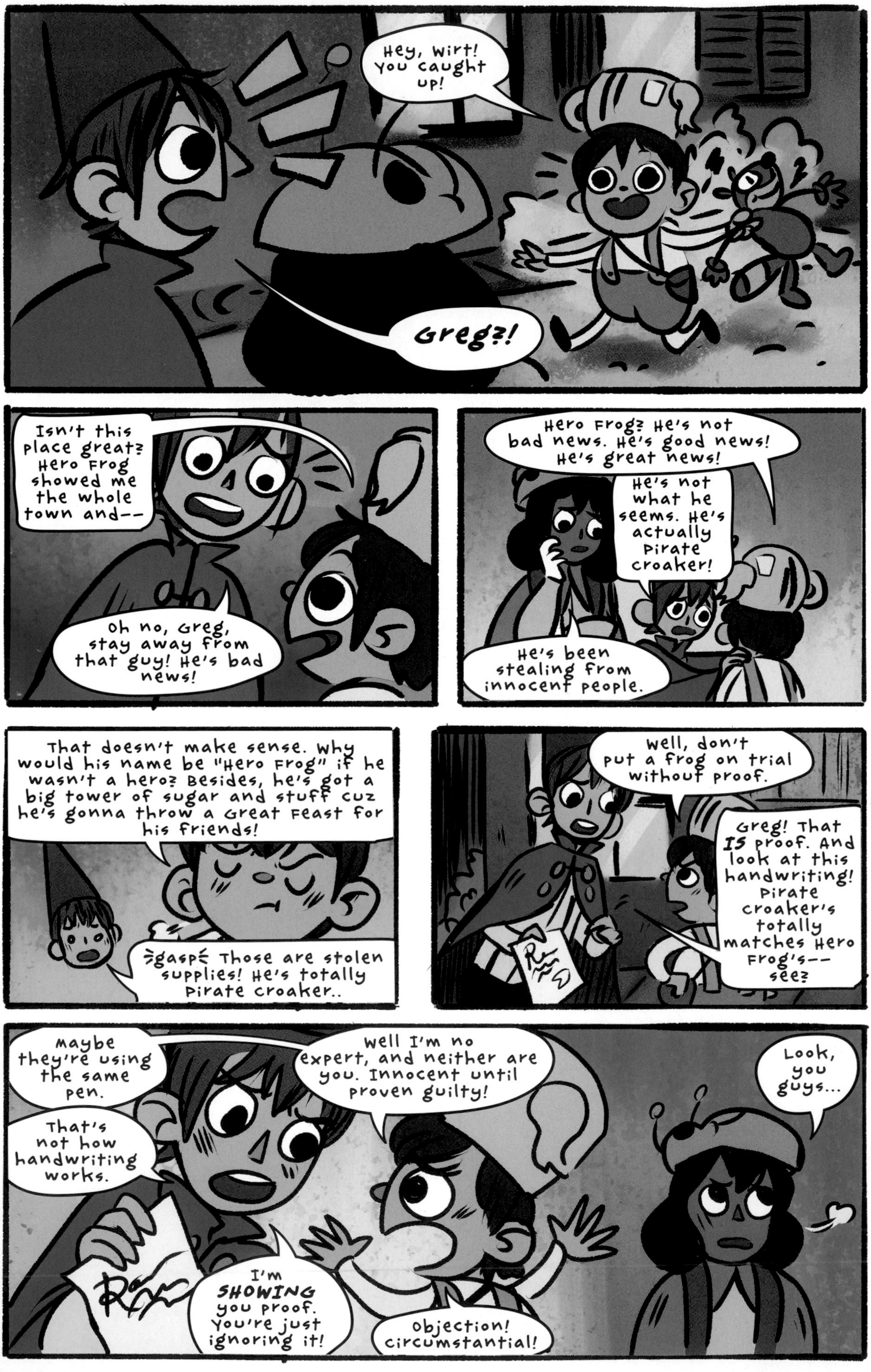
Hey, Wirt! You caught up!
Greg?!
Isn't this place great? Hero Frog showed me the whole town and--
Oh no, Greg, stay away from that guy! He's bad news!
Hero Frog? He's not bad news. He's good news! He's great news!
He's not what he seems. He's actually Pirate Croaker!
He's been stealing from innocent people.
That doesn't make sense. Why would his name be "Hero Frog" if he wasn't a hero? Besides, he's got a big tower of sugar and stuff cuz he's gonna throw a Great Feast for his friends!
≥gasp≤ Those are stolen supplies! He's totally Pirate Croaker..
Well, don't put a frog on trial without proof.
Greg! That *IS* proof. And look at this handwriting! Pirate Croaker's totally matches Hero Frog's--see?
Maybe they're using the same pen.
That's not how handwriting works.
Well I'm no expert, and neither are you. Innocent until proven guilty!
Look, you guys...
I'm *SHOWING* you proof. You're just ignoring it!
Objection! Circumstantial!

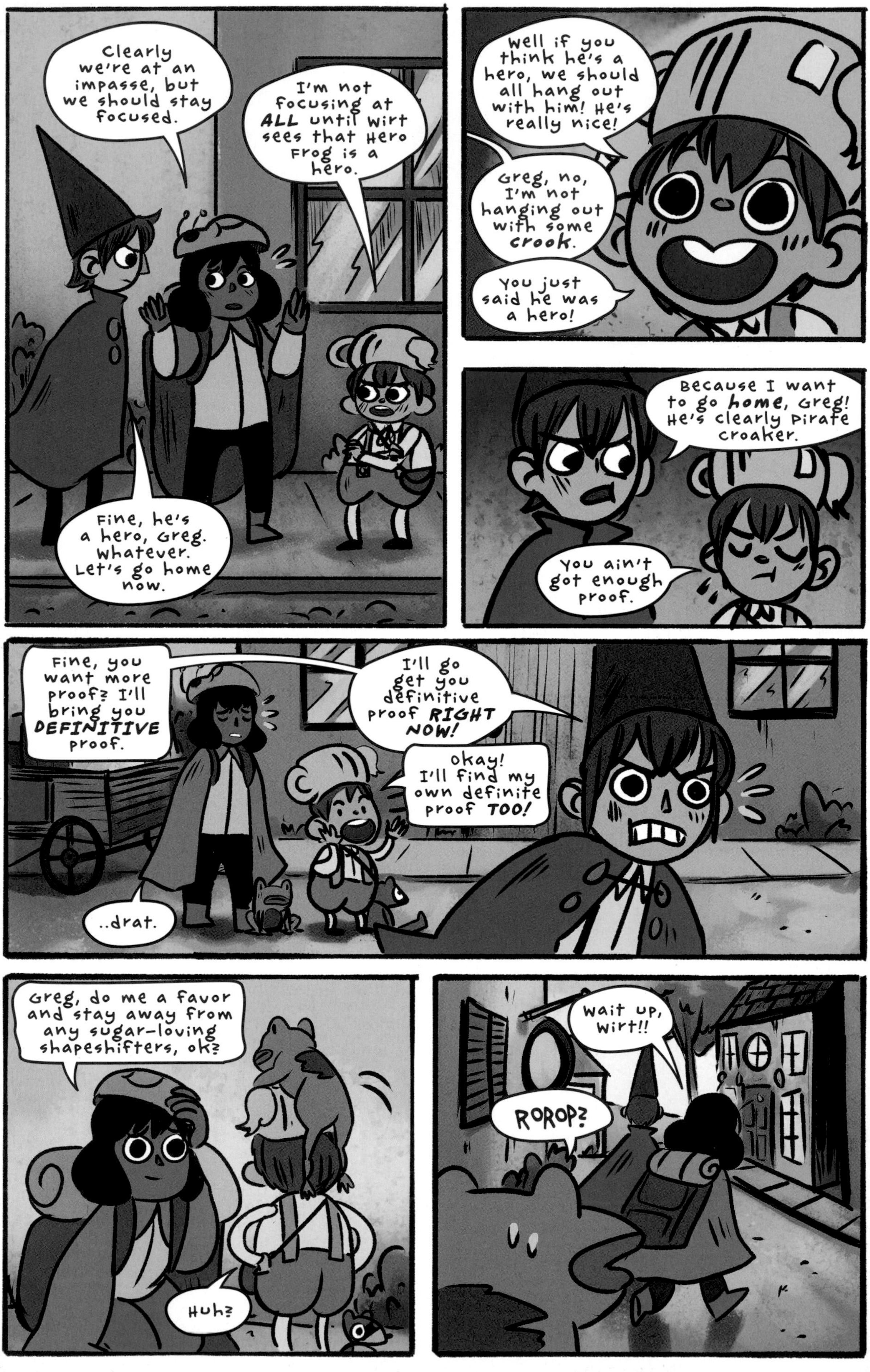
Clearly we're at an impasse, but we should stay focused.
I'm not focusing at ALL until Wirt sees that Hero Frog is a hero.
Fine, he's a hero, Greg. Whatever. Let's go home now.
Well if you think he's a hero, we should all hang out with him! He's really nice!
Greg, no, I'm not hanging out with some crook.
You just said he was a hero!
Because I want to go home, Greg! He's clearly Pirate Croaker.
You ain't got enough proof.
Fine, you want more proof? I'll bring you DEFINITIVE proof.
I'll go get you definitive proof RIGHT NOW!
Okay! I'll find my own definite proof TOO!
..drat.
Greg, do me a favor and stay away from any sugar-loving shapeshifters, ok?
Huh?
Wait up, Wirt!!
ROROP?

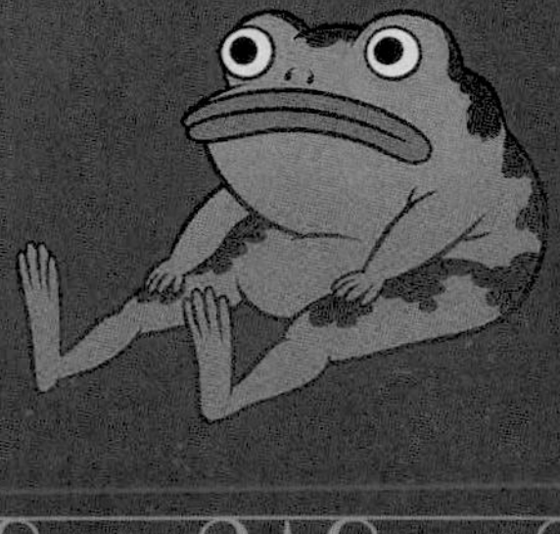

KITTY GOES TO SCHOOL

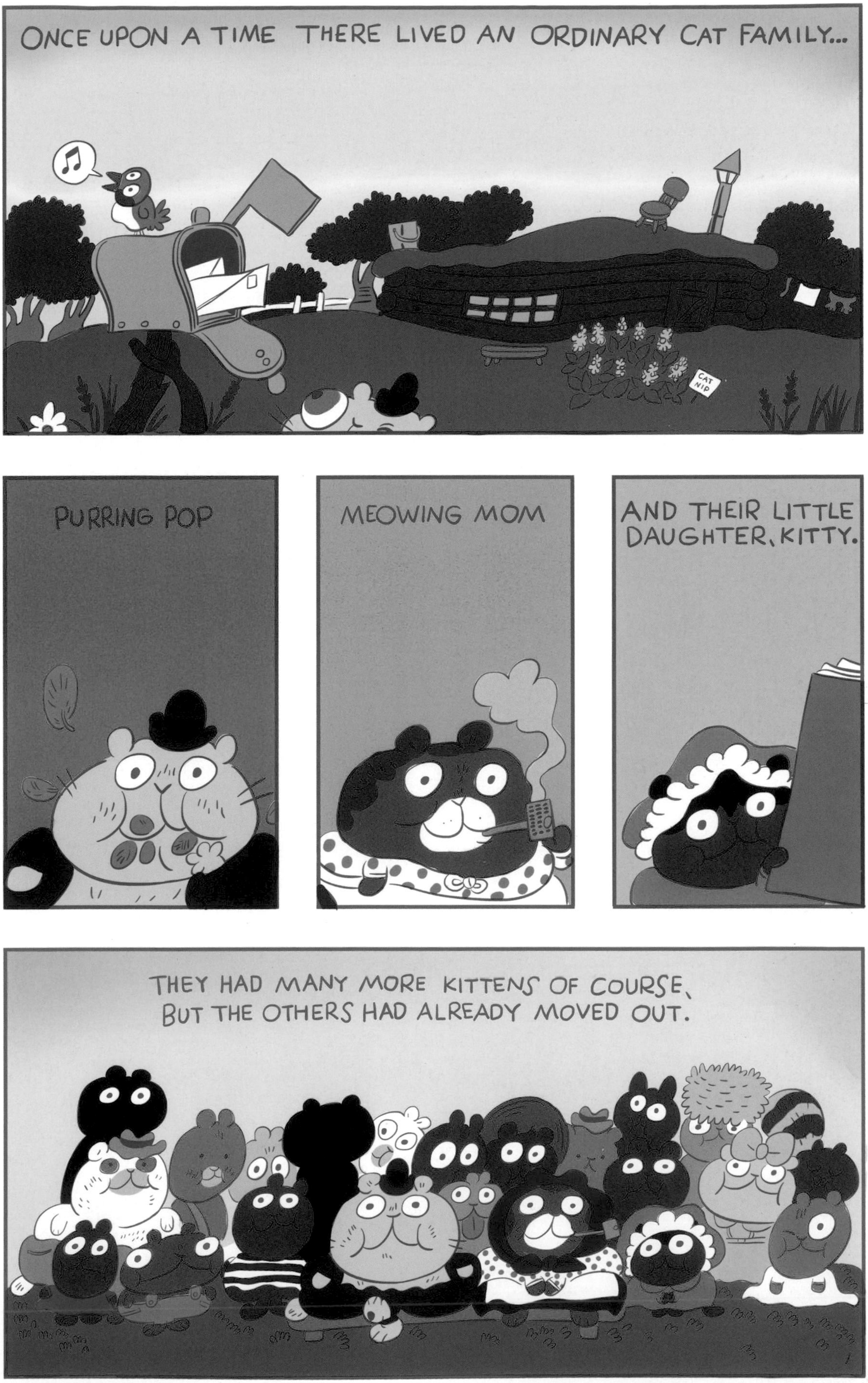
ONCE UPON A TIME THERE LIVED AN ORDINARY CAT FAMILY...
CAT NIP
PURRING POP
MEOWING MOM
AND THEIR LITTLE DAUGHTER, KITTY.
THEY HAD MANY MORE KITTENS OF COURSE, BUT THE OTHERS HAD ALREADY MOVED OUT.

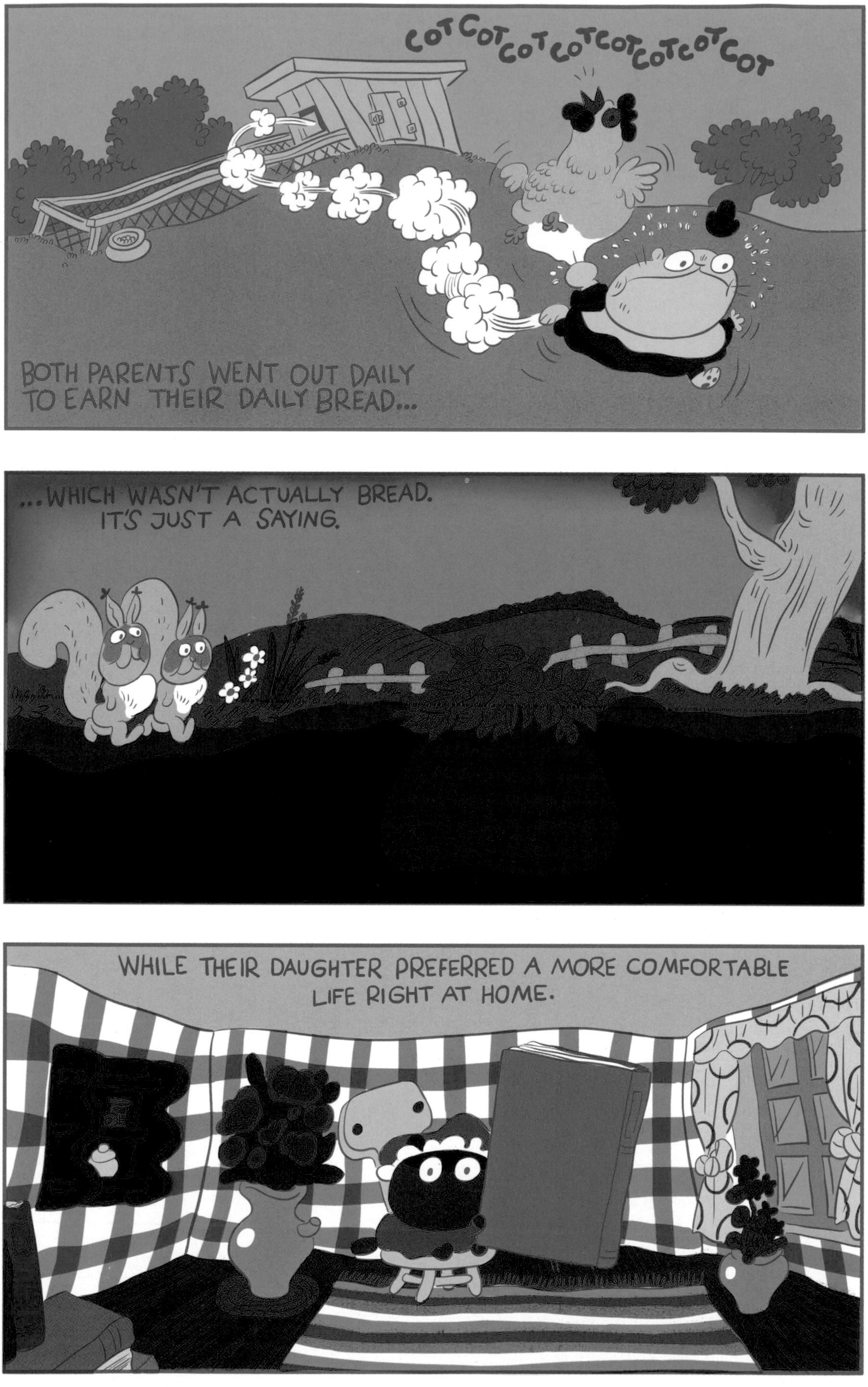
COTCOTCOTCOTCOTCOTCOTCOT
BOTH PARENTS WENT OUT DAILY TO EARN THEIR DAILY BREAD...
...WHICH WASN'T ACTUALLY BREAD. IT'S JUST A SAYING.
WHILE THEIR DAUGHTER PREFERRED A MORE COMFORTABLE LIFE RIGHT AT HOME.

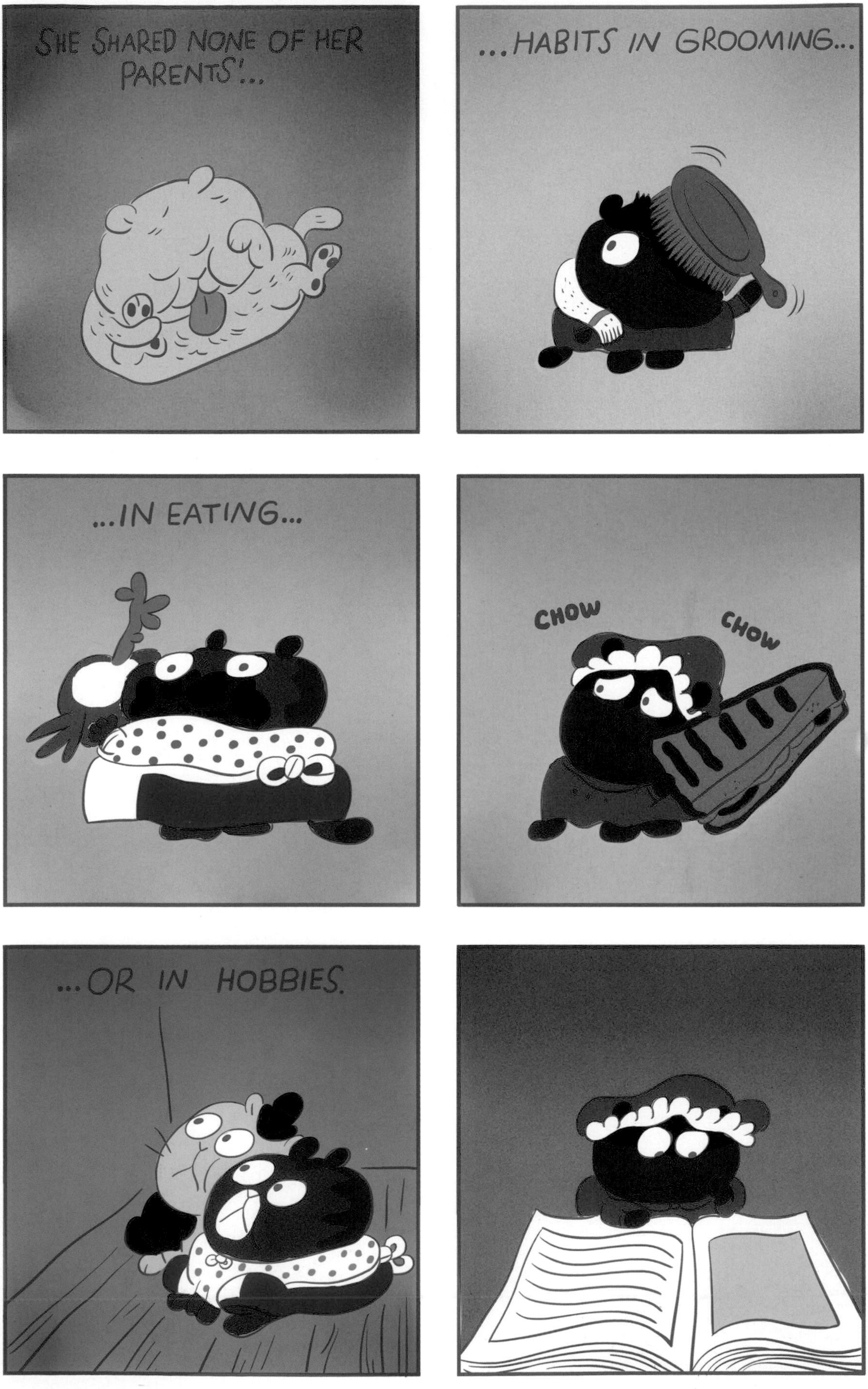
SHE SHARED NONE OF HER PARENTS'...
...HABITS IN GROOMING...
...IN EATING...
CHOW
CHOW
...OR IN HOBBIES.

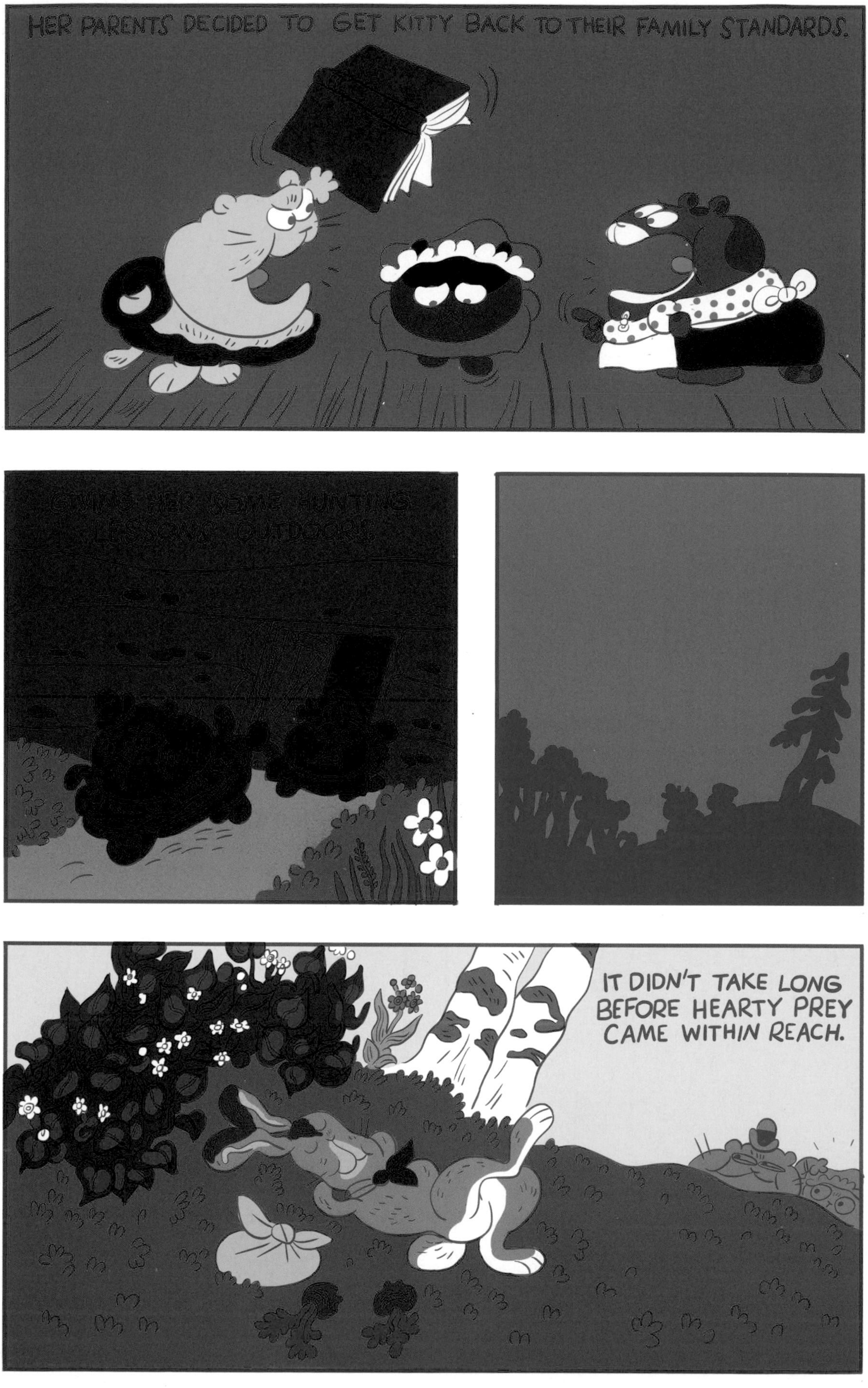
HER PARENTS DECIDED TO GET KITTY BACK TO THEIR FAMILY STANDARDS.
GIVING HER SOME HUNTING LESSONS OUTDOORS.
IT DIDN'T TAKE LONG BEFORE HEARTY PREY CAME WITHIN REACH.

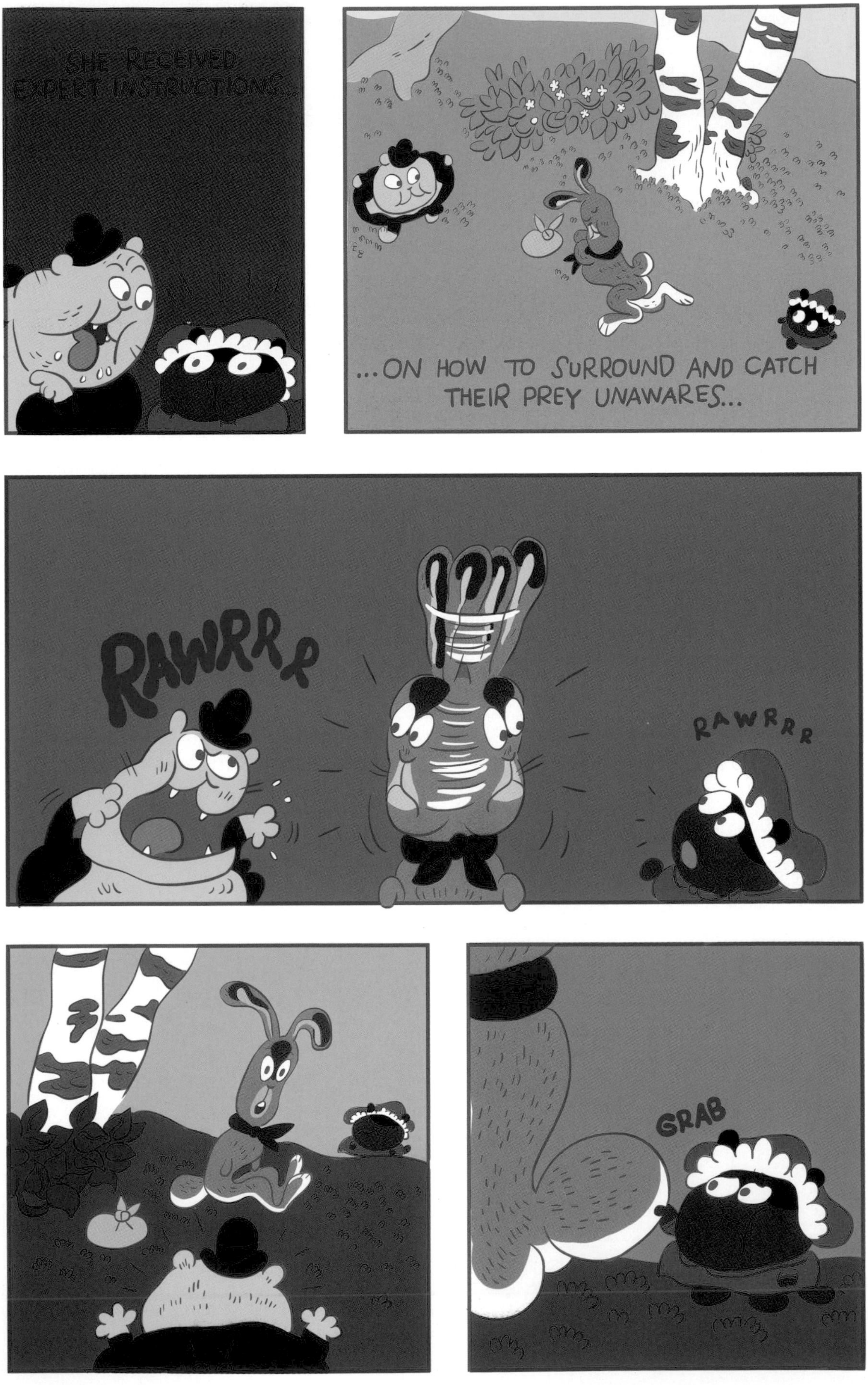
SHE RECEIVED EXPERT INSTRUCTIONS...
...ON HOW TO SURROUND AND CATCH THEIR PREY UNAWARES...
RAWRRR
RAWRRR
GRAB

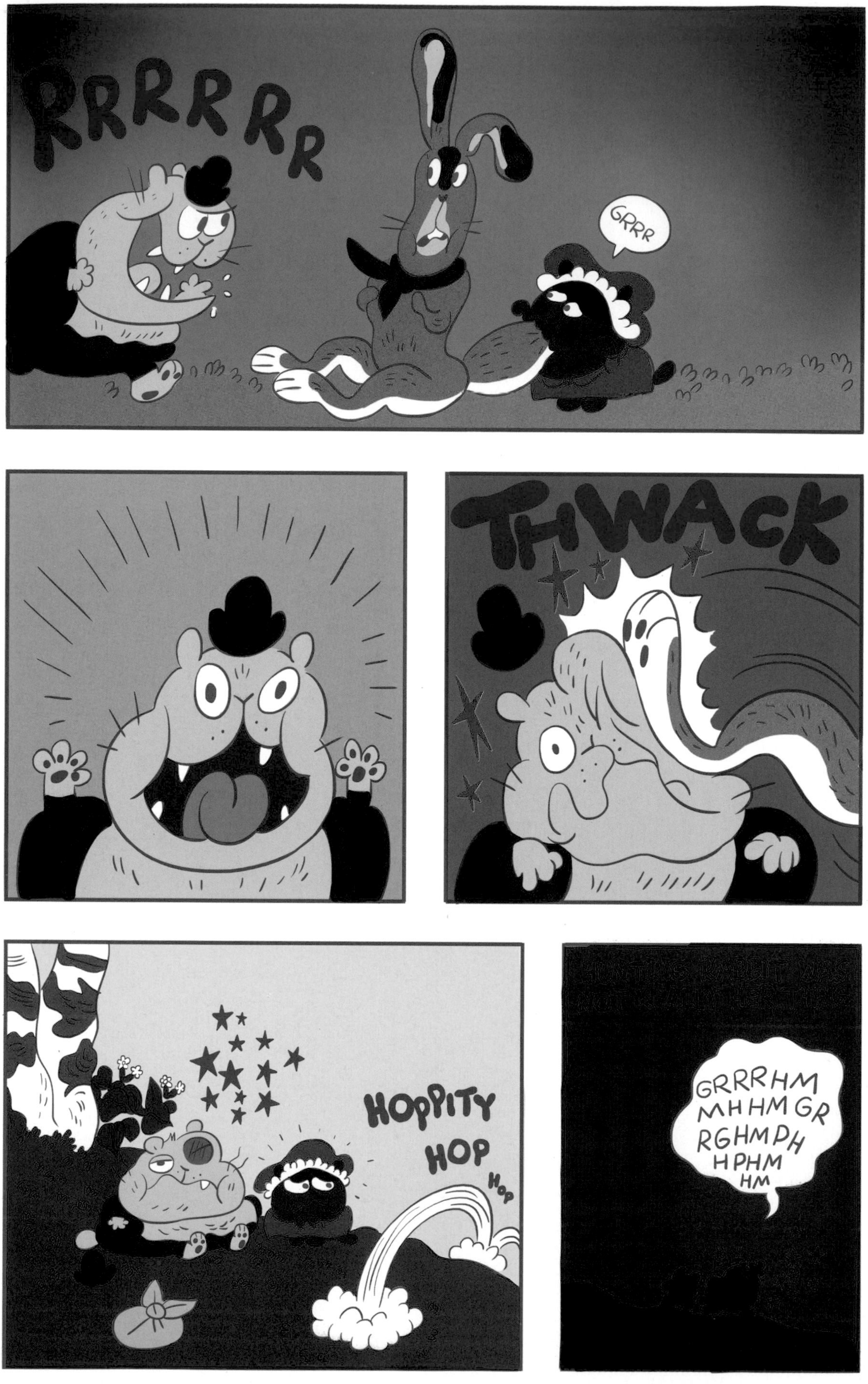
RRRRRRR
GRRR
THWACK
HOPPITY
HOP
HOP
HUNTING RABBIT WAS NOT REALLY HER THING
GRRRHM MHHMGR RGHMPH HPHM HM

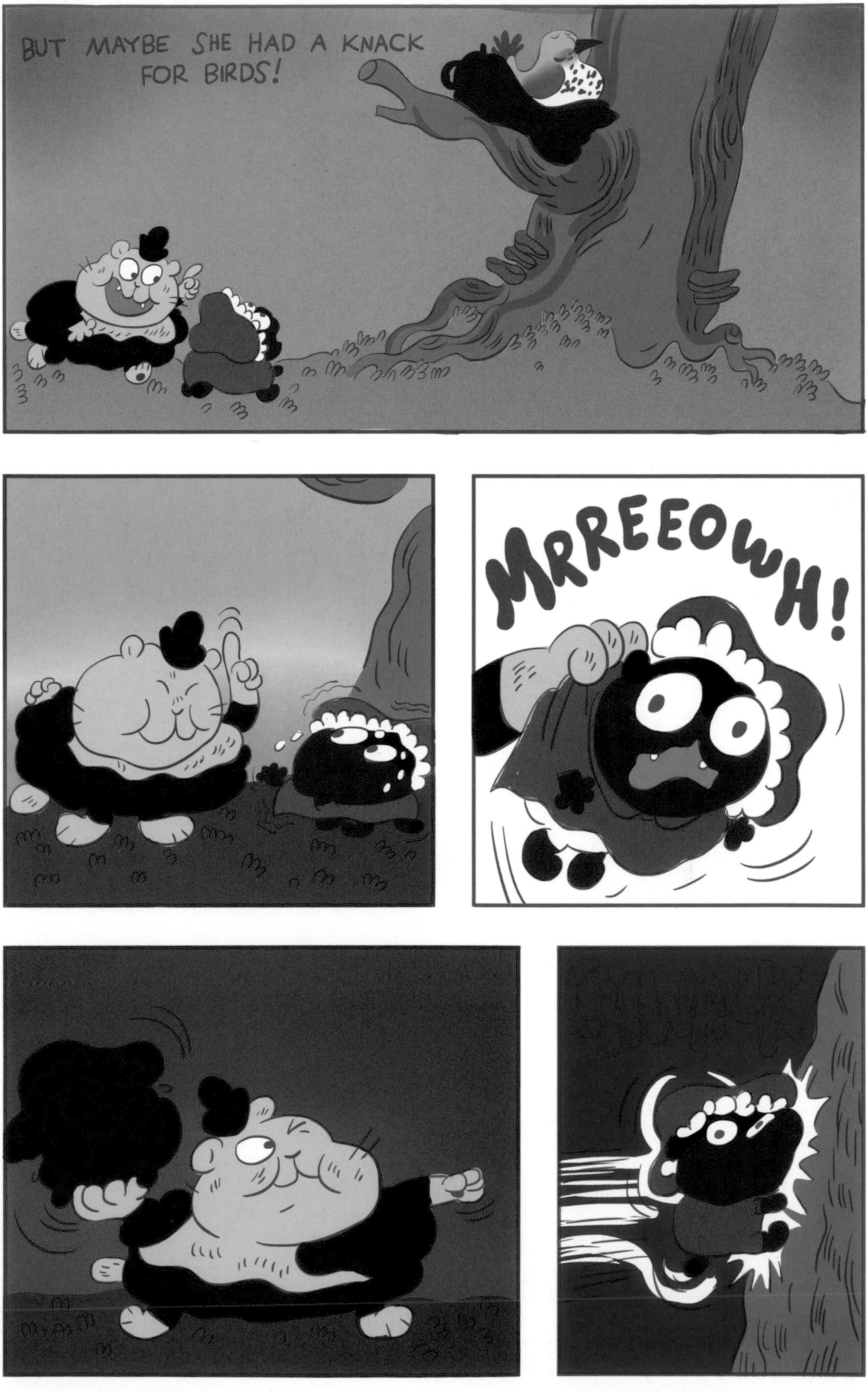
BUT MAYBE SHE HAD A KNACK FOR BIRDS!
MRREEOWH!

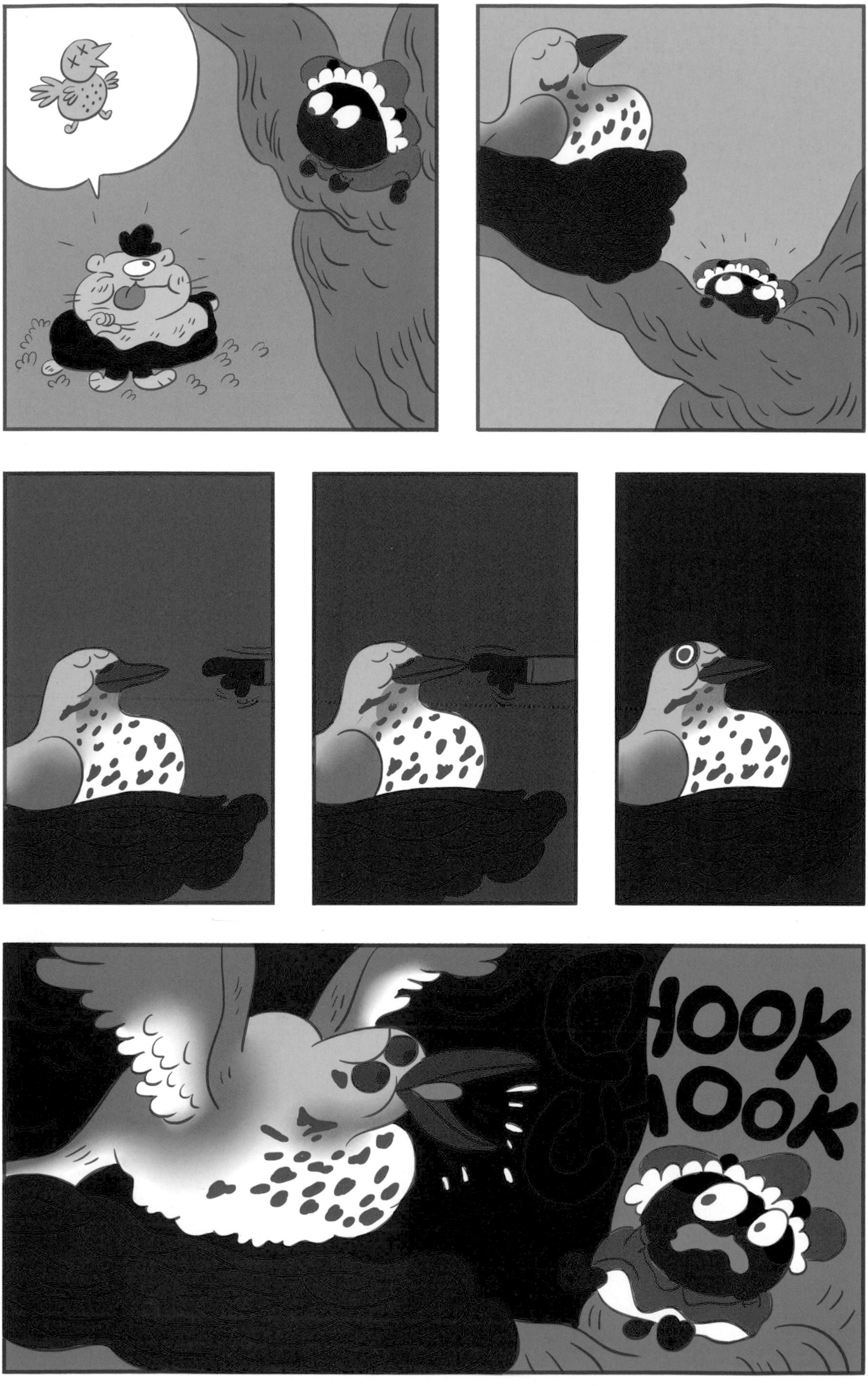
CHOOK
CHOOK

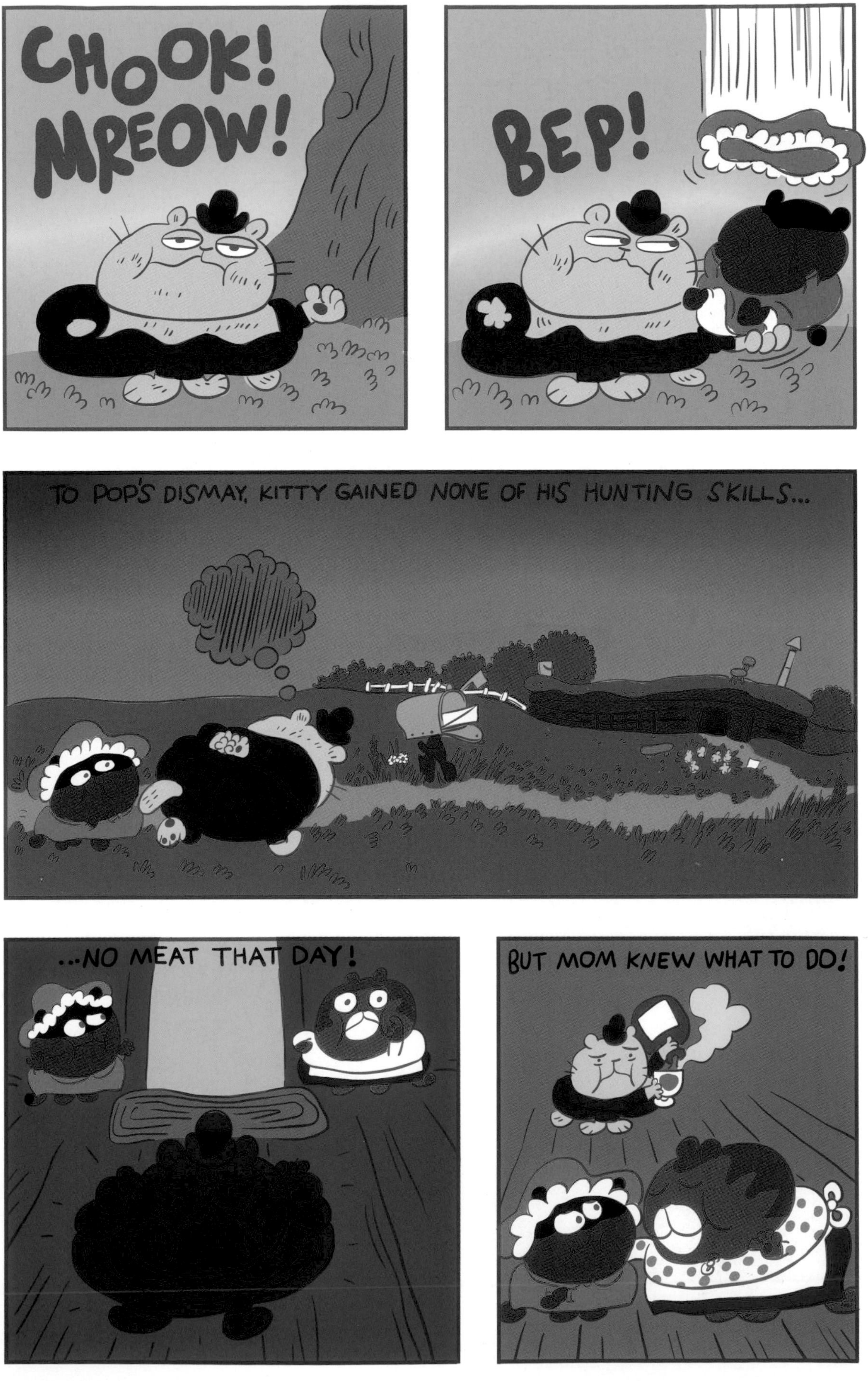

CHOOK! MREOW!
BEP!
TO POP'S DISMAY, KITTY GAINED NONE OF HIS HUNTING SKILLS...
...NO MEAT THAT DAY!
BUT MOM KNEW WHAT TO DO!

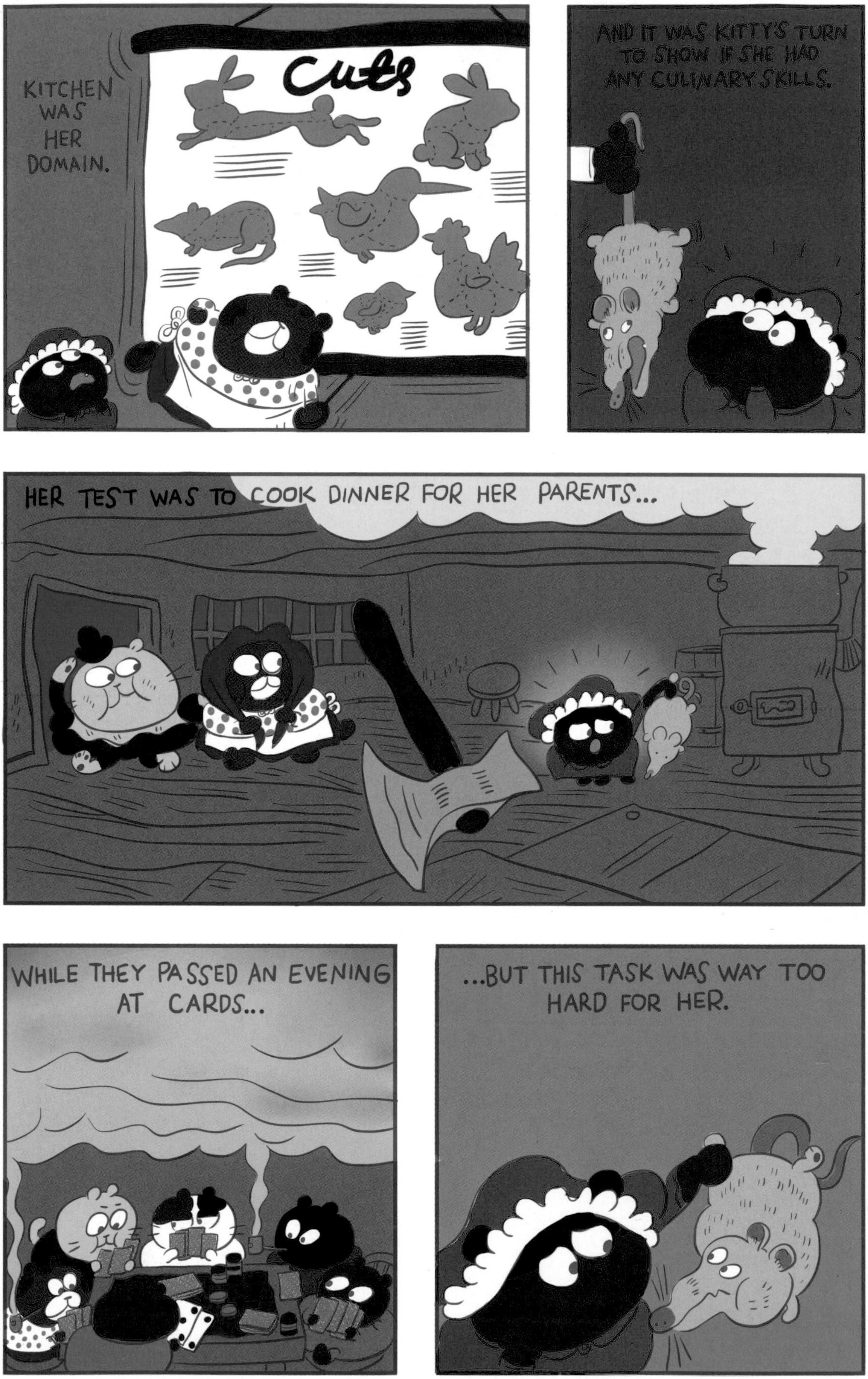
KITCHEN WAS HER DOMAIN.
CUTS
AND IT WAS KITTY'S TURN TO SHOW IF SHE HAD ANY CULINARY SKILLS.
HER TEST WAS TO COOK DINNER FOR HER PARENTS...
WHILE THEY PASSED AN EVENING AT CARDS...
...BUT THIS TASK WAS WAY TOO HARD FOR HER.

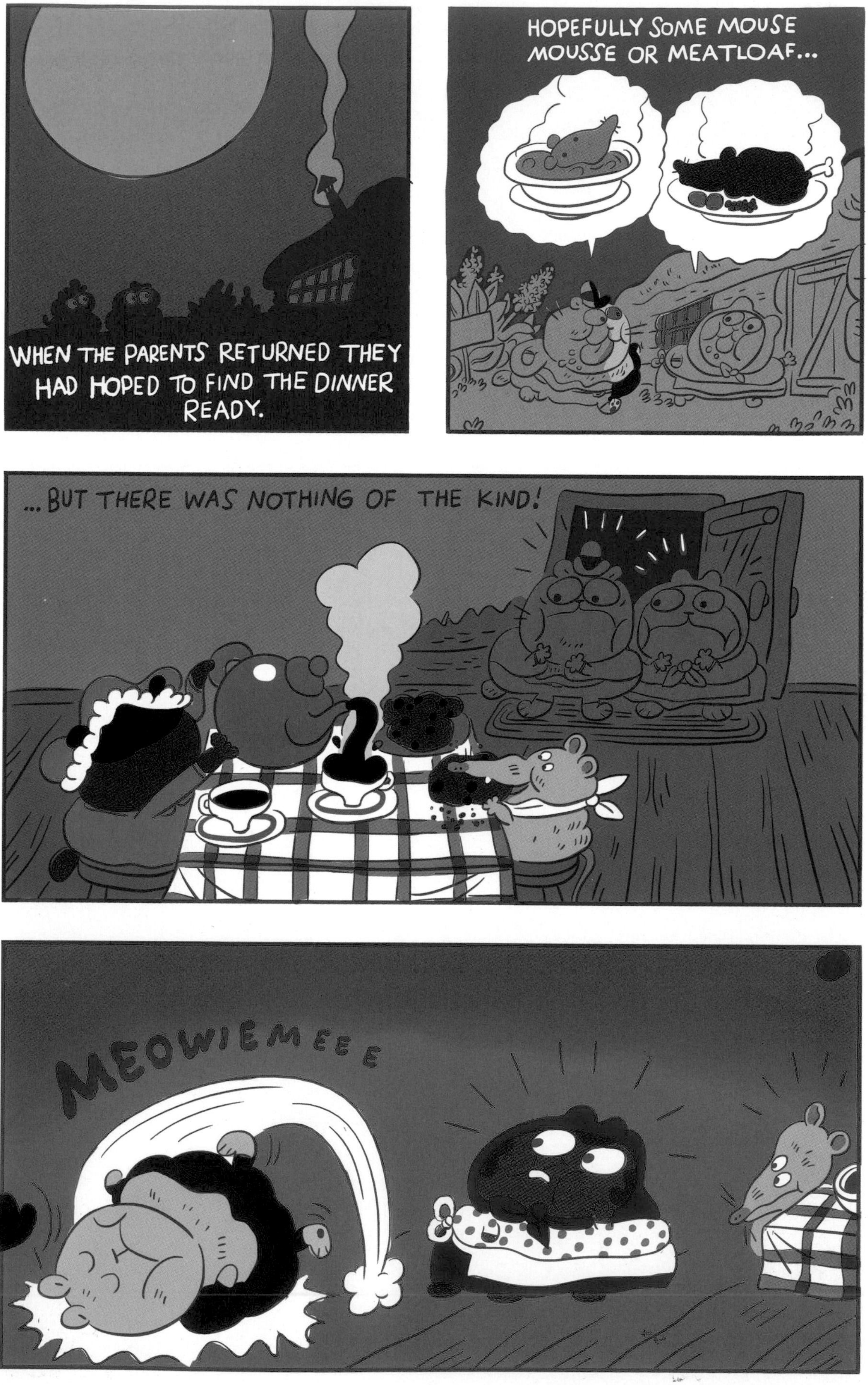
WHEN THE PARENTS RETURNED THEY HAD HOPED TO FIND THE DINNER READY.
HOPEFULLY SOME MOUSE MOUSSE OR MEATLOAF...
...BUT THERE WAS NOTHING OF THE KIND!
MEOWIEMEEE

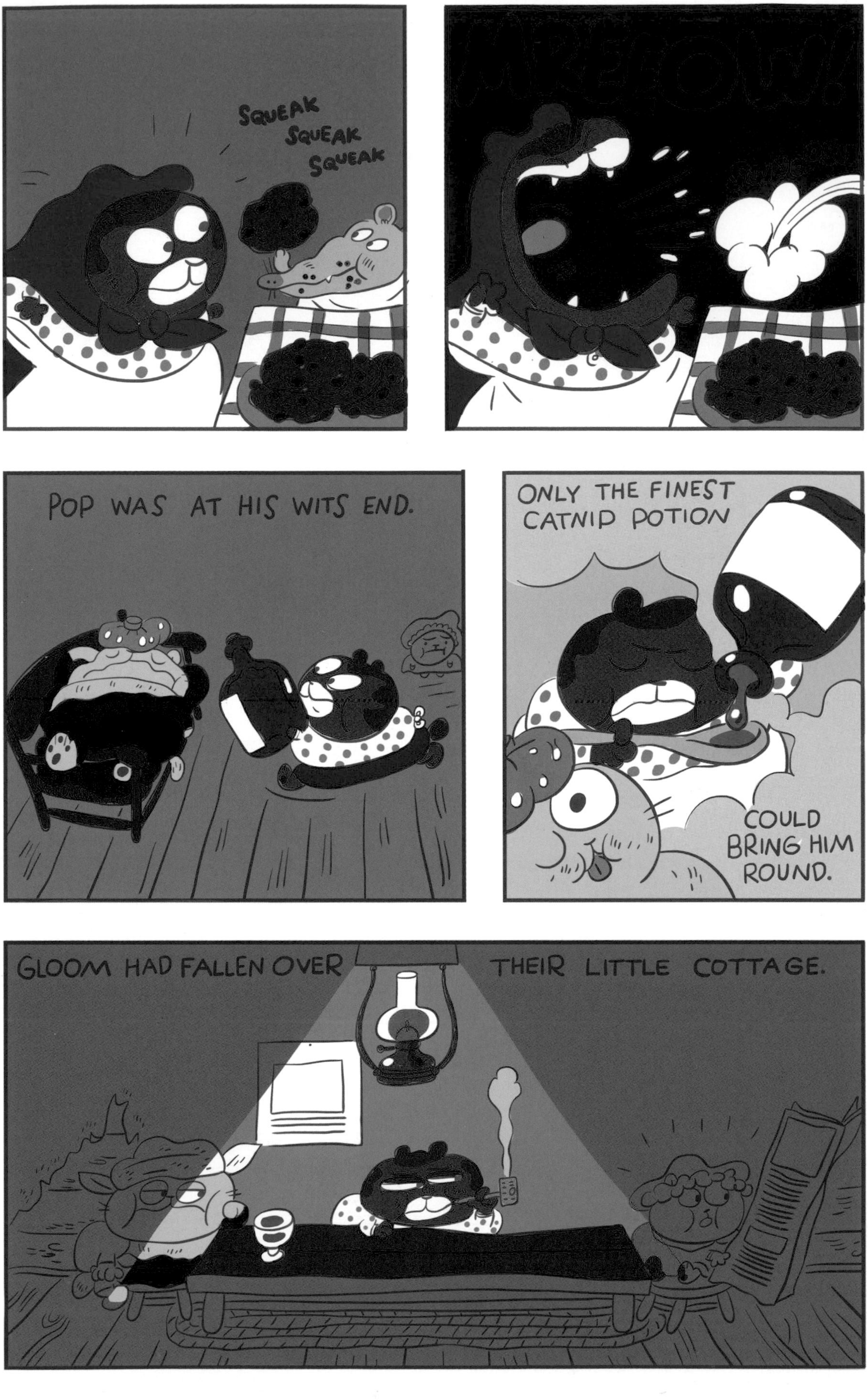
SQUEAK
SQUEAK
SQUEAK
MREEOW!!
POP WAS AT HIS WITS END.
ONLY THE FINEST CATNIP POTION
COULD BRING HIM ROUND.
GLOOM HAD FALLEN OVER
THEIR LITTLE COTTAGE.

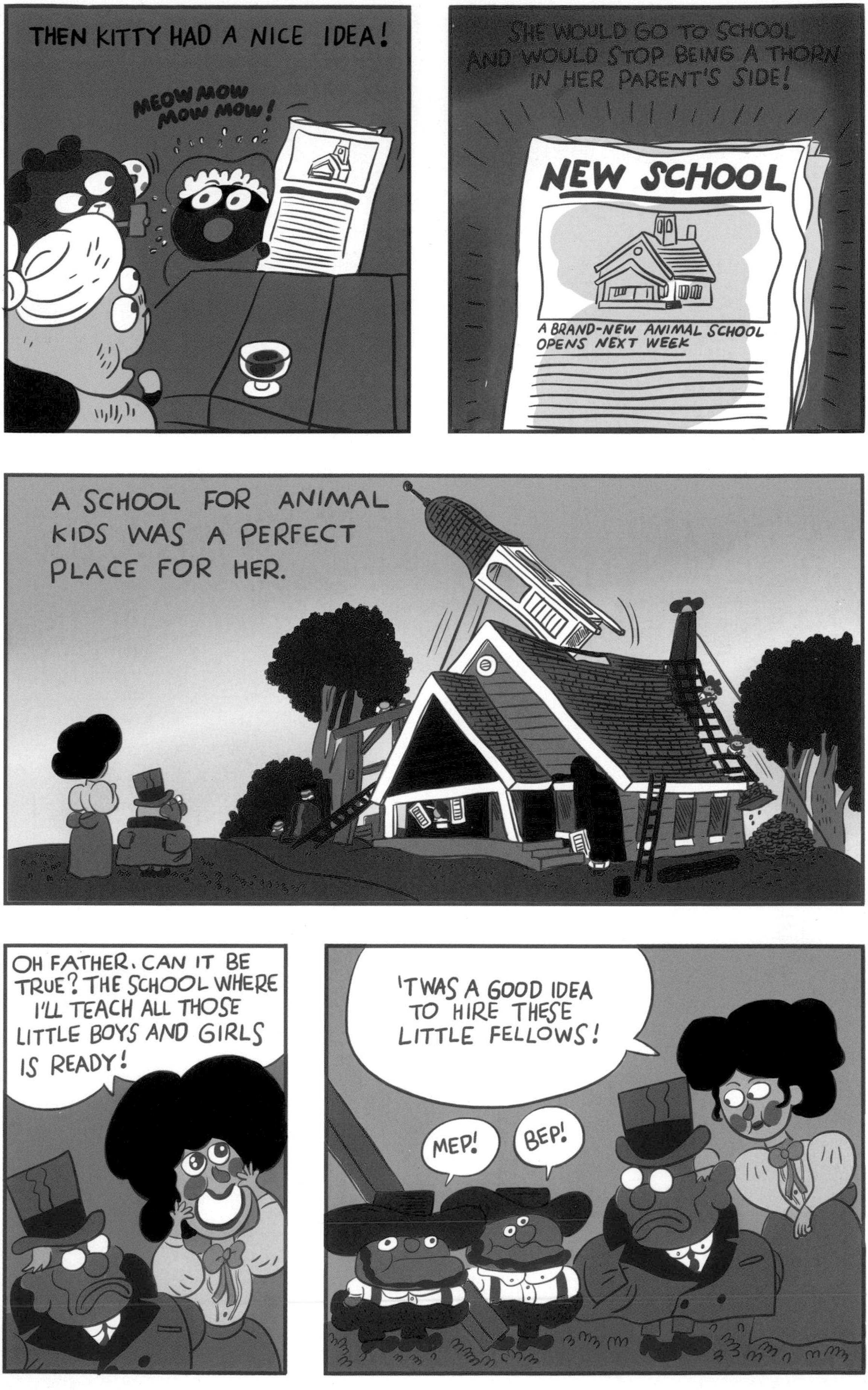
THEN KITTY HAD A NICE IDEA!
MEOW MOW MOW MOW!
SHE WOULD GO TO SCHOOL AND WOULD STOP BEING A THORN IN HER PARENT'S SIDE!
NEW SCHOOL
A BRAND-NEW ANIMAL SCHOOL OPENS NEXT WEEK
A SCHOOL FOR ANIMAL KIDS WAS A PERFECT PLACE FOR HER.
OH FATHER. CAN IT BE TRUE? THE SCHOOL WHERE I'LL TEACH ALL THOSE LITTLE BOYS AND GIRLS IS READY!
'TWAS A GOOD IDEA TO HIRE THESE LITTLE FELLOWS!
MEP!
BEP!

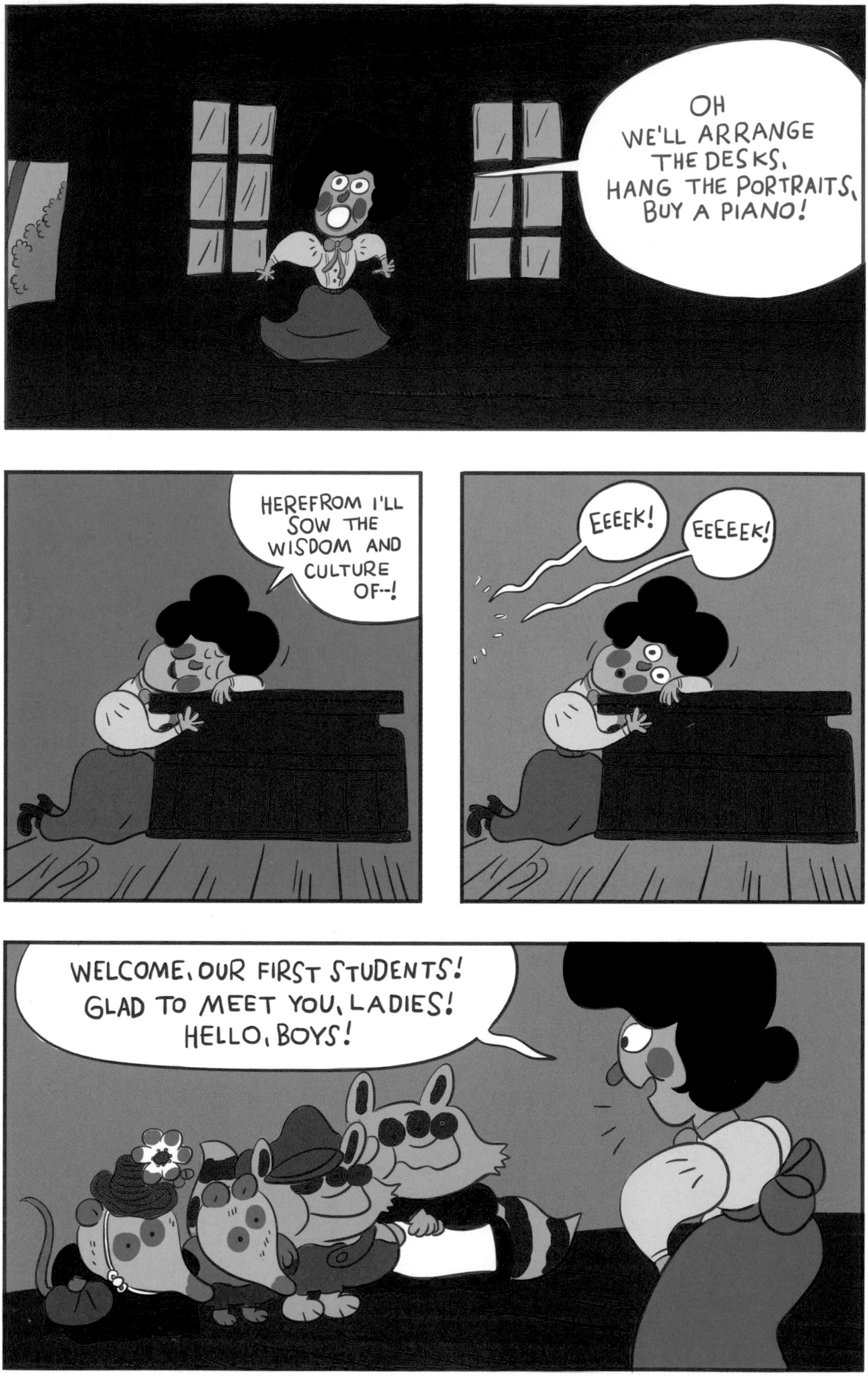
OH WE'LL ARRANGE THE DESKS, HANG THE PORTRAITS, BUY A PIANO!
HEREFROM I'LL SOW THE WISDOM AND CULTURE OF--!
EEEEK!
EEEEEK!
WELCOME, OUR FIRST STUDENTS! GLAD TO MEET YOU, LADIES! HELLO, BOYS!

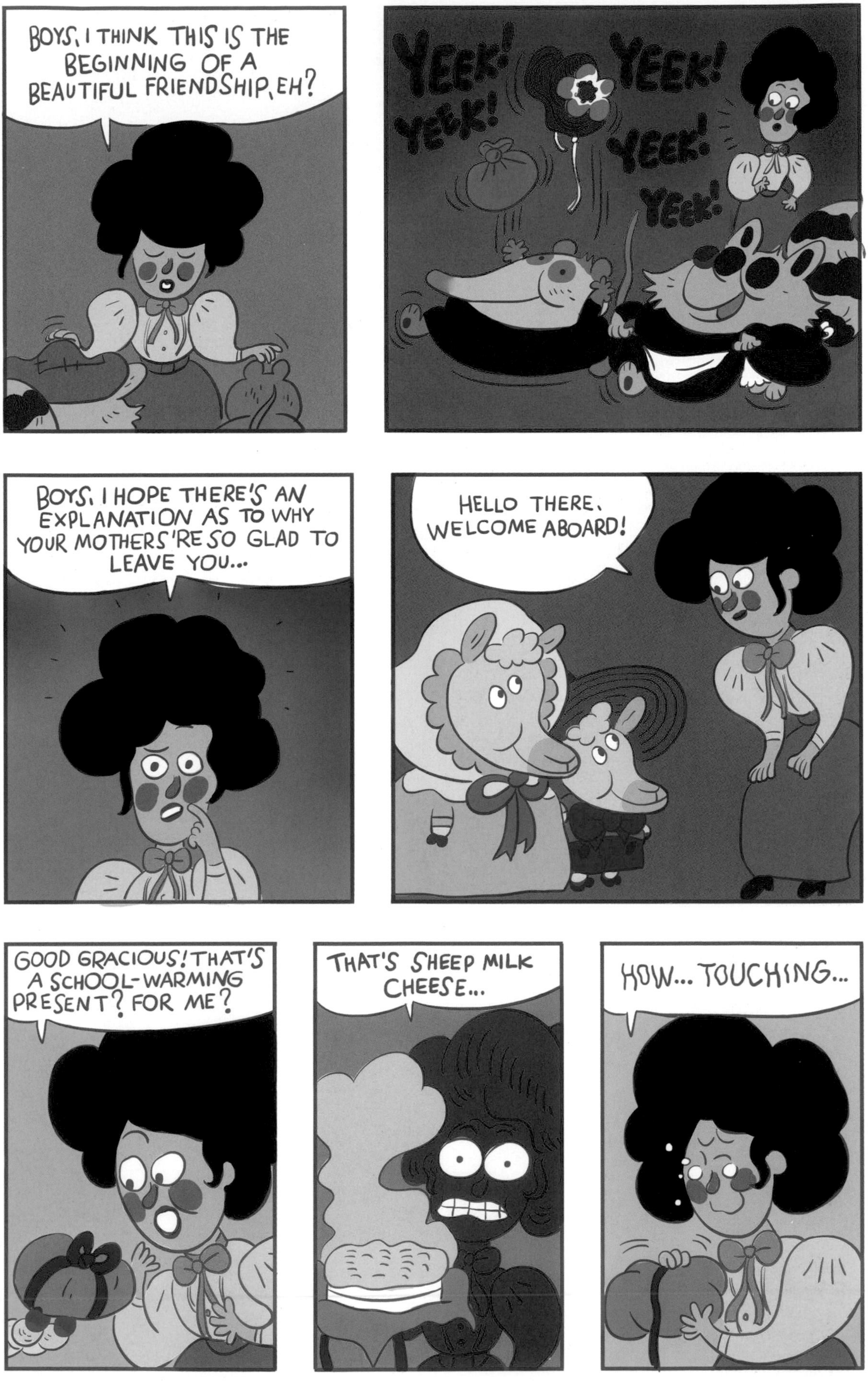
BOYS, I THINK THIS IS THE BEGINNING OF A BEAUTIFUL FRIENDSHIP, EH?
YEEK! YEEK! YEEK! YEEK! YEEK!
BOYS, I HOPE THERE'S AN EXPLANATION AS TO WHY YOUR MOTHERS'RE SO GLAD TO LEAVE YOU...
HELLO THERE. WELCOME ABOARD!
GOOD GRACIOUS! THAT'S A SCHOOL-WARMING PRESENT? FOR ME?
THAT'S SHEEP MILK CHEESE...
HOW... TOUCHING...

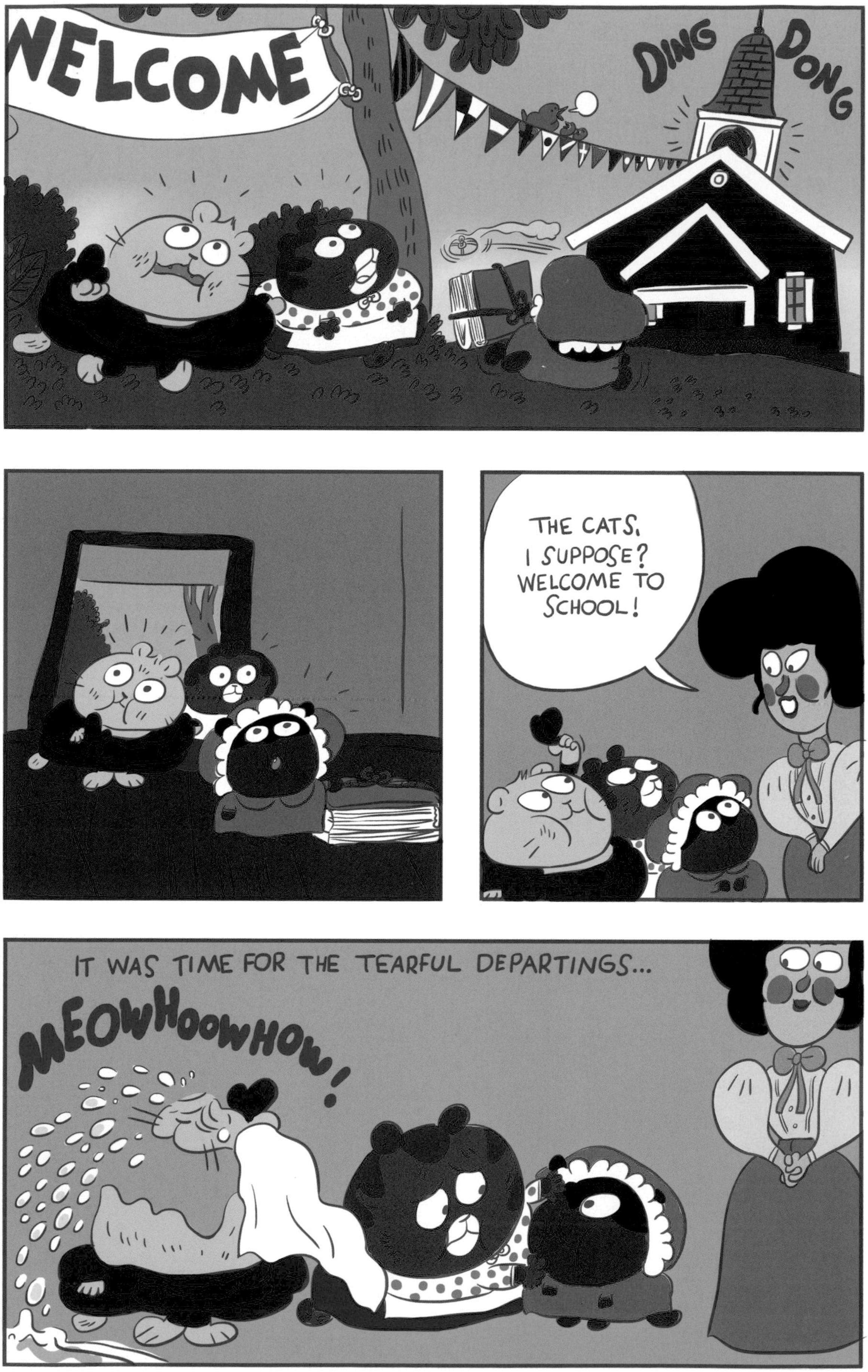
WELCOME
DING DONG
THE CATS, I SUPPOSE? WELCOME TO SCHOOL!
IT WAS TIME FOR THE TEARFUL DEPARTINGS...
MEOWHOOWHOW!

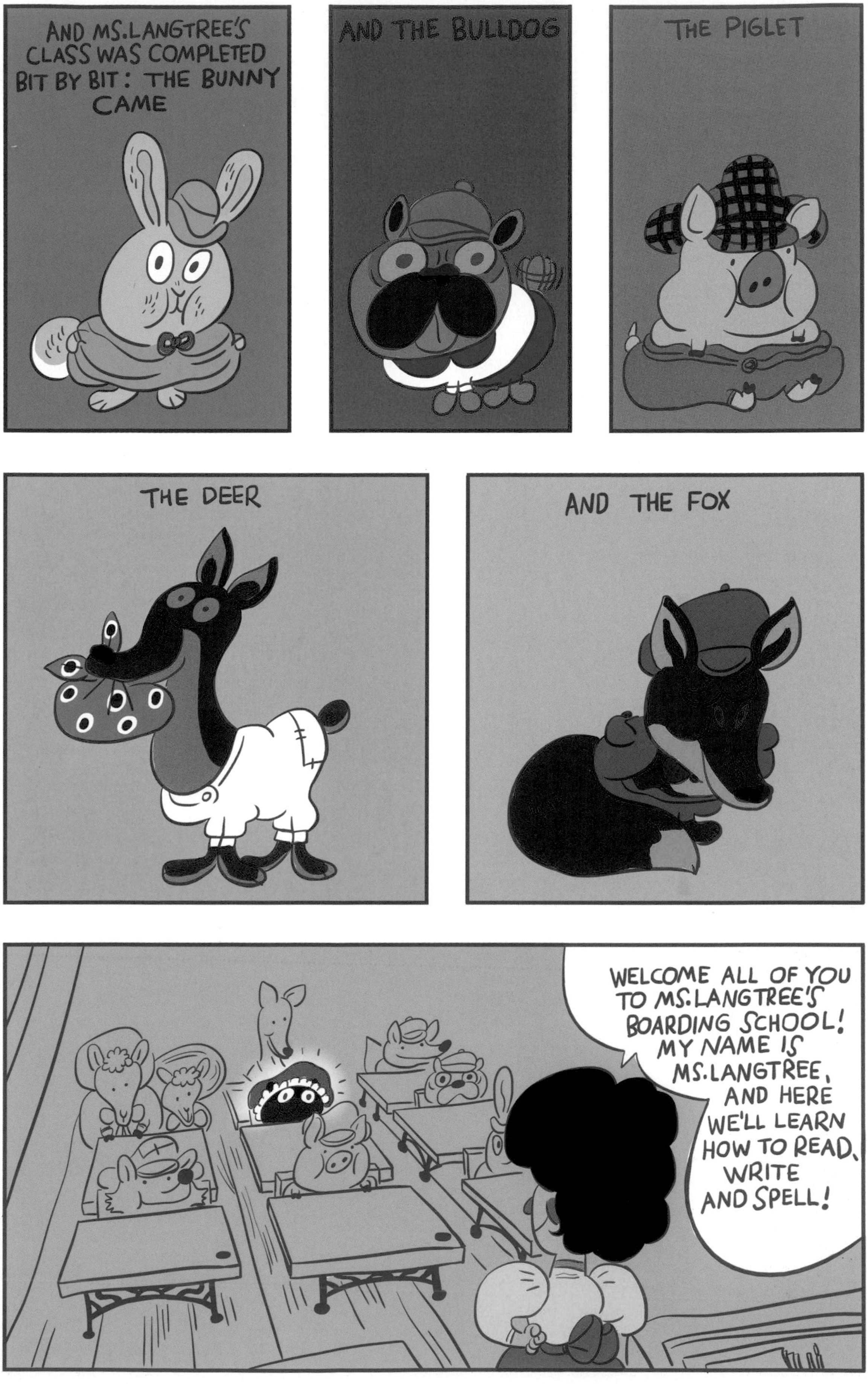
AND MS.LANGTREE'S CLASS WAS COMPLETED BIT BY BIT: THE BUNNY CAME
AND THE BULLDOG
THE PIGLET
THE DEER
AND THE FOX
WELCOME ALL OF YOU TO MS.LANGTREE'S BOARDING SCHOOL! MY NAME IS MS.LANGTREE, AND HERE WE'LL LEARN HOW TO READ, WRITE AND SPELL!

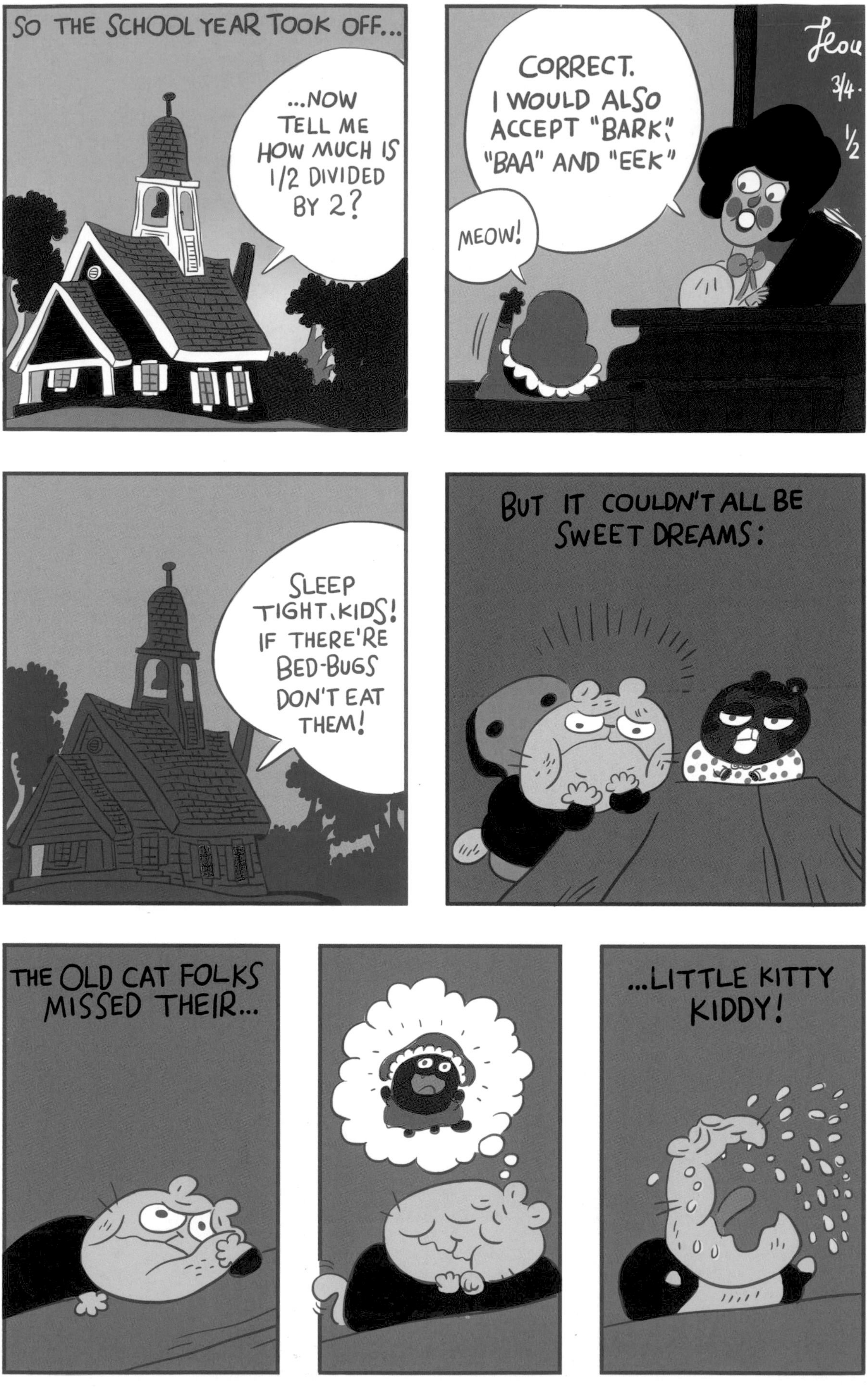
SO THE SCHOOL YEAR TOOK OFF...
...NOW TELL ME HOW MUCH IS 1/2 DIVIDED BY 2?
MEOW!
CORRECT. I WOULD ALSO ACCEPT "BARK," "BAA" AND "EEK"
SLEEP TIGHT, KIDS! IF THERE'RE BED-BUGS DON'T EAT THEM!
BUT IT COULDN'T ALL BE SWEET DREAMS:
THE OLD CAT FOLKS MISSED THEIR...
...LITTLE KITTY KIDDY!

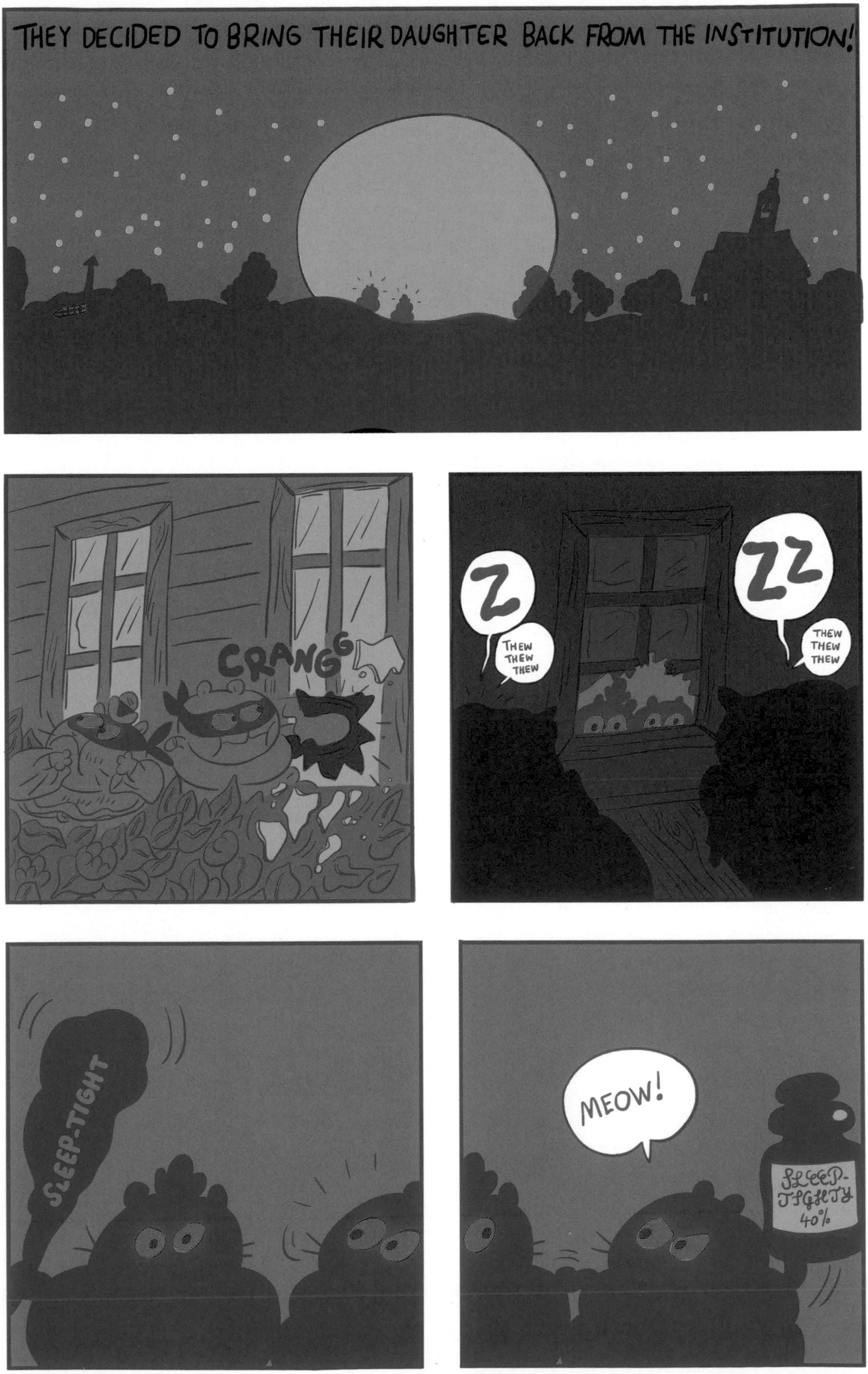
THEY DECIDED TO BRING THEIR DAUGHTER BACK FROM THE INSTITUTION!
CRANGG
Z
THEW THEW THEW
ZZ
THEW THEW THEW
SLEEP-TIGHT
MEOW!
SLEEP-TIGHTY 40%

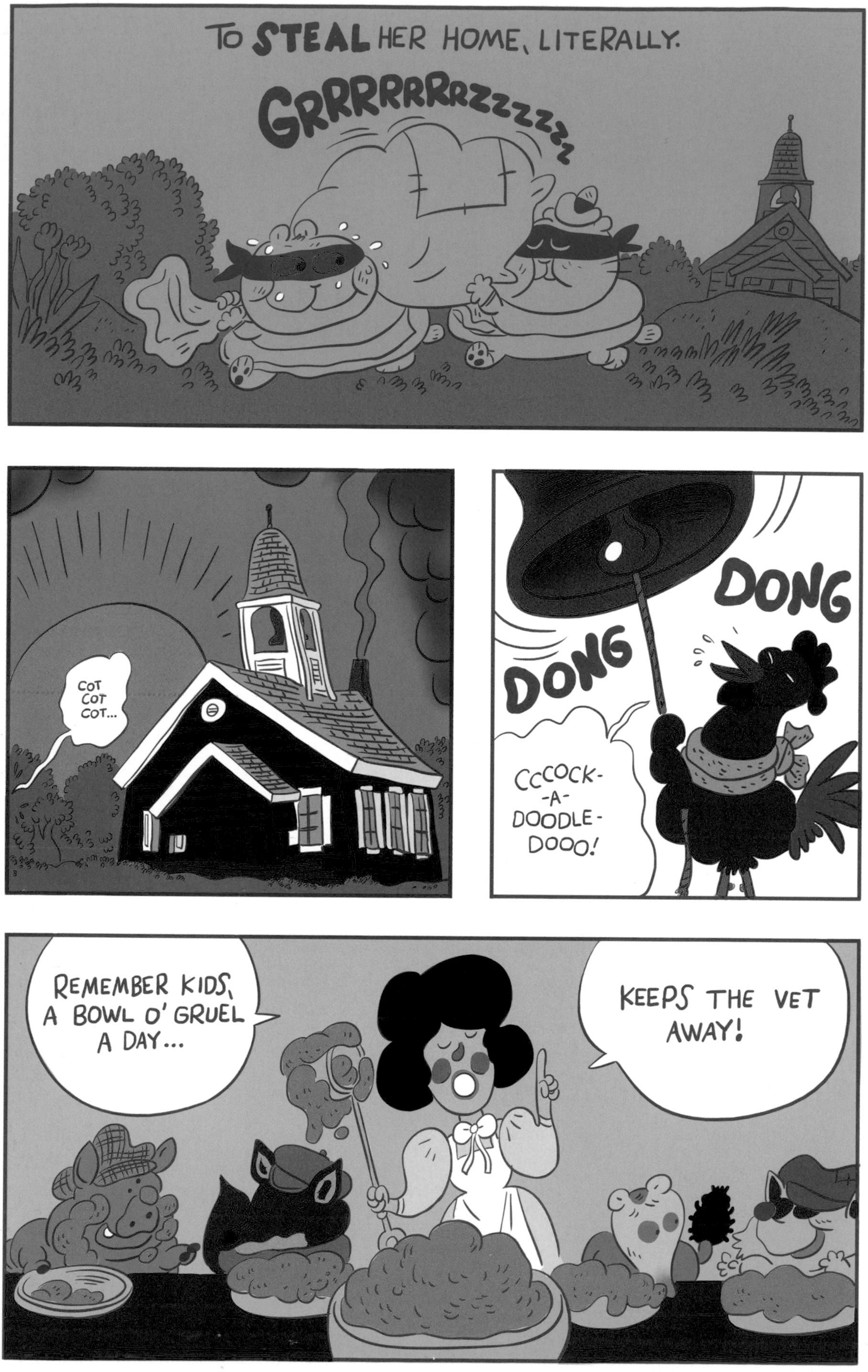
TO STEAL HER HOME, LITERALLY.
GRRRRRRRZZZZZZZ
COT COT COT...
DONG
DONG
CCCOCK-A-DOODLE-DOOO!
REMEMBER KIDS, A BOWL O' GRUEL A DAY...
KEEPS THE VET AWAY!

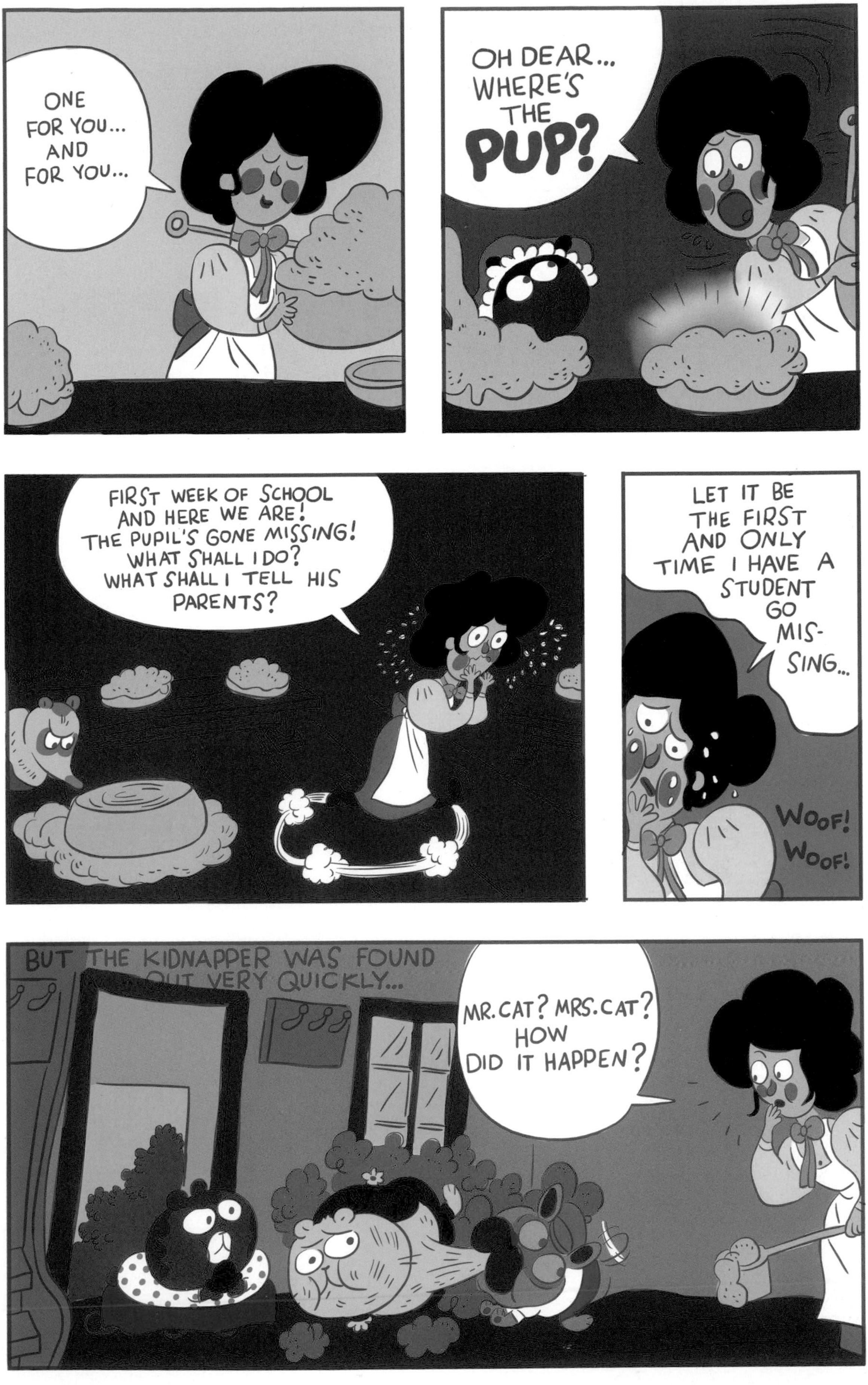

ONE FOR YOU... AND FOR YOU...
OH DEAR... WHERE'S THE PUP?
FIRST WEEK OF SCHOOL AND HERE WE ARE! THE PUPIL'S GONE MISSING! WHAT SHALL I DO? WHAT SHALL I TELL HIS PARENTS?
LET IT BE THE FIRST AND ONLY TIME I HAVE A STUDENT GO MIS-SING...
WOOF! WOOF!
BUT THE KIDNAPPER WAS FOUND OUT VERY QUICKLY...
MR. CAT? MRS. CAT? HOW DID IT HAPPEN?

COVER GALLERY

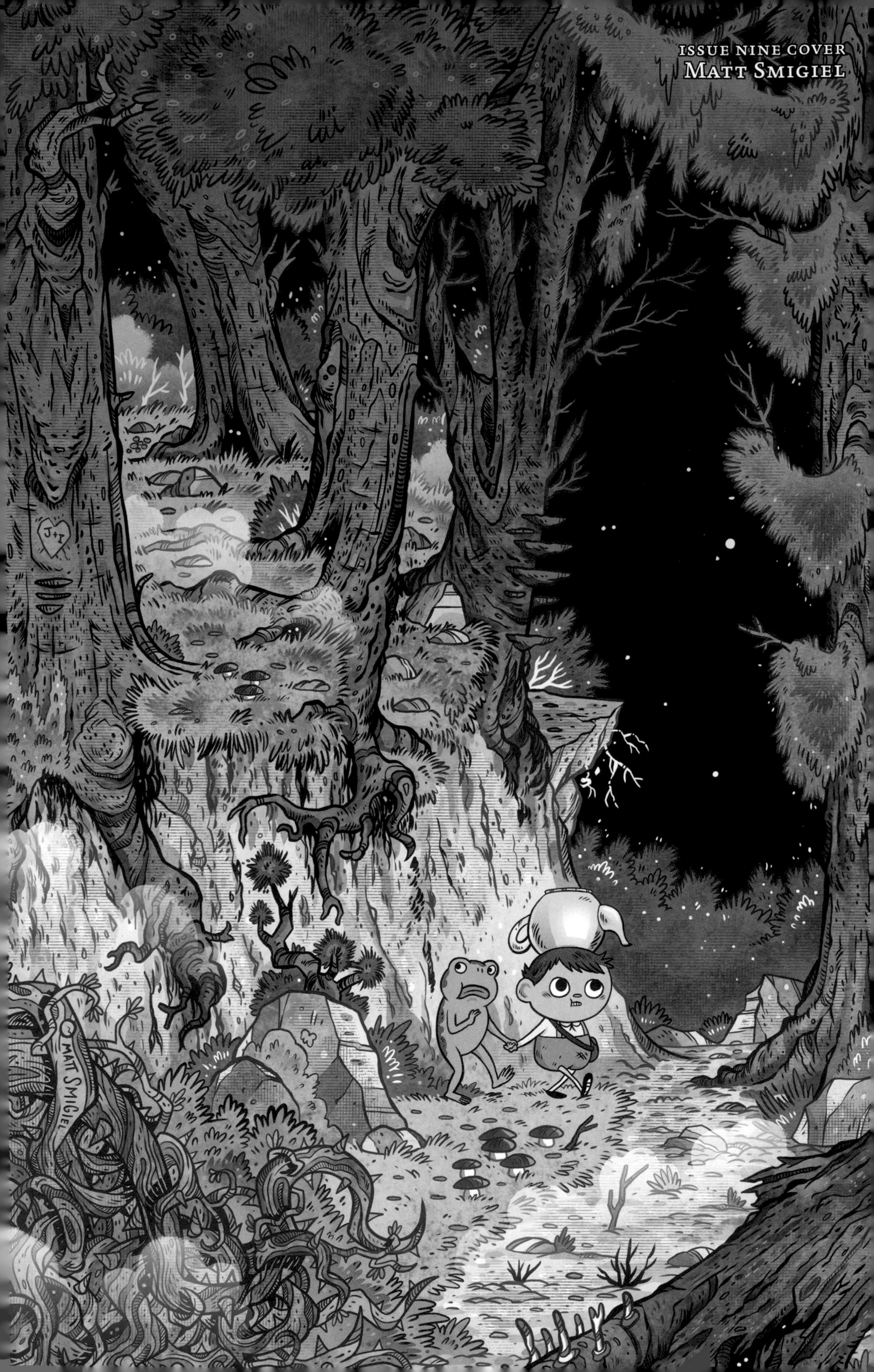
J+T
MATT SMIGIEL

ISSUE NINE COVER
MATT SMIGIEL

ISSUE NINE SUBSCRIPTION COVER
Kellye Purdue

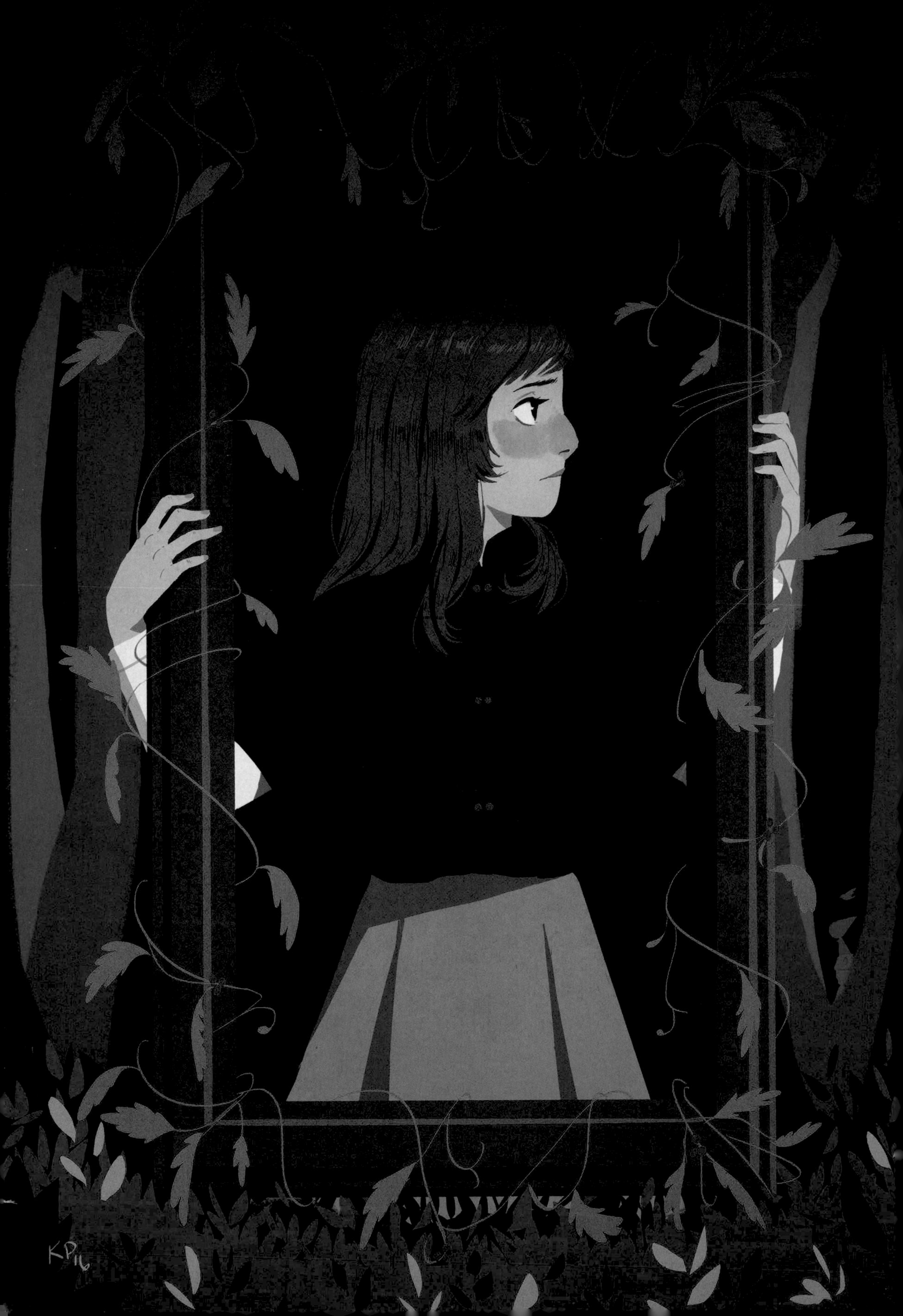
KP16

ISSUE TEN COVER
LAUREN DUDA

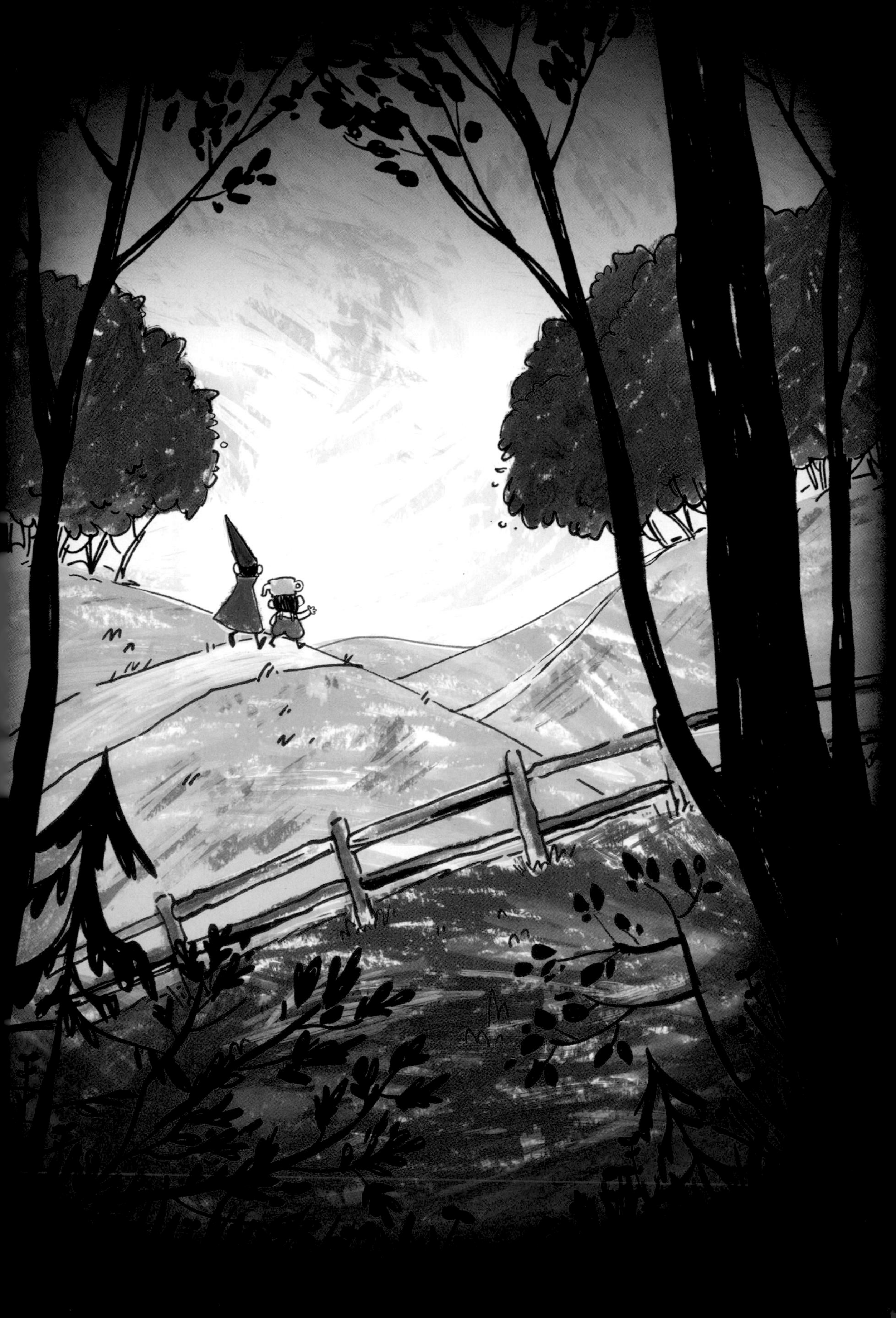

ISSUE TEN SUBSCRIPTION COVER
EMILY OSBORNE

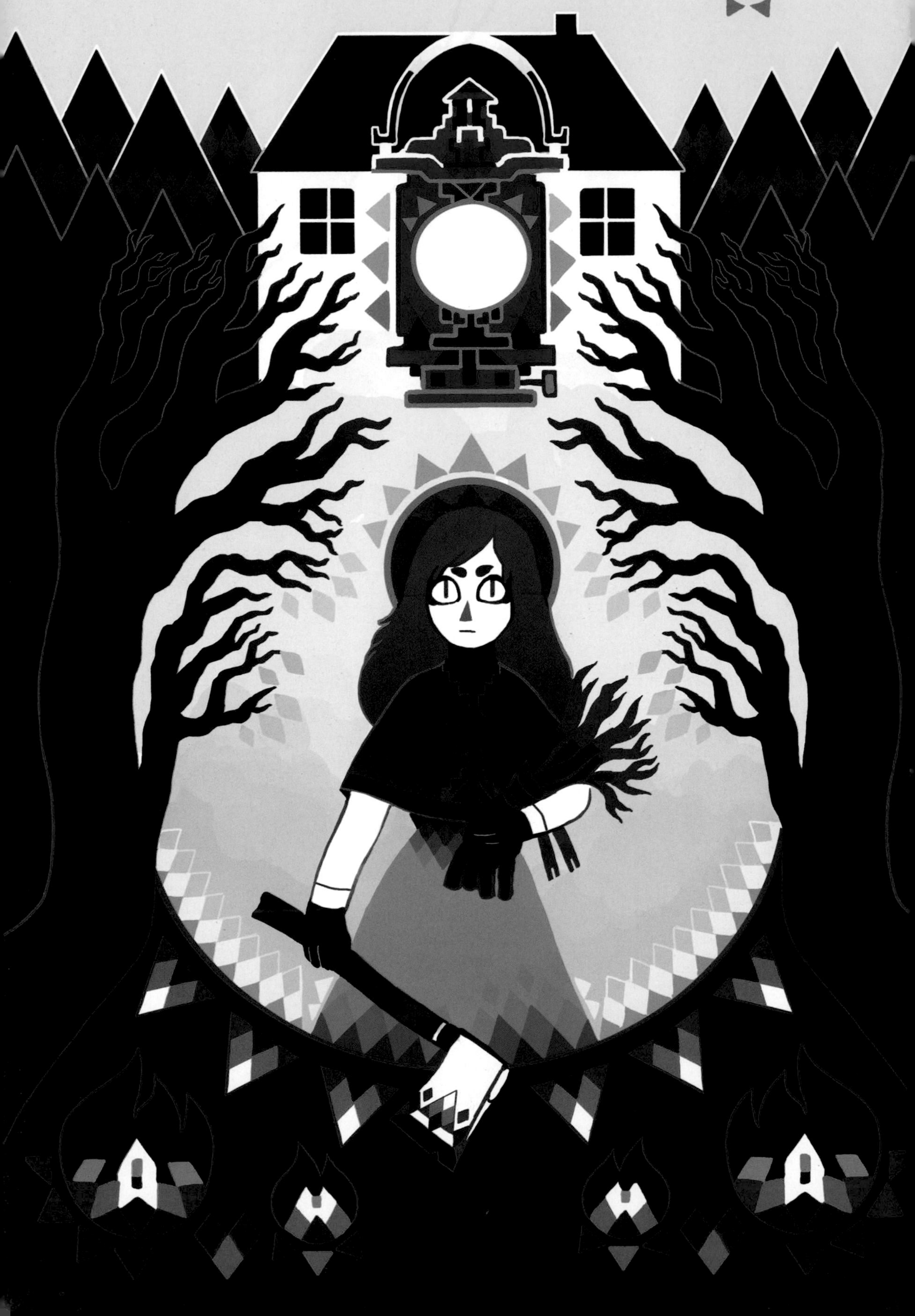

ISSUE ELEVEN COVER
KIERNAN SJURSEN-LIEN

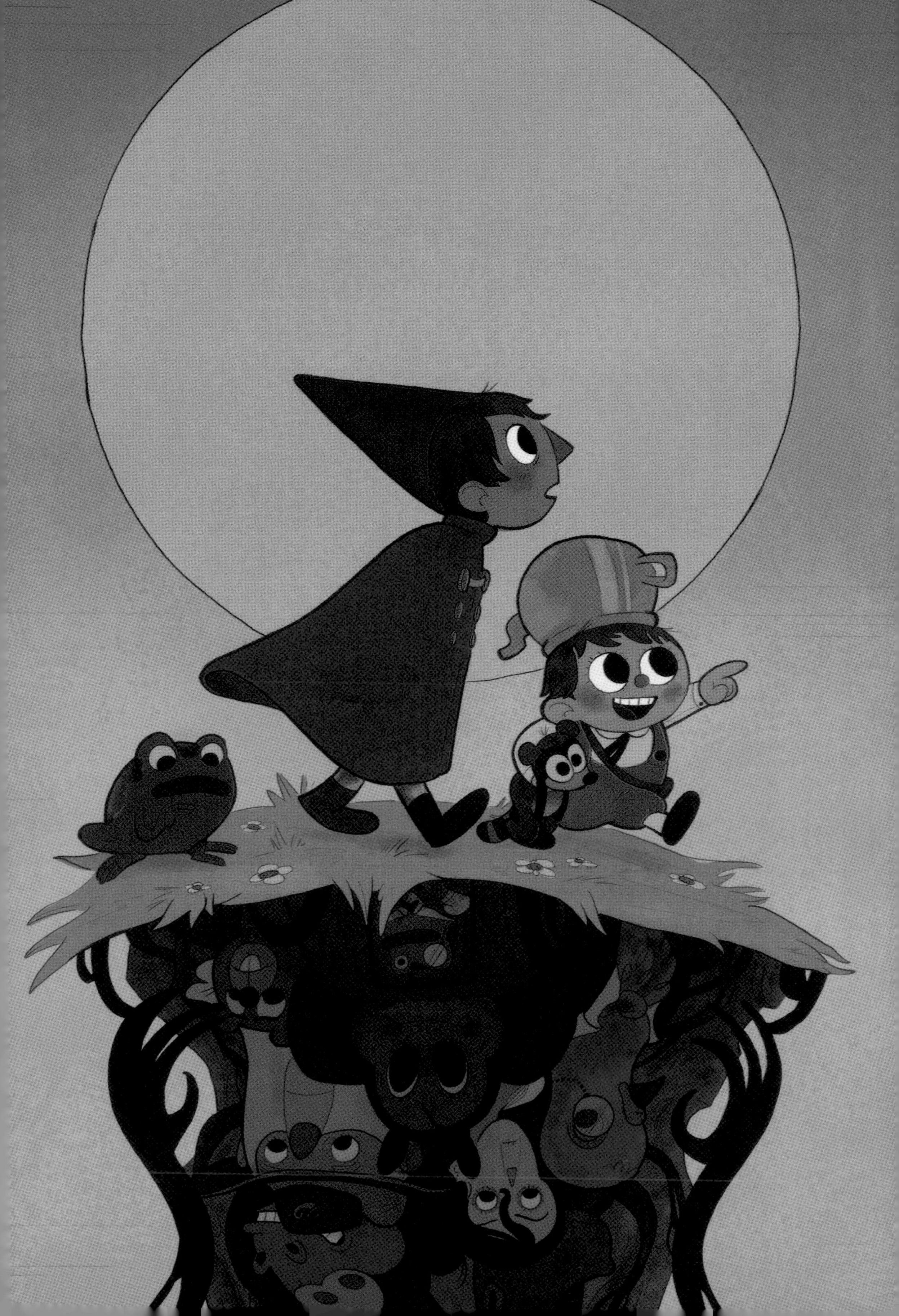

ISSUE ELEVEN SUBSCRIPTION COVER
CARA MCGEE

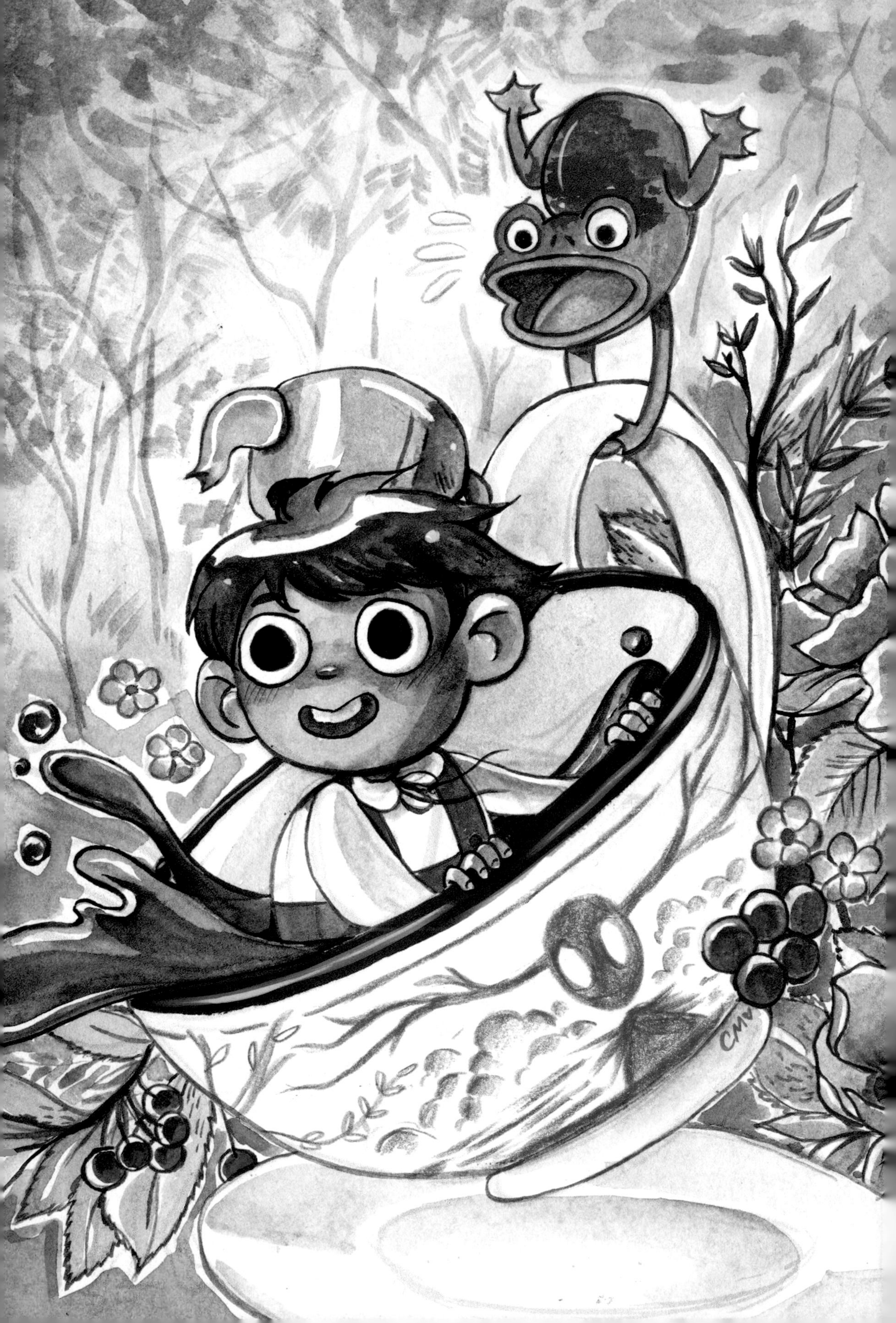

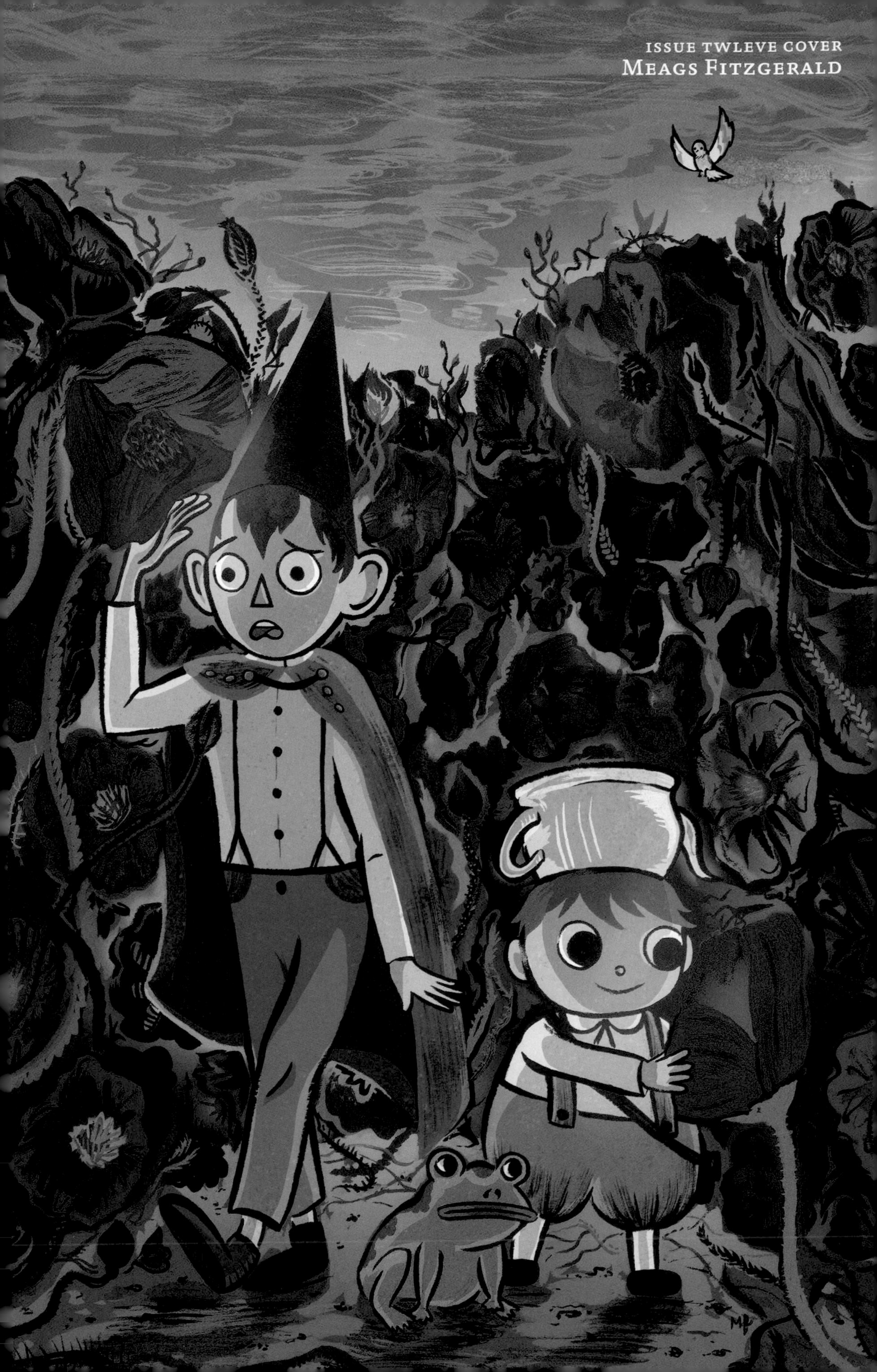

ISSUE TWLEVE COVER
MEAGS FITZGERALD

ISSUE TWELVE SUBSCRIPTION COVER
VICKI SIGH

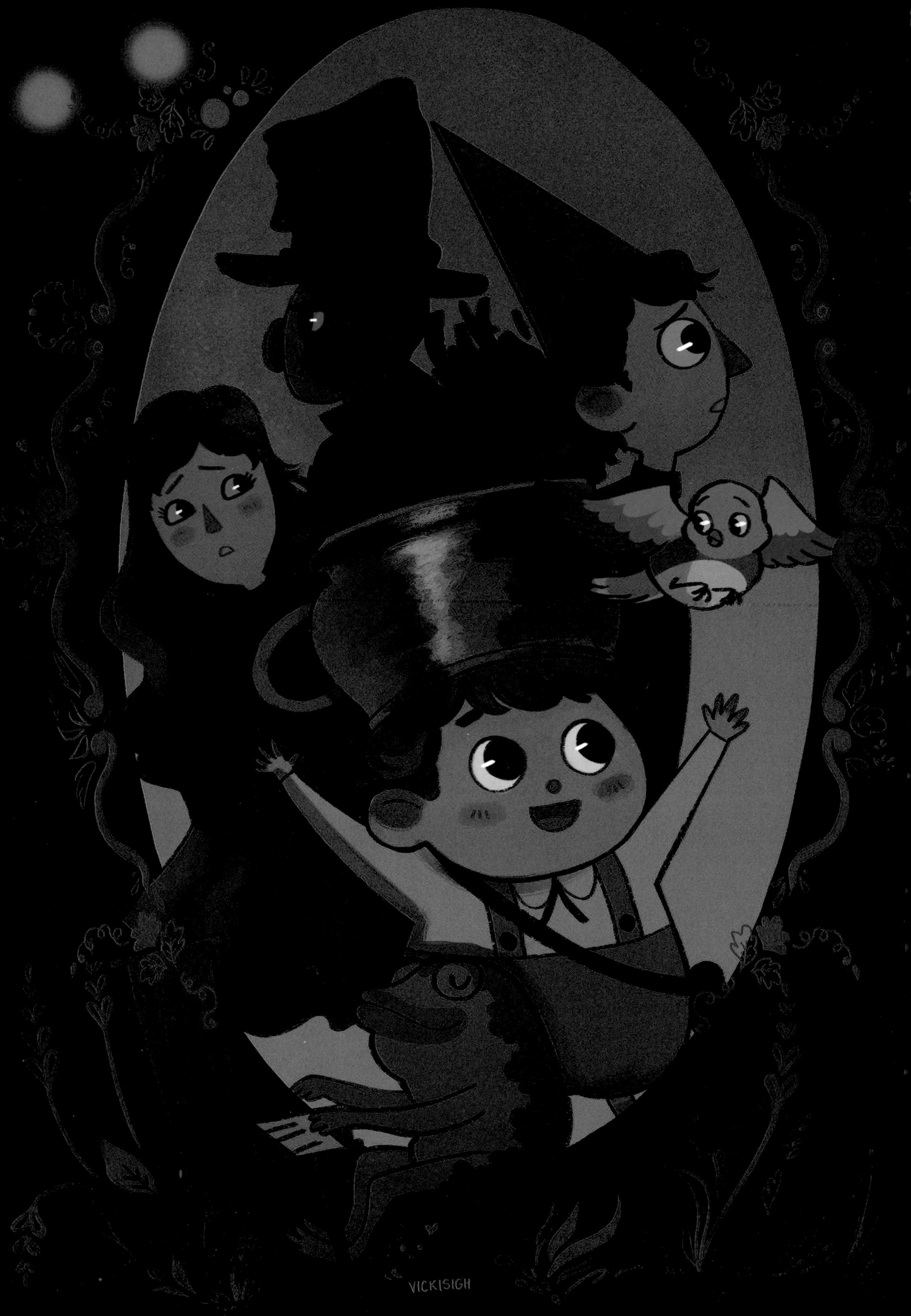
VICKISIGH

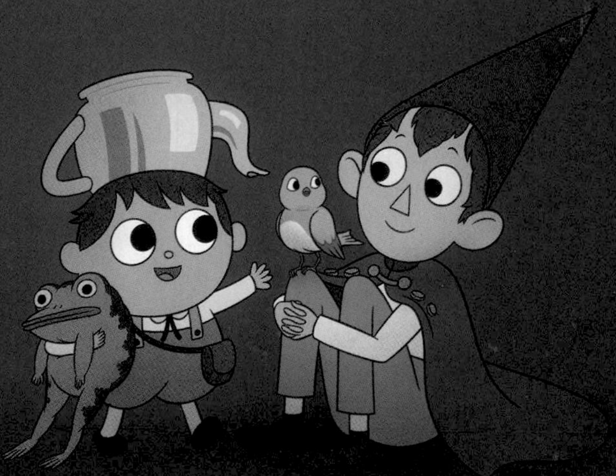

DISCOVER
EXPLOSIVE NEW WORLDS

ADVENTURE TIME

sam sykes · selina espiritu · sarah stern
Brave Chef Brianna

KELLY THOMPSON BRIANNE DROUHARD M. VICTORIA ROBADO
MEGA PRINCESS

THE NOT-SO SECRET SOCIETY
DALEY · CRAFTS · CLARK · BRUNI

OVER THE GARDEN WALL

STEVEN UNIVERSE
VOLUME ONE

kaboom!™

AVAILABLE AT YOUR LOCAL COMICS SHOP AND BOOKSTORE

To find a comics shop in your area, call 1-888-266-4226

WWW.**BOOM-STUDIOS**.COM

Adventure Time
Pendleton Ward and Others
Volume 1
ISBN: 978-1-60886-280-1 | $14.99 US
Volume 2
ISBN: 978-1-60886-323-5 | $14.99 US
Adventure Time: Islands
ISBN: 978-1-60886-972-5 | $9.99 US

The Amazing World of Gumball
Ben Bocquelet and Others
Volume 1
ISBN: 978-1-60886-488-1 | $14.99 US
Volume 2
ISBN: 978-1-60886-793-6 | $14.99 US

Brave Chef Brianna
Sam Sykes, Selina Espiritu
ISBN: 978-1-68415-050-2 | $14.99 US

Mega Princess
Kelly Thompson, Brianne Drouhard
ISBN: 978-1-68415-007-6 | $14.99 US

The Not-So Secret Society
Matthew Daley, Arlene Daley, Wook Jin Clark
ISBN: 978-1-60886-997-8 | $9.99 US

Over the Garden Wall
Patrick McHale, Jim Campbell and Others
Volume 1
ISBN: 978-1-60886-940-4 | $14.99 US
Volume 2
ISBN: 978-1-68415-006-9 | $14.99 US

Steven Universe
Rebecca Sugar and Others
Volume 1
ISBN: 978-1-60886-706-6 | $14.99 US
Volume 2
ISBN: 978-1-60886-796-7 | $14.99 US

Steven Universe & The Crystal Gems
ISBN: 978-1-60886-921-3 | $14.99 US

Steven Universe: Too Cool for School
ISBN: 978-1-60886-771-4 | $14.99 US

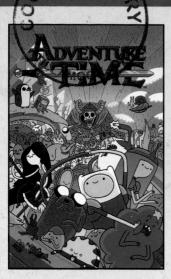

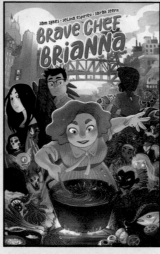

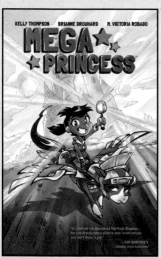

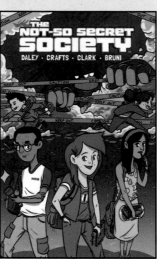

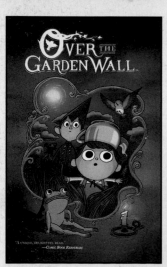

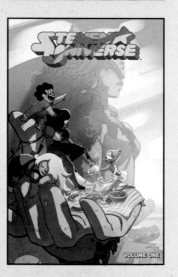

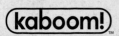